Home to Barcelona:
A Foreigner's Story

by Richard Manchester

Publicaciones Universitarias, S.A.
Diputación, 213, bajos - 08011 Barcelona

Second Edition
ISBN: 978-0-615-49789-1

ISBN: 978-84-477-1024-9 (first edition)

A portion of this novel appeared, in a slightly different form, in The Barcelona Review (thebarcelonareview.com).

Language book cartoons: Megyerine Kovacs Katalin, first published in *Hallo, itt Magyorszag!* *Akadémiai Kiadó,* Budapest: 1995.

Illustration credits: Jorge Sanchez

Lithograph reproductions: *Festes Populars A Catalunya.* Editorial HMB. Barcelona: 1980.

For Diane

PROLOGUE

SAN DIEGO

Nothing depressed me more than Mission Valley on a Saturday afternoon. I think it was the way the car dealerships and fast-food chains were piled up on either side, all that metal and glare. Reese, my mother's second husband, told me the river that ran through the valley wasn't always so dry. "Used to see cows all around here," he said, "grazing."

We were driving to the airport in Reese's old Saab. Without taking his hand off the wheel, he pointed to a huddle of brown townhouses at the base of a cliff. "Canadian geese used to make that their winter home. You could hear their quacking from Ocean Beach to El Cajon. I hate to say it Les, but San Diego was better then."

I never cared much for Reese. It probably had a lot to do with a kind of stepfather syndrome, though I had never really considered him that. I was twenty-seven that day he drove me to the airport, and was twenty-one when my mother and he began their relationship. Before that she was single for a long time. She had occasional boyfriends, but none of them could break the melancholy that had become her defining characteristic. My father left when I was five and my brother Tyrone was still just a baby. Reese Crapps came after all the hard parts of our lives were over, but he still acted like he rescued us, like whatever he said was golden.

"We all go through what you're going through Les, so don't go feeling like you're the Lone Ranger." I had wanted to avoid any kind of discussion with Reese about Svetlana, my ex-girlfriend. I wished Tyrone could have given me a ride to the airport, but his license was suspended—his license was always suspended—and he was still passed out when we left the house. "You've got an open-ended ticket, so come back whenever you want," Reese said. "No shame in coming home after a couple of weeks. See the Moaning Lisa, the Iron Curtain. Then stick a fork in it and come back home." Reese had brown but graying hair and wire glasses. He was a thin man, but nevertheless seemed out of shape, a little soft. "You can stay with your mom and I for a while. We'll put a cot in the garage for Tyrone, if he's still around, though he shouldn't be. He's getting a little old to live at home. He's going to have to be a man one of these days."

At five months, Svetlana Cimarron wasn't my longest relationship, but she certainly was the most intense. She was also the prettiest girl that I ever dated. People said that she was "voluptuous," and "sensual," and she was asked out all the time. Men would stop her in front of a 7-11, and then fumble for a question—the time, directions, the silliest lies. I'd seen that happen, and she told me about other times besides. "He was at least two hundred and twenty pounds," she said, "had a wedding ring and was driving a Ford Taurus." At those moments I was her confidant. But I knew that there were better offers for her out there—the ones she never mentioned, and the one that she finally accepted.

I met Svetlana right after her fling with an Italian architect. She used to tell me how the two of them passed romantic weekends just over the border in Ensenada, Rosarita, and San Felipe. He promised to take her to Italy some day, where they could build their own dream house on the Italian Riviera. She could learn Italian, take cooking classes, and pick out fabric for curtains, he said. But when the industrial park that he had designed in Chula Vista was completed, he went back to Genoa without her. He promised to return when the zoning permits for his next project were approved, though it had begun to dawn on her that he already had a wife, and probably children. She had been misled, she was sure, though she had let herself. "Everyone needs to have a fantasy," she told me. "So kill me for wanting to have a fantasy."

My trip to Europe was more a fulfillment of her dream rather than mine. She talked all the time about living on the Mediterranean, even after she learned that Fabrizio's permits were denied due to poor irrigation. "They take three hours for lunch over there," she said the first time we went out. "One for eating, one for fucking, and one for sleeping." Going to Europe became a way for me to get away from her and get closer to her at the same time. I chose Barcelona because I wanted to add my own stamp, and because it looked nice enough when I watched the Dream Team dunk their way to the gold in the '92 Olympics.

My first meal outside of the United States was a slab of salmon on a thick plastic tray. I was traveling on British Airways Flight #2319, Los Angeles to London. In the right, top corner there was a salad of limp lettuce, shredded carrot, and a single wedge of pale tomato. To the left rested a hunk of brown cake, the exact size and shape of a deck of cards. Next to the salmon, potato pieces were piled and coated with a pale-yellow sauce and sprinkled with something tiny and green, either parsley or dill. A spongy dinner roll fit snugly in a white plastic mug.

An ethereal screen in the front of the cabin claimed the plane was soaring 11,000 meters above Canada. No one else seemed to find this remarkable. We were also traveling at 867 kilometers per hour. The temperature was minus fifty-four Celsius—cold enough to freeze a man to death within seconds. I glanced back at my fellow passengers and they were fearless, hunched over their identical meals.

After her Italian affair, I was Svetlana's getting-back-to-basics boyfriend, a way for her to ground herself back in everything simple and American. She must have realized immediately that she had gone too far. I was too simple, too uncultured, too American. I had nothing at all to offer her. I was no doubt the low point in her dating history, and I credit her good breeding and overall sense of decorum for sticking with me for those precious weeks.

I was a short order cook. I drove a Pontiac Lemans—not one of the older hot rods but an '86 sedan that would have looked at home in front of a bingo hall or an Elk's club. I had earned twelve units of community college, and would have struggled to secure any old prize for Svetlana—a house, a family, or at the very least passionate sex, though with that I was trying my hardest. In the end I could offer her nothing but complete submission and unflagging attention.

When she called one Friday afternoon and told me that she didn't want to see me anymore, I tried to take it like a man, but was weeping in the car by sunset. I drank half a bottle of Southern Comfort and drove into a canyon over by Mesa College. I think I might have been trying to commit suicide, but since I was in a blackout, I can't say for sure. In any case, I woke up in the car with some deep bruises and a slice in my leg, the car tilted in a dry wash and invisible from the road. I saw the sun rise as I shuffled down the shoulder of the road; disheveled and alone, I must have looked for all the world like I was homeless, shaking off another scratchy night in the weeds, on my way to nothing.

When I reported my car stolen two days later, the cop said, "Who'd steal an 86 Lemans?" I told him I didn't know, but he didn't have to look for it if he didn't want to. I told him I never really liked that car anyway.

I had never flown before, but had twice traveled across the country. When I was fifteen, one of my mother's boyfriends drove us all to Wichita, his hometown, in a Dodge Dart. Charlie the pipe fitter mistakenly thought my mother would marry him in Nevada along the way. She feigned illness by the time we were in the Imperial Mountains, and sedated herself for almost the entire trip. In Arizona, Tyrone received a written warning for urinating on state property (a rest stop), though he was only thirteen. He kept it in a frame with a postcard of the Grand Canyon, which we didn't visit.

The other time I was seventeen, and I rode the bus seventy-two hours to be one of two attendees at my father's fifteen-minute funeral in a Catholic Outreach Program outside of Boston. The other character was a guy called Wes, a fellow Vietnam Vet, who was my father's "best buddy" on the soup kitchen circuit. "Your father told me he killed a man," Wes told me that night at a bar. "It was during Vietnam, but not in combat. Some sort of scuffle at the commissary." I paid the bar bill that night, and for some reason gave Wes twenty bucks. I've always considered that night the beginning of my hard drinking.

The Captain announced that we were encountering "mild turbulence." The seat belt sign illuminated with a "bonngg," and my journal began bouncing on the fold-down tray. A slight anxiety started to circulate among the passengers. The plane engines, however, did not even burp and their steady roar seemed almost soothing.

"You're not looking so hot," the guy next to me said. "Here, put a penny in your mouth and you won't get sick." I took his penny, but didn't say anything. "You wanna know something interesting about pennies?" He dug another one out of his cargo shorts. "The copper of these pennies was probably mined in Chile. The Chilean Andes. Amazing huh? I'm holding a little piece of Chile." He squeezed the coin between his chubby index finger and thumb, appraising it like it was some sort of fantastic relic. I finally put the penny he had given me on my tongue. I forced a tight smile, but it tasted like bad tap water and made me feel even more nauseous. I leaned against the window and watched the singular red light blinking on the wing.

It was my job at Snapperheads, as much as the breakup with Svetlana, that finally made me decide to get away from San Diego. Snapperheads was a restaurant in Pacific Beach that specialized in all-you-can-eat popcorn shrimp and forty-eight ounce Margaritas. One Friday afternoon before the early rush, Manny the boss came over to the walk-in cooler where I was sitting on an overturned bucket, smoking. "Ferry," he said, "Lupe wants to make you shift manager but can't because you don't speak Spanish. Why can't you learn some Spanish? Just a enough to yell at the dishwashers when they fall asleep in the pantry." Manny hoisted seventy-two pounds of butter onto his shoulder. I asked him if Lupe would teach me. "I don't think so my friend," he said. "She's too busy heating my ass."

Later in the shift, Manny happened to be slinking past when a clam detonated in the microwave, sounding like distant artillery. "Ferry," he said, "you can't fool with putting clams in the microwave. Shift managers do not fool like that. Besides, this is not some twenty dollar K-mart unit you're playing with," he patted its side like a salesman. "This is industrial grade—it costs about two hundred dollars." His face looked like oatmeal, and his shoulders slumped in front of him as if he was handcuffed. Manny himself had started two years earlier as a short order cook, and was moving straight up the ladder. But I could see it had more to do with fear than with ambition. "If I have to ask Lupe to approve another microwave," he said, "she'll be in everyone's shorts with a flashlight and ball-peen hammer. No one wants that." Manny, I realized, was afraid of his own imagination, and I was becoming just like him.

San Diego seemed to be slowly siphoning away my ambition. I didn't want to wake up someday and realize that I hadn't really done anything, that my whole life had been measured out in carne asada burritos and Tecate beers. I realized that so many immigrants wanted to come to San Diego for all the reasons I wanted to leave—safety, abundant jobs, a pleasant climate that lent itself to an overall family snugness. I daydreamt about meeting these characters at the border, wearing their modest but smart clothing. They looked at me with contempt mixed with incomprehension—why leave a place of comfort and freedom? What, if not that, do you search for in this world? I told them that I just wanted a little experience, I pointed at the cloudless blue sky, as if that would somehow explain my position. The matriarch responded crisply by saying that "experience is of value only to gain comfort and freedom." How did she know all these answers? "When you have comfort and freedom," she recited, "then there is no need to gain experience. Experience is merely a tool to gain comfort and freedom." Then the patriarch of the immigrant clan declared "enough of this nonsense" and roughly pushed me aside with a hairy, outstretched arm; his children bounded onto the grassy space of land that I just vacated. These children ran and cheered, and ignored me completely.

"You know I never told you about my first wife," Reese said. "It's bad form to say those kinds of things to your new wife's son. I read that in a man's magazine. But you're a man yourself now Les, and I'm afraid you don't have anyone to really talk to." Reese was driving, like he always did, with both hands gripping the steering wheel. "My first wife decided that she wanted her freedom. 'Her freedom,' she said, as if living with me was like living in jail. Anyway, I thought we'd have a little separation, three months tops." Reese had gotten off the freeway and was taking his signature shortcut near the VA hospital. "Well Les, I was naïve. Two weeks later I saw her driving around with the fellow who had installed the ceiling fan in our den." There was a line outside the VA—they were probably handing out meal coupons or prescriptions. I thought about my real father, about how he probably stood in a lot of lines like this one. Reese kept talking. "But it all turned out fine in the end. It turned out that I eventually met your mother."

PART ONE

VOICES OF THE OLD SEA

CHAPTER 1

At twenty-seven, I was worried that I'd be the oldest one at Barcelona's George Orwell Youth Hostel. But the place seemed to be a kind of shelter for international drifters. The Australian guy who slept on the bunk above me, Roger, was easily past thirty. Deeply tanned with receding blonde hair, he looked like a rock singer rehabbing from heroin. He rolled joints on the cover of his dog-eared travel guide. A green bottle of beer was always within arm's reach. His feet and hands were calloused yellowy-white—he told me that he worked on boats. He exuded the exact kind of salty worldliness that I hoped to gain on my trip.

Roger also cooked elaborate meals in the hostel's industrial-sized kitchen. Everything he did was a smiling, let's-get-to-know-you production. "Got heaps a pasta," he said to an American girl holding a frying pan. "There's sauce in the pan and a bit of cheese, I think it's Gruyere."

I sat in a folding chair some distance away from him, and read the sports page of an eight-day-old International Herald Tribune. "Wanna dried chickpea?" he asked the girl, who was still holding the frying pan. Her brown hair bobbed on top of her freckled shoulders. She was wearing a tight orange sundress without a bra. Roger showed her the package of peas, and they both appraised it at arm's length. "I bought them at one of the little shops on the other side of the park. Lotsa these little shops."

The two of them sat down with their pasta, just out of earshot. Another girl walked in a minute later, her black hair matted down from the shower, a look of weary surprise on her face when she saw her friend sitting with the guy wearing the salesman smile. Roger spoke to her and pointed at the pot and pan on the stove. She shuffled over and reluctantly took a plate from the drying rack above the sink. There was a practiced forlornness in her movements, as if she were not only preparing to eat a meal that she didn't want to eat, but that she was somewhere she didn't want to be, with people she didn't want to be with, and was used to it. She glanced suddenly in my direction, maybe feeling the weight of my judgment on her. I tapped a pen on my chin and looked at the greasy cabinets behind her, trying to give the impression that I was thinking about something fascinating and totally unrelated to her. The drying pasta fell onto her plate in a single sticky lump.

The men and women slept in separate rooms at the Orwell, but all fifty or so travelers shared one bathroom. It had six or seven toilets, and the same number of showers, but they were shoved into a space for half that many. The toilets stalls were more like little rooms with regular doorknobs, and were so narrow that I couldn't lift both elbows at the same time. It was odd to step out of the stinky little closet and see a couple of sunburned girls in sleeveless t-shirts brushing their teeth.

And everyone but me seemed to have the lifestyle down pat. They had cheap shower shoes and plastic soap containers; I got a wicked case of athlete's foot and kept my bar of soap wrapped in toilet paper. They also could undress, shower and redress in the 2' by 2' shower stall. And most of all they did not seem to confuse the sharing of bathroom space with a more profound intimacy. Not that I made any passes at anyone. I looked blankly at those girls brushing their teeth, at the one twisting a washcloth in her ear, the one with the downy hair on the small of her back.

I only planned on staying at the hostel a week or two, then finding a roommate situation, something the guidebook said was pretty easy, though my cavalier guidebook made everything sound easy. If nothing panned out, I planned on packing the rucksack and heading to France or Madrid. In other words, I had utterly no idea what to do.

I saw Roger the next afternoon in the dormitory we shared. He was wearing a t-shirt with the sleeves cut off, showing off his tattoo—a wavy band with thorns around his bicep.

"Got a root last night, wish she spoke Australian but."

"But what?"

"But she didn't. Got a root just the same." I had not had many conversations with Australians, but I got the feeling that Roger hammed his accent.

"You a lifer here?" I asked.

"Would love to be. Get a real steady diet here. But I'm due in Mallorca next week. Me chick's coming on a forty-foot Hatteras. Then we're off to Bali. Been?"

"Not recently," I said sourly.

"C'mon now, cheer up mate. Why not try and get laid? That'll do ya good. Melissa's traveling with a friend. Not my taste, but maybe you could have a go at her. Everyone wants to get a root in these places."

I thought for a moment that maybe Roger was right, that very well could have been a suggestive look from the girl with the washcloth, and that maybe what I needed after all was just some female company.

Roger was sitting cross-legged on the floor, giving himself a pedicure with a Swiss Army knife. He was actually using the blade to carve the formidable nail on his big toe. He was biting a smoldering cigarette in the corner of his mouth. For a moment, I imagined that we were in prison. There was a little Steve McQueen in this randy Australian. Roger, to be sure, would have been incarcerated for committing some act of larceny that was both clever and romantic, the kind of crime that wins a private smile from the police, and has film producers flying to Leavenworth to visit him. His crime would have been without flaws; he would have been betrayed by a jealous stool pigeon.

On the other hand, my crime would be born from sloth and simple mindedness, maybe some pilfering from a factory, or buying a BMW out of the company slush fund. My downfall would simply be my lack of attention to detail, my big face a banner of stupidity on some warehouse security camera, all ten of my fingerprints inside the safe. Only my mother would come and visit me. My mother behind the bulletproof glass, holding the oversized telephone. My mother would finally have something to cry about.

The Irish girl that worked Orwell's desk suggested that I look for a room to rent on the bulletin boards at the university. She was studying Catalan Literature, she said, and had found a cheap place to stay there herself a few months before. She looked gaunt, with severe cheekbones slicing beneath her eyes, and I wondered if she was eating enough. I asked her about the slim book with the Catalan title that lay splayed on her desk. "*Pointy Hearts*," she said. "They're poems."

The students at the Universitat de Barcelona stood around smoking in expensive shoes and square-rimmed glasses. Everyone looked younger than me, unlike at Mesa College, where in my evening English class I was one of the young upstarts at the age of twenty-six. The university itself was a complex of old stone buildings and tree-shaded courtyards. Next to the stairway that led down to the cafeteria, there was an enormous corkboard covered with pins and paper messages. When the wind blew, the notes fluttered like frightened birds fleeing a bush.

The flyers with words that didn't end in vowels, the ones in Catalan, I ignored. I assumed that they were written in Catalan to discourage people like me, a hapless foreigner, from calling. From the boxy blue payphone, I called a number from one of flyers written in Spanish. A recorded Catalan voice came on the line and spoke quickly and elegantly. The message repeated and was followed by a loud and desperate-sounding busy signal. I put the receiver back on its cradle and listened to my money tumble into the coin tank.

As I stood there searching my pockets for more coins, a woman walked up to the message board, took a tack from another announcement, and pushed a flyer onto the corkboard: *busco persona alquilar…*

She had a plaid luggage cart on wheels, the kind I had seen older people use for groceries. But she wasn't so old—probably only a little older than me. Her golden hair was stretched back so tight that it seemed to pull the skin of her face back too. I got the fleeting impression that this woman might have been a little crazy, like someone who has twenty or thirty cats, or cries during televised parades. I knew immediately that I was going to rent her room, though not by any feat of intuition, but because I just wanted to cut short the whole process of looking for a place to live. I grunted and stammered and pointed at her flyer, and in a minute she was turning down streets, and I was following.

I followed her down Carrer de Pelai, crowded with afternoon shoppers, and then through a network of crooked streets. We crossed Via Laietana and walked passed the Santa Caterina Market and into an area called La Ribera, a place my guide book suggested was becoming a haven for Eastern/Central European gangs. As we got close to the apartment, Paz pointed out a store called "DIA," and she explained that the store was for "*los pobres*." She also pointed out the tobacconist, the bakery, and the Pakistani store. Just before the entrance to her building, she motioned to the neighborhood restaurant, El Fondo. I saw the hams hanging around the perimeter of the bar, the bottles of sherry lined up on the shelves, and the paunchy bartender who stared at Paz's lower half as we walked by.

The room was not really a room, but more like a converted closet—though for a closet, it was pretty big. The bed was pushed against the back wall, barely fitting from head to foot. A thin sheet hung over the sides, but it didn't quite reach the bottom edge and I could see that the mattress was just yellow foam. There was room enough to stand, but not to walk even a step: a dresser blocked the way to the left, and to the right a tiny desk—a desk that was, in fact, made for a child. A window above the desk opened onto the central ventilation shaft and I craned my neck and saw a piece of the sky. At 22,000 pesetas a month, it was by far the cheapest place that I'd find—less than half of most of the other places I'd seen on the flyers. "There's another renter, " she said, stepping away from the stuffy room, "and the bathroom is right across the hall." I was free to use the kitchen, she said in Spanish, but implied with her tone that she wouldn't want me in there all the time, that there were limits to my privileges. Paz stood behind me with her arms folded, like someone accustomed to confronting disappointment and rejection.

When I lugged my duffel bag to the apartment the following afternoon. Enrique, the other renter, was watching television. He greeted me without taking his eyes off the TV. He was watching a Spanish variety show—men dressed as women acting ridiculously among voluptuous real women. The laugh track was gushing every other second, but Enrique just stared stoically at the set, in what seemed a deliberate attempt to ignore me. Paz had taken two steps into the kitchen area and was pointing at the refrigerator and the cabinets, rambling through sophisticated explanations of which I understood virtually nothing. She then addressed Enrique directly. Without taking his eyes off the TV, which had shifted to a commercial, he asked me in smooth, barely-accented English: "You don't have any questions about how to use the sink or the refrigerator, do you?"

"No, I don't think so," I said.

"No," he said to Paz. "*Claro que sí.*"

In the Ciutadella Park, a tiny old man in a beret and dark slacks sat holding a water glass half full of sherry. I imagined that he might be able to remember the days that I read about in the "History" chapter of my guidebook, the days of homemade bombs and police beatings, when gangs prowled the streets intent on menace, the executions carried out in the neighborhood plaza, the mummies piled up in the jambs. *Back then they didn't care if you had a family, or were just in the wrong place at the wrong time: put him against the wall, untie his hands and let him leave this world as a man.*

CHAPTER 2

Another reason that I chose to go to Spain was because I was born there. My father was stationed at Rota, on the Atlantic coast near Cádiz, just before his dishonorable discharge. Our small family moved back to the United States before my third birthday, right before my brother Tyrone was born, so I had only vague memories of the place. Yet I've always had this image of a dark man—who I believed was my father—sauntering across a sweltering tarmac, the blurry heat waves rising in the bright, blinding sun. I had no other childhood recollection of the man. I never mentioned this memory to anyone because I supposed it would not be the least bit interesting or remarkable to anyone else. It would be the kind of thing someone tells a lover in the throes of intimacy, just another meaningless piece of pillow talk.

It was only after I paid Paz for a month's rent that I began to imagine that I would actually live in Barcelona. Up until then, I had the depressing suspicion that sooner rather than later I'd be meeting Reese on the tarmac of Lindberg Field, that strange way that San Diego makes passengers disembark from the plane directly onto the airstrip, descending the staircase like a politician or a rock star. Reese would probably walk all the way out to the plane in his stupid straw safari hat, the default witness to one more humiliating episode: $800 of airfare just to detach from my girlfriend for nine or ten days.

I went right back to the university sign boards and began looking for a job. I had seen all kinds of postings there, though I didn't take the time to try and decipher the messages with my dictionary. I decided that I'd take a job as a cook if nothing else presented itself. I wanted something a little more exotic, grittier. Loading crates on a ship, for instance—something physical and mindless, where I could learn Spanish profanity. Years later, I imagined, I would be able to call someone something like a lousy armpit in rugged Spanish, and would then have to explain to whomever overheard the remark that I had learned it as a stevedore on the Barcelona docks. I would then show this person my anchor tattoo gracelessly etched on the inside of my forearm.

The university boards were in fact filled with a bunch of miscellaneous messages. I sensed something romantic about these notes, even the ones I couldn't read, the ones in Korean or German, Japanese or Hungarian. The faraway voices pinned to a corkboard waiting for the singular reader, all the while getting ripped and rained on and pinned over. Some of them had fallen to the ground and lay with crushed cigarette butts and beer caps.

There weren't a lot of jobs pinned to the university corkboard, though I soon found that there were plenty of other bulletin boards all over the city. Visiting them became a way for me to structure my days, a way to navigate the chaotic urban sprawl, a way to feel at home however remote and fleeting that feeling was. I found little boards in the back of bakeries. People taped notes to the front window of the DIA near my apartment. There were even little notes pasted directly onto the sides of buildings, though mostly those were for apartments to rent or buy.

After a couple days of wandering, I discovered a municipal building just off the Ramblas on Carrer de Ferran. A four-foot tall woman arranged index cards on a large board in the foyer. Even with a stepladder, she seemed overmatched by the job. I took a chance and asked if she spoke English.

"Of course I do," she said. "I worked for ten years in Birmingham."

"Alabama?"

"For heaven's sake. England you poor dear."

"That's sort of why I came here for help. I need some kind of employment."

"This is not an employment agency—but sometimes people post jobs on this board. What are you looking for?"

"I was hoping to get work on the docks, down by the boats, with a dark wool hat."

"You can't work at the docks. They're unionized."

"Maybe a grocer then. A mom and pop one. Stock shelves, learn vocabulary. Deliver to invalids."

"You're not going to get a proper job like that without working papers."

"I'll get papers."

"No, you won't. It would take a lot of money and time and you would probably not get them anyway. You must explain why you want to work in Spain. You must have some kind of reason. Do you have one?"

"Not one that would look good on paper."

"Then I am afraid that your sentimental little grocer is out."

"Taxi driver?"

"No, this isn't like Manhattan. They're the Mafia besides. Why not just teach English? That's what all you people do. There's a big demand for it."

"What kind of credentials do I need for that?"

"That is something I don't know. But I see people come in here all the time that don't look like they could have credentials in anything. They write down numbers from this section." The woman pointed to the bottom left of the board, where there were in fact three advertisements for English teachers, though they were all dated more than a month ago. "You might want to try the English bookstore," she continued. "It's a kind of civic center for you expatriates. They have jobs posted outside there, free coffee, and once in a while a poetry slam. I'm not quite sure what a poetry slam is, but I believe it involves heavy drinking."

In the Eixample, near Avinguda Diagonal, the Come On! English bookstore had an enormous message center. The board itself was outside the bookstore, but locked in a glass cabinet like hard liquor at a twenty-four hour gas station. The index cards were arranged in reverse chronological order, and were almost all soliciting English teachers. The first card was dated that same day.

Urgent!
English Teacher Needed Immediately!
The Hello Its English Time School
76 Enric Granados
2 blocks from Come On!

The Hello Its English Time School was halfway up a marble staircase, on what's known as the *entresuelo,* in a gorgeous old building. The cavernous office was empty except for a dark-haired woman scribbling behind a counter.

"I'm here for the job. I saw the job for the English teacher." I approximated the size of the advertisement with my thumbs and index fingers.

"Just a moment," she said in stilted English, and walked into a back room. The office had cheesy, framed posters of London, Dublin, and St Louis. The smell of microwave popcorn hung in the air.

From a chewed-up wooden end table, I picked up an old *Time* magazine with a picture of Ross Perot on the cover. Before I could even begin the article about his second presidential campaign, a tall man in a tie was bounding into the room. "Hi! You're an English teacher. I'm Darnell, you can call me Dan, or Darn if you get mad at me," he forced a chuckle. Darnell was about six feet tall, had short-cropped hair and a dark mocha complexion.

"I'm Lester Ferry. But call me Ferry, everyone does."

"Ferry huh? You bet. You been teaching long?" Darnell sat on the couch across from me. He began to cross his legs, but the couch was too soft and he sank awkwardly backwards at the attempt. He instead leaned forward with his elbows on his knees.

"Well, no. I just got to Barcelona a week or so ago. But I took some classes at college and I like to read."

"Wow! You don't hear that much anymore. Reading, that is. What kind of things do you like to read?" Darnell's sleeves were rolled to the middle of his forearms.

"I read a book last year about a guy who went camping all over Alaska with his dog, but then the dog died. He kept on camping though, kind of like that's what the dog would have wanted."

"Wow, that sounds pretty interesting."

"And I sometimes read car magazines. *Hot Rod*, *Low Rider*, *Motorhead*."

"You know a lot about cars?" Darnell wore metal-framed glasses that either had no lenses, or lenses so thin and clean that they were invisible.

"I can drive."

"And it sounds like you like to read and know a thing or two about English. A lot of people know about English, but don't know that they know it. You know what I mean?"

"People think because they can talk, then they know what it all means."

Darnell nodded emphatically. "Let's say I'm a student of yours," he said seriously, "and I ask you, 'Mr. Ferry, why do you say *in* the evening but *at* night?'"

"Jesus. That's a good question. I'm embarrassed, but I don't know. I never really thought about that. It's weird, isn't it?"

"It *is* weird. Excellent response. I like how you're not afraid to answer right away. The fact is, I don't know either and I've been teaching English for going on ten years! That's the thing about English—it's kooky. Tell your students they just have to memorize the idiosyncrasies. And don't worry about all that 'I'm embarrassed' business. Just speak with authority. The only thing to be embarrassed about is if you would start saying 'in night,' or 'at the evening.'" Darnel laughed self-consciously. "Know what I mean?"

"Yeah, I got it."

"So here's the deal. I've got about twenty hours a week that I need covered starting yesterday. We pay seventeen hundred pesetas an hour, no traveling expenses. I'm not sure if you've made the rounds, but that's what everyone pays. We'll give you the books. The only thing I ask is that you try and dress a little professionally."

"I didn't even know I was coming here today," I gushed, looking down at my t-shirt and jeans. "I had no idea, I just saw the posting at the bookstore—" Darnell interrupted my explanation by stretching out his hand.

"I understand, I understand. That's how I dress when I'm not teaching. You're perfect. Don't worry. I'm teaching these classes today, but I'd like you to start tomorrow. Isabelle will give you the books, the schedule, and the addresses. All of Dmitri's classes are off-site which means that you have to go to them."

"Who's Dmitri?"

"He's the guy you're replacing. Good luck."

Isabelle was the dark-haired woman behind the desk. She spoke good English but with a thick French accent. Once she learned that I had no idea where I was going or what I was doing, she spoke more slowly, with a slight air of condescension. She explained that I could use the same book for every class, though there were several different levels. She gave me the book—*Headstrong*—to take home. She said to come back the next day and she would have directions to each class, and that she would find out from Darnell the chapters that each one was currently working on.

As she was explaining all this, another man came in and began using the photocopier. He slammed the plastic paper drawers, cursed loudly under his breath, ripped open a ream of paper. Finally he got the machine working, but he didn't close the cover, so the whole room was filled with periodic flashing.

"Clarence," Isabelle called. "Clarence this is Lester Ferry. He's taking over Dmitri's classes. Could you show him to use the photocopier?"

"If you hired someone to teach a class and that person can't operate a photocopier then you've got a big fucking problem."

"Clarence," she said wearily, "please just show him where is the paper." She patted me on the forearm. "I'll see you tomorrow.

Come in about one to get prepared. Your first class is at 2 PM. Very close by."

I walked over to Clarence, who wore thick horn-rimmed glasses with a piece of white tape on the bridge. "There's the fucking paper," he said. "Right in the fucking paper drawer."

I was so pleased with my new job that I decided to celebrate with a beer at the bar below the school. What Dmitri did to lose a job like this, I could hardly imagine. I pictured mental patients in straight jackets screaming "at the evening, down the morning, over the night."

Clarence came in and walked directly over to me with his briefcase. "So you're an alcoholic too. You're going to fit right in."

"I like to think of myself as more of a hard drinker."

"That can only help you. I'm more of a binge drinker." The bartender brought Clarence two beers without being asked.

I watched him drain one of them in one tilt. "So are you on a binge now?" I asked.

"Yes. I've been on a binge since 1993. It's how I ended up here."

"You make it sound like we're in San Quentin."

"We are, in our own way. But we have unlimited commissary. Infrequent conjugal visits. Top-notch transportation."

"How long you been at the school?"

"Less than a year. Since I got fired from my last job."

"Why'd you get fired?"

"They say I assaulted one of my students. I shoved an eraser into his mouth. It wasn't even my fault." Clarence had oily, brown hair. He wore a long-sleeve blue shirt that looked faded—maybe it was the fraying collar and cuffs. He had a normal build, except for his head, which seemed too big.

"The one you have to worry about here," Clarence continued, "is Isabelle. Keep track of your hours. Your other concern is attrition, so keep drinking steadily." He lit a cigarette. "You ever taught before?"

"Well, not exactly. I mean, I told Darnell that I had been in school, but I never said that I took any English teaching classes or anything. The fact is that I'm confident that I'm going to be able to—"

"Look," Clarence cut me off, "I'm just making conversation. No one gives a fuck. Least of all me. Or Darnell. Darnell is the administrator and doesn't get paid to sub the classes, so he'd have hired you if you had Tourette's. The last replacement was a complete clown. He wore skin-tight chinos and women's blouses. And even he went MIA."

"Well then no, since you're asking, I never taught. I don't have the slightest idea how to teach or what to teach. In fact I never even imagined that I would teach. I have a feeling that I'm going to be a terrible teacher."

"OK, don't overdo it. If you feel that pathetic, you can sit in on one of my classes. I'm starting an intensive class here tomorrow morning at ten." He drained the second beer and slapped a couple of coins on the bar. "I've gotta run now. I've got a two o'clock class in Les Cortes."

The next day, I saw him back at The Hello Its English Time School, copying a list of false-friend cognates. Clarence was preparing for his Beginners Two class, which assumes only the most rudimentary knowledge of English. I took a seat at the back of the classroom. Although the students seemed to be mostly young teenagers, none of them looked twice at me.

Exactly at the top of the hour, Clarence walked in, turned on all the lights, and slammed his briefcase down on the counter. "The first rule in this class," he boomed, so loudly it was almost a yell, "is you don't fucking touch me. Not on the leg, not on the arm, not on the back. I don't go in for all your friendly Latin bullshit, rubbing my fucking arm after class. Let me say that right from the get go. First person who touches me, gets poked in the eye with a dry erase marker." He clicked open his briefcase and pulled out an unopened pack of markers. He tossed them on the desk and started to walk stiffly up one of the aisles, his hands tucked in his pockets. "Let me be absolutely clear. Under no circumstances should any part of your body touch any part of my body, intentionally or otherwise. This includes all manner of clothing and utensils; for instance, you should not poke my coat with your pencil." The students looked around anxiously at each other, afraid they might be in the wrong class, or that they were the only one not understanding Clarence's diatribe. Clarence affected a high-pitched voice that he crudely-accented to sound like a foreigner and said: "*But what about today...our first day,* some foolish, quizzical student may want to ask." He stopped pacing. "Today is no different than any other day—you should just sit down and shut the fuck up. You're in class to learn English, not make friends. If you want friends, go join a fucking cycling club." He pointed out the window, and all the students looked. "Clarence Burns gets paid to teach you English, and not to rub your fucking arm and ask you about your fucking weekend." A few students started to write in their notebooks, but most just stared blankly at Clarence, who had resumed his position in the front of the class.

"No, I am not suffering from some horrible maladjustment or from mental illness. I'm simply Anglo Saxon. My blood runs colder than the North Sea. My body has evolved to perform optimally on potatoes and lager. I rarely have sex, and when I do, it's in the dark. I eat two meals a day, alone, in front of the television. I hit men in pubs for trifling reasons. I haven't seen a member of my immediate family for eleven years. Affectionate, casual touching has no place in my world.

"Some of you may be wondering—*what about each other? Can we touch each other?* While I cannot prohibit you from touching each other, at least I cannot prevent you with the same delicious fury that I prefer, but I can quietly loathe you. Yes, that would suit me fine."

I had started leafing through *Headstrong*, trying to ignore Clarence's rant. This class was not making me feel any better about teaching. And then suddenly Clarence was in front of me. "Looks like someone thinks they're ahead of the game," he said with clenched teeth. He then punched me, hard, on the upper arm. I slid off my seat and had to catch myself on the adjacent desk. One of the girls gasped, and another kid said "*joder*."

"That's right," Clarence said. "*Joder.* Three weeks. *Intensivo*. Non-refundable. *Joder*."

CHAPTER 3

I started drinking a lot of DIA BRÄU—the cheapest beer on the planet, far as I could tell. The umlaut was the portal to another realm, a remnant of Saxon ancestors, pillagers and marauders. I chugged, and saw buxom maidens swing their blonde braids, I heard the clank of metal steins, I smelled the urine and beer splashed on the canvas pants of rugged men. *Partake the kidney of the fresh-slain beast/We crushed the foe on the storm-swept beach.*

Growing up, we sometimes got someone to buy us beer from the Ocean Beach Bottle Shop. They always had stacks of cheap German beer—often names with umlauts. They must have fallen off the forklift at the port and purchased at a steep discount, because these cans were always dented—sometimes they opened without releasing carbonation. We drank them all the same. We drank them under the 805 overpass, at Dog Beach, and in a ravine by the zoo. We knocked them down and threw them up. Tyrone came with us the night we broke into the maintenance shed of the Presidio Park recreation center. I can still hear the clatter of cans as Tyrone cleared a place to lie down and pass out. At thirteen, that may have been the beginning of *his* hard drinking.

The Internet Cafe on Gran Via was dark and lurid, a place where young travelers spent otherwise bright afternoons pecking away at their left-behind relationships. Svetlana finally responded to my email, in which I explained that I wanted "to possess" her—though I went to some pains to explain that I didn't mean in an overbearing, domestic-abuse sense, but if she was thinking *picnic*, I wanted to be present with potato salad and a thermos of Kool Aid, wearing a novelty apron.

She countered my deranged plea with what I felt was a typical Svetlanaesque phrase: "necessary distance." Then she emphasized this point with her trademark smiley face, cleverly created with a parenthesis and a colon. I felt a certain sadness when I thought about how far mankind had devolved emotionally; we went from blunt, unambiguous caressing in caves and adobe huts, to exchanging cryptic symbols, separated by vast oceans, while sipping cold coffee in the neon-lit midst of strangers. I realized that the Internet might well be the new bane of traveling, and that I was probably never going to talk with Svetlana again.

Some of the teachers of Hello Its English Time School met every weekend at the Quiet Man, a bar tucked into a corner of the Raval, which I learned roughly translated as the "suburb," though it couldn't have been more different than San Diego's El Cajon, La Mesa, or Rancho Santa Fe. The Raval was also known as Barrio Chino, Chinatown, though there were no Chinese people living there, only Pakistanis and Moroccans. The whole old quarter, the part of Barcelona once contained inside the old walls, fascinated me. Twisting medieval streets, wrought-iron balconies, yellow lights reflecting in puddles and shop glass—it is what I imagined the fifteenth century was like. But that was mostly on the other side of the Ramblas. On the side of the Quiet Man, all the romance and charm were muted by the dismal effects of poverty and crime. Post-menopausal prostitutes sat around in beat-up lawn chairs drinking wine out of coffee cups. The younger hookers—mostly transvestites, cross-dressers and African women—were on their feet and a bit more solicitous. And there were scores of addicts, covered with sores and track marks, sprawled on the sidewalks and huddled in doorways. A putrid, open-sewer smell hung in the air of the Raval, and the place seemed damp even when the sun was shining.

The Quiet Man was a jewel of a bar. Brass light fixtures lit up vintage Guinness posters in gilded frames. The perimeter of the ceiling was lined with a shelf of clean, green and brown bottles, all full and sealed, as if awaiting an inevitable quarantine that would keep us in good spirits as we endured the end-of-the-millennium plague.

I sat at the bar made of polished oak drinking a Damms, the Spanish equivalent to Budweiser. On a stage near the restrooms, a band was strumming and tooting some Irish folk music. At first I was put off, almost embarrassed, by the singsong melodies and the earnest lyrics. The whole scene would be impossible back home, I thought. Maybe at some funky bar in Ocean Beach, where everyone smoked clove cigarettes and wore homemade sweaters. But the Quiet Man was full of well-dressed Catalans and urbane expats.

"Once in a while Ferry, you have to go top shelf," Gordon said. He was the teacher with the most seniority, after Darnell. From the English Midlands, Gordon was tall and lanky and moved his limbs very slowly, as if he was being careful not to seem too awkward. He had patches of acne, and he tried to hide some of it with shaggy brown bangs. The effect was that he seemed almost a teenager, though he was twenty-nine. "If you keep drinking that swill, you'll have no bladder left. They make that with seawater you know," he said. He ordered himself a Guinness and turned to me with a wry smile screwed onto his face. It always seemed that the next thing out of his mouth would be a punch line.

"You know, I haven't seen the sea since I got here." I said.

"You'll love it," Kylie said. "It's got turds floating in it." Kylie was from Sydney, and had arrived in Barcelona some six months before me. I got the impression that she was trying to mute her natural good looks. Her dirty blonde hair was either unkempt, or when she was teaching, pulled back into a knot. She wore jeans, sneakers, and a large, orange blouse. "When the waves crest it looks like a school of ebony minnows."

Gordon had turned his back on Kylie and me and was trying to wedge himself into a conversation with nearby girls.

"In junior college they told me that the Mediterranean is a dead sea now," I said, "that all the fish are gone, that all the fish have been fished out. Nothing left but plankton."

"I don't think it's been flushed out that badly. The fish might just be a bit dodgy."

"When I was a kid I used to watch those Jacque Cousteau programs," I said. "Did you have Jacque Cousteau in Australia?"

"What, do you think Australia doesn't have TV? You think we sit around beating a cactus with a stick, waiting for a kangaroo to hop by?"

"And listening to AC/DC."

"Oh, you're going to be prat like the rest of them."

I heard Gordon force a laugh, though he still had his back to us. I watched his head move up and down, emphatically agreeing with the girl whose pained face he exposed with every bob.

"I just thought maybe he wasn't popular there," I said. "Maybe there was a better, Australian Jacque Cousteau."

"Dear, Jacque Cousteau is Jacque Cousteau. He invented the underwater lung. Besides, he filmed a heap of his programs off the Reef."

"I'd like to have something like that. I'd like to invent some special kind of lung. Just have something I'm known for, something I'm good at. Something people in a bar would talk about me doing, you know, after I'm gone."

"You're going to assassinate someone, aren't you?"

"I doubt it. I don't know enough about politics."

"You don't have to limit yourself to politics these days. Let me have a look at you for the biographer." Kylie touched my chin and turned it side to side. Her hand stirred a warm feeling in me. "Boyish like all Americans. Baby crow's feet around either eye. Dirty ears," she said.

"It's not so much about being famous. It's about having that kind of purpose."

"You poor sod. So much growing up to do."

"Because I want to have some kind of purpose in my life?"

"Why not make TOEFL your purpose? You could be the Jacque Cousteau of TOEFL."

"I know TOEFL means something about teaching. But I was never clear on what exactly that stands for."

"Or maybe it's not too late for you to go to a college that isn't a junior one. A lot of Americans are late bloomers."

"I think I actually would like to be Jacque Cousteau. I want to be the Jacque Cousteau of marine documentaries.

"Then I insist you visit the sea."

"I read something about Tossa del Mar," I said. "That's supposed to be nice."

"Yeah, for tossers," Gordon said turning back toward us. The band crashed into another song. Kylie grabbed the plastic bag that I had crumpled by my feet. "There's no shame carrying a shopping bag around," she said, "but for fuck's sake not a DIA bag. Get one from El Corte Inglés." She pulled out the book that I bought earlier at a second hand bookstore in Grácia.

"What's that Ferry's got?" Gordon asked, grabbing it from Kylie. "*Under the Tuscan Sun,*" he said pompously.

"I've heard of that," Kylie said. "Some lady from the U.S. moves to Italy and thinks it's so wonderful and charming. As if Italy didn't exist before she arrived."

Gordon appraised the back and the front before opening it to the first page. He began reading: "And so, at the beginning of our fifth summer here, we now dig the potatoes for our dinner. They come up so easily; it's like finding Easter eggs. I am surprised how clean they are. Just a rinse and they shine." He practically sang the last bit, trying to lay on the mockery. "Digging potatoes for sport," he said. "A bit bourgeois for you, isn't it?"

"Ferry where do you go off buying rubbish like this?" Kylie said. "You have as much in common with Frances Mayes as with Juan Carlos"

"Who's he?"

"He's the bloody King of Spain," Gordon said.

"That is just so precious," Kylie said. "Albanians are in southern Italy making three dollars a day digging potatoes. I bet they think they're fucking Easter eggs."

I liked the book, what little I read of it. I even felt a pang of greedy protectiveness about my new life as an expatriate, afraid it might become too popular. I had been fantasizing of living not just for the next few months in Spain, but the rest of my natural born life. I could work hard for the next twenty or so years and then retire to the countryside. And I didn't want the throng of tourists on the Ramblas corrupting my little country home.

Barcelona would surely be one of the first places to be overrun, if it wasn't already. I'd have to go to Girona, a place that I read had one foot firmly in the last millennium. When the hordes invaded there, I thought, I could go to Zaragoza, and then smaller dots on the map, until I reached an isolated barn, archaic tools hanging on rusted hooks, the language of the townsfolk known only to their kin and scholars in faraway libraries.

A surly bartender replaced our beers. The band stopped playing and a few girls stepped onto the riser with glasses of beer. The band's singer stepped to the mike and announced that they were selling CDs. I rolled a cigarette on the bar.

"Did you come down Drassanes?" Clarence said in a huff as he arrived. "It's completely covered with trash. My feet never touched the pavement. This fucking city is like a compost heap. And the fucking junkies just lie around in it."

Clarence seemed to take some measure of delight from the filth and decay—why else would he live here? I tried to imagine what kind of life he'd have back home: if he managed to stay out of prison, he'd work in a slaughterhouse, raking the bones off the grated floors, punching cartilage through the clotted sluice chutes.

"I got propositioned for a wank on the way in," Gordon said.

"Giving or receiving?" Kylie asked.

"She did look a little broad in the shoulders."

"We wouldn't be caught dead in place like this in America," Clarence said. "These people need a lesson in civilization."

"We're teachers," I said. "We're just the people to give it to them."

"For fuck's sake," Kylie said. "We could only teach these people to masturbate and wear second hand clothes. We could teach them how to piss their life away with pints. "

“That sounds nice,” Gordon said. “You make a pint sound nice.”

“It’d be nicer to march them off to Morocco,” Clarence said. “Or kill them and burn their corpses in the plaza. Hose the blood and vomit off the buildings and start over. That’d be really nice.”

CHAPTER 4

I awoke the next morning and took a train into the mountains. I wanted to catch a glimpse of this anti-modern wonderland that Frances Mayes was raving about. The mountain village, hardly touched by time: a place where they bottled water and made cheese, where the villagers donned their rustic clothes on festival days, and where anxiety found no purchase.

The train chugged through the mountains. I saw underbrush that was the darkest green that I had ever seen. Thunder cracked in the west. "We have a motto in Catalunya," the old woman on the train said to me in clipped English, "If you don't like the weather, just wait five minutes." All these years in the countryside, and that's all she can say? They say that everywhere.

I got off at what looked like a quiet, sleepy village. A weary mountain shower dotted the sandstone walls, a church bell rang, a moped accelerated, and the sun seemed to be nowhere behind the clouds. I imagined myself as the estranged convict returning to his village to make amends for a terrible crime, committed some long ago December. As I walked down a cobblestone street, I heard the sound of music from an open window, and could identify a handful of Catalan words: *Cobriu-me de flors, que d'amors me moro.*

Not long before I landed in Barcelona, I imagined that I was going to end up like everyone else. Before I got the job at Snapperheads, I submitted my resume electronically to a large aircraft parts manufacturer, hoping for an entry level, white-collar job. Reese suggested that I follow up in person, so I ironed one of his nice shirts and went to their sprawling plant down by the airport.

Tamika, the human resource associate, told me that my resume did not print out for review, so there would not be an interview.

"Why didn't it print? I brought a hard copy," I said, pulling several cream-colored resumes from a binder.

"That won't be necessary. You see, we scan all the resumes and eliminate some seventy percent based on the appearance or absence of certain words. If you like, you could submit your application and resume for consideration on what we call the floor, the factory. Their parameters are more generous."

"No, that's OK. But what kinds of words do you scan for?"

"All kinds. PhD, MIT, Cal-Poly all go to the top of the stack, so to speak. The automatic rejections are obvious—felony, probation, methadone."

"What if I worked at a methadone clinic?"

"That would hardly qualify you to work as a junior executive in a industrial manufacturing plant. "

"What if I volunteered, as a teenager, at a methadone clinic?"

"That would be unfortunate. But really Mr. Ferry, methadone clinics don't have teenage volunteers. Clinic on its own would be OK. Crisis, asylum, shelter—none of these words are preclusive. Points are in fact generated when these words appear in proximity to volunteer, public service. But methadone is a stopper, even on the floor. "

"But why was my resume rejected? I'm not stupid, even if I was taking methadone I wouldn't put it on my resume. "

"Well you're required by law to disclose that information. But maybe there was something on the application that you submitted. We of course scan that too. Did you go to college? "

"I went to community college for a year. "

"Of course. High school diploma or GED? "

"GED. "

"Well there you go."

"You rejected me because I have a GED? Jesus, what if I got it when I was fifteen so I could work and help my mother pay a mortgage? "

"Did you get your GED when you were fifteen to help your mother pay a mortgage? "

"No. "

"When did you get it? Nineteen, twenty?"

"Twenty-one. "

"Exactly. People don't get their GED and then start working double shifts—that's a myth. You're thinking about *Good Times*.

The only instance when GED doesn't get rejected is if you were in the military. I take it you weren't in the military. "

"No, I wasn't. "

"Granted Mr. Ferry, we realize that some decent candidates never get printed, but this process saves us the time-consuming task of interviewing a lot of undesirables—parolees, drug users, or just some of the twenty-something bums down in OB who suddenly get it in their head that they want to get on the beam."

As I walked down the auxiliary stairs of the main plant annex, I could hear the screaming of the machines, the rumble of production, the dying screech of a descending jet.

I thought of that interview as I was underground in Plaça Catalunya. The doors hissed shut, and the train hummed forward. I stared at the people in the adjacent car, the windows scratched and blurry. I saw a girl with Svetlana's short henna hair staring back at me through the dirty window. If I call out to her, I thought, she wouldn't hear me, and even if she could, she wasn't Svetlana. I got on the next train and rode it out to the end of the line. *Marina, Glóries, Clot.*

The market across the street from my apartment was referred to as the Pakistani Market, but only because the proprietors were from Pakistan and not because of the kind of merchandise they sold. In fact, their chief item seemed to be alcohol.

I went there for some beer one night at eleven, as all the other neighborhood markets had long since closed. There were three guys behind the register, and they were talking in a kind of hushed, reverent way. I always felt uncomfortable in there, as if these guys were judging me, or talking about me, perhaps discussing how I was a profound symbol of America—drunk and self-centered, soft and plodding, dumb but smiling. I didn't even know if they knew where I was from, or if they cared at all. I just knew that I felt self-conscious around them. And that I envied them. I envied their camaraderie, their sense of belonging. They had a little clique in this foreign world. They were a community in a land of communities, in a place that valued community over the individual, and they were succeeding there in a way that I never could. They traded in bread and beer, coffee and tomatoes. My currency was simply competence in my native language, which just happened to be popular.

I got back to the apartment with a couple of big bottles of beer. Enrique was relaxing on the couch, chain-smoking the Ducados that I had left on the table, and watching his favorite late night talk show. It seemed to be a cross between David Letterman and Howard Stern. The host's resident sidekick was a well-dressed midget. They were engaged in a mock-serious discussion about the pros and cons of artificial breasts.

"Cosmetic surgery was invented in the U.S." Enrique said. "Anything bad in the world, you can bet came from the U.S."

"What about tobacco? Or chocolate? They came from America. They're good."

"They were before Columbus. And he brought back syphilis with them."

"What about corn? Corn came from America."

"Corn will be the end of agriculture. They use it instead of sugar. Cows go to slaughter in half the time because of corn. You can't say anything good about corn. Also, you should say the U.S.

and not America. You can't just call yourself by the name of the whole hemisphere."

"What are you talking about?"

"America. The U.S. is only one out of three countries in North America. Then there's South and Central America. How can you call yourself an American?"

"I never really thought about it. It just sounds better than saying the U.S."

"Well maybe you should have said that to Washington and Jefferson. They thought of that lame name when they were done raping their slaves."

"It's the United States of Mexico," I said, "but everyone just says Mexico."

"Are you sure you want to start talking to me about Mexico?"

"I'm just saying that it's no big deal. If we say we're Americans, who are we harming? It's not like the Bolivians are really Americans and they have to change everything to call themselves Bolivians. We're not really taking the name from anyone else. I don't think there is any bad intent."

"Aggression can be born from ignorance the same as bad intentions. Face it, it's arrogant. It's the failure to realize all the other people that share the continent."

"You can't make United States into an adjective or a personal noun. It's awkward. I don't want to be a United Statesian."

"That is not my problem."

"Well, I'm American. That's the way it is. If you don't like it, tough shit."

"Perfect. I couldn't have said it better myself. You have proven to me everything I have always thought. Yes, that's excellent."

The midget sidekick pushed his oversized glasses up the bridge of his nose and inspected a transvestite's breasts like a marine scientist might inspect a whale carcass washed up on the beach. He turned to a real woman, who dutifully pulled up her top. Her tits spilled down in a sudden rush, momentarily ruffling the little man. The audience gasped and laughed. The midget quickly collected himself and inspected the real woman's breasts in the same deliberate manner. The woman's breasts were not as pert as the transvestite's, but they seemed to strike a chord with the small co-host, who had begun rubbing his hands together.

"There is genius in the feminine geometry," Enrique said. "What do you think? You probably prefer the artificial ones."

"No, I don't. Those breasts are on a man. It's hard to disconnect the breast from the person."

"Not in the abstract. Not if you have imagination."

"There is just something missing in implanted breasts. There's something intangible missing. Robert Frost said poetry is what's lost in the translation. It's the same with implants."

The midget and audience agreed with me. The transvestite, clearly versed in the art of public humiliation, pouted and stridently made a case for his own breasts, going so far as touching those of the woman. He lifted one and let if fall. The crowd continued their campaign against him, jeering and mocking him. He was effectively sealing his own doom, as the woman's breasts gained esteem with each poke and caress.

I called my family from Paz's clunky old telephone. Tyrone answered.

"I'm on house arrest," he laughed.

"What happened? What's that?"

"The jails are full, so the probation department put this steel band around my ankle. They can monitor my whereabouts. Like radar." He lit something and inhaled. "Beats being in the hole," he said.

"Why are you even on house arrest? Did you start smoking crack again?"

"No, hell no. I was just walking through the parking lot of Denny's," he pulled deeply off his smoke, "and this guy had left a Skil-saw right in the back of his truck."

"So what?"

"So what? I lifted it. You can't just leave shit like that laying around."

"What the hell do you need with a Skil-saw? What's a Skil-saw?"

"It's for serious cutting. Good ones go for a few bills."

"What, did you try and pawn it?"

"I wish. These rednecks came barreling out of the restaurant, all yelling. I ditched the saw and bolted through the back of the parking lot. I got wedged trying to squeeze underneath the cyclone fence."

"Why did you go under? Why didn't you go over?"

"Everyone goes over. Besides, it was a fifteen footer."

"Did they kick the shit out of you?"

"I wish. They sat on my calves and called the cops on a cell phone. What the fuck is that? What's the world coming to? Twenty years ago they would have dragged me back into the parking lot, whacked me around, given me body bruises. No *cops*."

"Maybe."

"Hell yeah. After they were through they'd probably buy me a beer—say 'hey punk, you know how to *steal* a Skil-saw, but can you cut with one?' I'd be working with 'em for chrissakes."

I'm certain my mother and Reese were disappointed that Tyrone was not finally condemned to jail. At twenty-three, his house arrest would have been like a sentence *for them*. Over the years, he stole their stereos and televisions; he ripped out checks from the back of their checkbooks. He pawned their CD collection, Reese's fishing tackle, our mother's Teflon cookware. He never lived away from our mother, except when she remarried and moved in with Reese. Tyrone relocated himself into a storage unit next to Interstate 5. After three weeks, the overnight security guard smelled pot smoke coming from Tyrone's "storage" bay. When the old man lifted up the garage-like door, he trained his flashlight on Tyrone, who was naked and sitting on a duffel bag, holding a water pipe. That was four years ago

"Mom and Reese aren't home," he said. "They went on an old person day cruise. Shuffle board, swing dancing, prime rib." He laughed derisively, my only brother. "I'll tell 'em you made it to France."

CHAPTER 5

DIA manufactured their own brand of generic goods, labeled in Spanish, Italian, Portuguese, and Greek—the short list, Gordon told me, of European Union lightweights. The claustrophobic aisles were scenes of constant disaster—broken jars of beans in smelly fluid, burst sacks of flour and rice, abandoned infants screaming for the world to end. The chaos increased toward the end of the month, as the entire stock dwindled to nothing, and "shoppers" fought over the remaining cartons of milk, the final jars of white asparagus, the last filet of frozen hake.

DIA gave me the sinking feeling that it was the last stop on the block, abject poverty and despair waited for me to make one more mistake to play their advantage. This was the exact opposite of the feeling that I got at Barcelona's more upscale markets, Caprabo and El Corte Inglés, where it seemed the world was a place of unlimited abundance.

In the midst of all this disorder, the women who worked in my local DIA maintained a detached, unsentimental attitude. In filthy red smocks, they focused on their job without indulging each individual customer. They were like relief workers expediting supplies to a sleepy fishing village in the aftermath of a tidal wave. And they were young—not one of them older than thirty. I maintained a sneaky admiration for their ability to endure the unglamorous circumstances. Not surprisingly, I developed a crush on one of them, the butcher girl. She spoke a rapid-fire brand of Catalan to her coworkers, and I imaged that she might one day teach me to love that language.

"*Bon dia,*" I said.

"*Hola, com va*?" she said and whacked the head off a scrawny chicken that had a few feathers left on its body.

"*Bona bona*," I said eagerly, fidgeting with a package of vacuum-packed sliced chorizo. I proposed to her that we "take a cup" after she got off work. Kylie had written the phrase down in Spanish, but I tried to make it sound Catalan by lopping off the last vowel.

"*¿Cómo*?" she said. I got the feeling she understood, but was hoping she had not. So I simply read the question in Spanish, like some dim third grader reading his book report to the class.

She blushed, this time clearly astonished. "*No, no. No puedo,*" she said, sliding a purple organ into a pile of gizzards. She had a "mountain" of things to do, she said. She had shifted into slow, precise Spanish to ensure that I understood.

Catalans don't meet people this way, I thought. Of course, I had no idea how Catalan people met each other. For all I knew, the butcher and patron could be the prototype of Catalan romance. "*Yes, he used to come in everyday," she reflects with relaxing, attentive relatives during some future holiday. They have heard this story countless times, though always enjoy the telling, as it has become part of the family lore. "Finally I agreed to go out with him, just so he'd stop pestering me." She feigns exasperation. I walk into the room holding a cocktail—no a baby. I am immediately awash in feelings of respect, admiration. I am responsible, committed, one of them. My frank opinions and American can-do attitude are valued by this family. Her brothers confide in me their own amorous travails. The father is forever pulling me aside, warming me with a joke, soliciting advice for his modest but consistently profitable hardware store. I sense that he wishes his own sons were more like me, more capable, more debonair.*

The cleaver thumped down on the counter, separating a chicken from its wing. The DIA girl had emphatically resumed her duties. My cart with two bastard wheels lurched and jerked as I pushed it away from the meat counter and toward the freezer. I selected three pizzas and five-hundred grams of breaded squid rings. I thought about another lonely meal, as I piled them onto my usual staples—potato chips, cartons of wine, and a dozen loose cans of DIABRÄU.

Pizza con Chorizo

Preheat the oven to four hundred degrees Fahrenheit, or whatever that is in Celsius. Of course, if your Spanish oven is

> like mine, it will simply have an on/off switch. Carefully unwrap your DIA frozen pizza. Top pizza with DIA olives, DIA chorizo and DIA oregano before placing on the oven rack. Begin reading the lifestyle section of the USA TODAY INTERNATIONAL EDITION. When you have reaffirmed that you will never, under any circumstances, move back to that stupid country, your pizza will be ready. Serve with DIA lemon soda and DIA gin.

For me, the most unexpected difficulty of living in Barcelona was the Catalan's insistence on speaking Catalan. At first, I imagined that Catalan was just a dialect of Spanish, but as my ear developed, I became aware of the language's sheer power—its ubiquity, its difference. The city itself spoke Catalan, not Spanish. The swarming geometry of the streets and buildings whispered messages that overlapped and interfered with one another. Only the announcements on the metro reached me uncorrupted: "*Correspondencia amb linea cinc*," a woman said. This recorded voice echoed in my head at night, as I tried to fall asleep in the summer heat, wiggling my limbs on a foam mattress.

Catalan justified my inability to learn Spanish, which was one of the reasons that I told everyone I was going to Spain. It didn't help that I only hung out with other English speakers—all my fellow teachers. It seemed like we spent all of our free time tilting beers in one of Barcelona's Irish bars. In my apartment I hardly spoke to Paz at all, and when I did I used a lot of hand gestures. Enrique never spoke to me in Spanish because he spoke excellent English. He was studying anthropology, but seemed to have only tenuous ties to the University of Barcelona. A professor there was helping him shape his dissertation about the socio-economic impact of Latin American expatriates on the Iberian Peninsula. But I only saw him reading novels and pornographic comic books.

Still, there were plenty of opportunities to speak Spanish. Paz herself could only mutter a few words in English. From Andalucía, she didn't speak Catalan either. She stayed home, alone and foreign as anyone from overseas, and basically lobbed me conversation starters in Spanish: *this summer is hotter than last summer; Sevilla is more beautiful than Barcelona because it has more churches; Enrique likes tortilla de patatas—do you like tortilla de patatas?* I just nodded or shrugged, or just ignored her completely and watched television.

Kylie, on the other hand, talked incessantly with Montse, her drunken landlady. Soon after we met, I stopped by her apartment on the way to the office. Kylie and Monste were standing in the cavernous kitchen, Kylie holding a fistful of silverware, Montse a tumbler of gin. "I have a spoon and I carry it to the room," Kylie stammered in Spanish. "No, a knife. I carry a knife. Because I have to cut a piece of fruit. Not an apple, but like an apple. Green. Like a woman."

"*Pera*," said Montse, glassy-eyed and wearing pajamas. She nodded patiently, pleased to provide a word to end a sentence. She'd like to do this all the time, I thought. And with Kylie, she practically did. Kylie told me that she literally planned lessons for herself, and then hunted Montse down. I thought she might be taking advantage of the poor woman, who probably imagined that the conversations were spontaneous, sincere and practical. On the other hand, maybe Montse knew Kylie's design and didn't care, was simply happy to have the company.

"*Montse, quiero un vidrio*," Kylie said. I could hear her Australian accent through the clumsy Spanish sentence.

Monste shuffled to a kitchen chair, moaned—she was only around fifty—and sat down with an exaggerated exhale. She grinned mischievously at Kylie, lifted her tumbler and rattled the ice cubes. "*Este es un vaso, la ventana de vidrio*."

In my own quiet way, I envied Kylie. She had a plan. She could wake in the morning and say to herself, this is the day of kitchen nouns.

"We gotta get going," I said to Kylie in English, "or I'll be late for my class." I tried for some reason to make my words difficult to comprehend, even though Montse couldn't understand a word of English.

Kylie went into her bedroom to collect her things. Montse leaned back in her chair and lit a cigarette, a picture of Latin disrepair. She gazed at me, as if to say "You want to try? Go ahead, I know it all: table, chair, closet, broom, gin, smoke, death."

When Kylie came back, looking attractive in pressed black slacks, she handed me half a pear. "Let's *vamos*," she said.

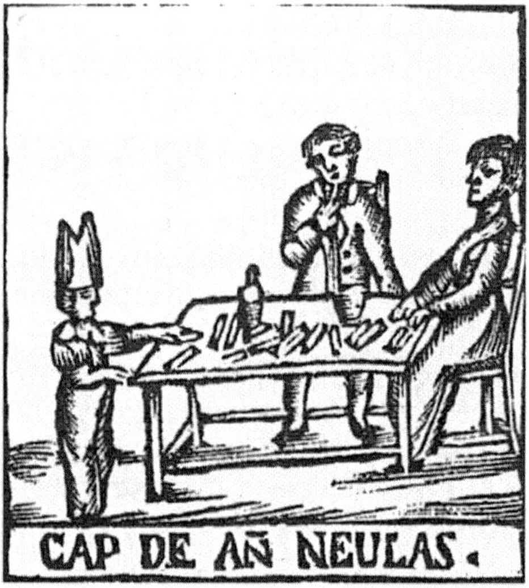

We walked up Rambla Catalunya to the Hello Its English Time School. Clarence and Gordon were already at the copy machine. "So what," Gordon said, "you just leave your garbage piled on the street at night?"

"That's right," Clarence said, seething, "it's the new Ajuntament's sanitation plan, the imbeciles. They come around and collect it in the morning. After all the dogs and addicts and hookers have rummaged through it."

"What happened to the dumpsters?"

"They were sick of people setting them on fire, so they've gotten ridden of them."

"Gotten ridden?" Kylie said as she entered the room.

Clarence looked at her, appalled. "What did you say to me?"

"Gotten ridden? You're an English teacher for fuck's sake. What language is that?"

"There's such a thing as colloquial speech you stuck up bitch."

"Wanker."

Clarence gave her the finger with both hands. Kylie contorted her lips and tongue into an obscene gesture. These were my kind of people. I had learned quickly that the office was a place for complaining, insulting, and the general airing of random and various grievances. Griping about your students seemed to have particular value.

"Today's the big day," I announced.

"What do you mean, big day?" Gordon said.

"Crunchtime. Paydirt. Rubber match."

"What are you on about?" Kylie asked.

"The battle of the behemoths, no holds barred, steel cage match with no referee."

"Fight? Where?" Clarence asked, all-too-ready to indulge a violent metaphor.

"Guimerá." I said dramatically.

Gordon looked up from his haphazard stacks of copies. "Oh, that geezer at Anderson," he said. "Dmitri called him the Catalan Homer Simpson."

I nodded sagely. "Guimerá and I are pitted in a heroic battle—who can better express through body language their displeasure of the English lesson." Clarence offered a rare smile. Although I had been there only a few weeks, the self-proclaimed most cynical man in Spain had taken a shine to me.

"Guimerá won the last battle by scraping his scalp with his fingernails," I said. It was very involved and drawn out. He really had to dig around." I demonstrated Guimerá's technique. "Then he studied the encrusted booty beneath his fingernails and some of it flaked off, right onto his chart of irregular verbs."

"What did you do?" Gordon asked.

"What could I do? It was sophisticated. He totally disarmed me. I conceded on the spot."

The day had become quite warm. I stood beneath the washed-out sycamore trees on Diagonal, waiting for the number seven bus to take me to Guimerá's office. My chest and back began to perspire, and I could smell the sweet pungency of last night's beer seeping out of my pores. When the bus finally arrived,

I took one look at the distressed, sweaty driver, and knew the air conditioning was broken. Some people shuffled on, others peered down the street to see if another bus was on the way. My lesson with Guimerá started in exactly ten minutes, and I was far too cheap to take a cab, so I got on board.

For some reason, all of the windows on the bus were sealed, and no one tried to open them, so the bus was like a casserole dish. By the time I stepped off at Plaça Francesc Maciá, the polyester shirt that I had bought at DIA was soaked with smelly sweat. I was already a few minutes late, and still had to walk two hundred meters to Anderson Consulting. Rushing past the well-groomed executives on their lunch-breaks, my second-hand slacks felt a little tight in the thigh. I calculated in my head that my earnings for this lesson would only come to fifteen dollars—enough to eat one of these fancy lunches, buy a paperback book, or get a haircut.

Ten minutes late, I strode past Guimerá's heart-stopping secretary and into his office. A portly man with jowls like a St. Bernard, Guimerá was sitting motionless at his desk with his hands folded, a picture of contrived patience. I must have looked seriously disheveled, though he merely offered a cursory remark about the heat and humidity. I tried to render the events of the last fifteen minutes into rudimentary English so he could appreciate my situation, and because I had nothing else prepared. Guimerá nodded along, but then glanced at his books arranged neatly on the desk. He looked especially crisp and attentive. It dawned on me for the first time that Guimerá was an important executive whose days were full with significant business. He occupied the corner office on the tenth floor, the city a haze of bright below him.

I improvised the whole class. Guimerá seemed keenly aware of my lack of preparation. I vowed to myself to be ready for the next lesson, but then I remembered that I had made that same vow two days before, squirming in the very same seat. Sweat began to tingle on my back again, like the cold touch of an executioner come to wake me for the guillotine.

About twenty minutes into the lesson Guimerá asked where I had been trained. He had assumed an air of objectivity that made me nervous. "Did you had a special classes to learn teach?"

"I went to school in California," I said. "I went through the TOEFL program at UCLA," a bald-faced lie. "It's one of the top five TOEFL programs in the U.S."

He looked at me coolly, skeptically, as if I had claimed royal ancestry.

I made him read one of the paragraphs for advanced students at the back of the book and corrected every single pronunciation mistake.

CHAPTER 6

Frank Sinatra died. Just a few days before, Gordon and I sat in the Quiet Man and discussed all the where-were-you-when celebrity death moments of recent vintage. Our conversation became a kind of ironic competition, where the winner was the one doing the most inane thing at precisely the time the news reached him. It offered, Gordon believed, a measure of our standing in the society at large. "Moments are like the nucleus of a cell," he said "They contain the genetic plan for the whole organism. Moments are the map of our entire lives. They tell us what sort of creature we shall become."

I won Kurt Cobain handily. I remembered working for minimum wage at the popular fish taco concession stand inside Jack Murphy Stadium. It was hours before game time, and I was draining the deep fat fryer. When the radio DJ announced in hushed tones that "the body of Cobain was discovered by an electrician," I was trying to dislodge chunks of burnt debris from the drainpipe with a wire hanger.

Gordon, on the other hand, was driving his grandmother to a bulk food distributor to buy industrial-size cans of stewed tomatoes. By the simple virtue that his actions involved service to another human, he lost, though he tried to make it close by piling insults onto his grandmother. "It was the silly woman's special Italian sauce," he said. "She always made such a bloody big deal about it. Run to the Sainsbury, clean that pot, chop that onion. But it was horrible sauce. It always had too much oregano or basil. Some magazine put it in her mind that she had to become this traditional grandmother. So she cast herself into this role of the great matriarch and we suddenly had to become her underlings. As if she had this vast mothering experience. It had been better when I was a child—she sat around watching game shows and drinking sherry, nice as pie."

Yitzhak Rabin was a tie. Gordon was shopping for orthopedic insoles (he had a foot condition) at a Sheffield mall, while I was searching my car for a clipped joint that I had misplaced a few weeks before.

Princess Diana was a little controversial, though I gave him the nod as a gesture of national respect. I never had a handle on how British people felt about the Royal Family—wasn't there at least a little irony seeing them prance around in their fancy get-ups? For my part, I reported to Gordon that "I was in the Azteca Cantina, a dumpy little place in the Normal Heights section of San Diego. I liked the bartender, a short Mexican girl, even though she called me 'Ferret' instead of Ferry. I told myself it was an ESL issue, though the way she giggled, I had my doubts. I ate two baskets of fried tortilla chips. I drank several Coronas with limes squished in them. I watched baseball highlights on the television above the bar. Then the bartender got a whiff of the news from one of the waiters, and she stood on a milk crate and changed the channel. 'I can't find the remote control Ferret,' she said. The waiter laughed. She stood with her back turned, her floral print shirt bunched around her waist, full of elastic. I watched her stretch to find the volume knob, and I imagined her reaching toward a kitchen cabinet in *our* home, reaching for a pair of plates on which to serve the two of us a pile of enchiladas. 'Can you watch now?' I imagined the padding of chubby little feet, the sunset on the prairie porch, the American-made tools arranged in the shed. 'Tell me Ferret, can you watch it now?"

"Princess Di has been in a serious car accident in Paris..."

Although her death was not finalized for a few hours, Gordon and I agreed the key moment was when the information first appeared on the radar screen. For him, that moment didn't arrive until days later, an astounding forty-eight hours after Diana was pronounced dead. "I was near Alicante, with a German girl," he said. "We met at the International House, during one of the teacher training seminars. I ended up dropping the course after the third consecutive day of language bingo. At the same time they realized that I wasn't going to be able to pay. So it was more or less a mutual parting. Miriam had stopped by to look for a motorbike on the signboard. Anyway, after suffering through a couple hot weekends in Barcelona together, we decided to go down the coast. It was August. The both of us had been lonely, the way you feel after a few months away from home. We talked a lot about being lonely at first, the way you do. The kind of lonely that you feel walking down a strange street. The way you look up into the windows of the homes and wonder about the people's lives—you know, how they spend their days. Anyway, that's the sort of drivel we said to each other. That's the point of the relationship we were in. She was on about finally finding someone she could talk to. All the German blokes she knew were either too soft or too hard, she said, but she fancied I was in between, which is something I still have mixed feelings about. Kindred spirits let's call us.

"We took a cabin near the beach, no phone, no TV. German birds like that sort of thing—you know, walking around naked all the time. Bottles and bottles of Portuguese wine. Muesli, salads, crisps. It was hot. We saw a few people, but we didn't talk to anyone. On Tuesday, she covered her face with mud and said she wanted to lie in the shade for four hours. We were already reaching a different stage of the relationship, the stage where you can say more or less flat out that you'd prefer not spend time with the other person for a whole day. And everyone knows that it is only a matter of time before that feeling becomes a permanent condition. So I took the bus to the English pub five miles into town. When I got there, they were all watching the telly above the bar, the way they do when there's a match, though it was August and I knew there was no match.

"The first thing I saw on the television was a car. Then it was the flowers. The sound was way up but the broadcasters were mum. Everyone was staring at it like they were in a trance. The bartender was the only one not looking at it. He was pulling the taps, and asked me what I wanted. 'Who fucking died?' I asked him. He looked at me disappointed, like I was trying to be funny but wasn't. A few people saw me out of the corner of their eye. 'Whaddaya drink smart guy?' he said. I asked for a Guinness. I felt a little uneasy. That's the moment for me, Ferry, that breath between knowing and not knowing. Knowing that everyone else knows too, just that you don't know. That's fear, that's what they say depressed people feel like all the time, or alcoholics when they're sober. I couldn't take it, not for two minutes. 'Who fucking died?' I said to him, louder. Everyone at that point turned their dumb faces towards me. "Who fucking died yer asking me?' the bartender said, like he was itching for a fight. 'Yer fuckin' Princess. She fuckin' died and now we're watching her fucking funeral. And if you don't shut up, we'll be watching yers.'

"Watching the cars drive around on the telly was for me the *enactment* of her death. Like they were performing some kind of interpretative dance. I was looking at the limousines that contained her remains when I heard that she died. I felt the slightest bit guilty, that I let someone down, that if I could have kept abreast of all this, it would somehow be different. What it was, was that the world was different and I missed the change. There were a few days that couldn't be recovered. It was like I was part of a primitive tribe and I walked out of the jungle and into Piccadilly Circus. You know that story. One minute I'm happy as a clam eating grubs and sleeping on grass, and then the next thing you know I'm crapping in my trousers over a bad real estate deal.

"Needless to say, I immediately became the center of attention in this stupid bar. They wanted a distraction. I was a kind of celebrity, a folk hero. At first they thought I was putting them on. But you could never carry that kind of lie for very long, so they knew. Blokes came over from the dartboard and just stared at me, didn't say a fucking word, but just stared me, like they were waiting for me to tell them some kind of special information, to explain the magic of what it was like to be living with Diana alive for an extra few days. A girl without saying anything touched a bit of my shirtsleeve. Maybe she thought that by touching me she might get the same kind of charm. There was a charm not knowing about it, having those two extra days, as it were. Diana was remote for me, a distant satellite, but she was there, twinkling. Not knowing about it was a blessing, the people in the bar were right. They stood me pints all day."

As I watched my favorite, sexy newscaster provide details of Frank Sinatra's death, I surveyed my personal scene for its own outstanding details, as it might prove to be the tiebreaker. I was sitting in my underwear eating ham-flavored ruffles, and my fingertips were coated with the ham flavoring. There was a ribbon of smoke hovering above the television and the rattle of a not-too-far-away jackhammer. I thought of calling Gordon, but then considered that if I were the one to tell him about Sinatra, it might disqualify me.

And there was something ironic, after all, about Frank Sinatra dying. What piece of news could matter less? I thought about a poem that I read in high school, "The Day Lady Died." My teacher, Mr. Wisterman, went on and on about how Billie Holiday's death in 1959 had ended an era. His tone and demeanor suggested this was a rather fantastic era, and that we were then living in a terrible one. Then he said it outright: his generation had Billie Holiday, and we had Ozzie Osbourne, Madonna, and Michael Jackson. To most of us these were just product names, meaningless nobodies, forgettable notes of music. But to him, these names meant something different and profound—they represented us, the kids in his high school English class. A thin, single man in his fifties, Mr. Wisterman seemed naturally disposed to melodramatics and sentimentality. His personal dissatisfaction with the political and cultural climate was the foremost theme of the class. I felt a pang joy when my mother told me a few years later that Wisterman had been arrested on Christmas Eve for soliciting a prostitute along the Mile of Cars in National City.

I changed the channel. There was a special report on the Balkan conflict, in which the footage of recently unearthed mass graves in Bosnia was particularly gruesome. I called Kylie.

"I'm watching some blue helmets poke around a mass grave in Bosnia," I told her.

"They knew they were there the whole time," she said dismissively.

"Probably."

"Too bad they're not showing what's happening in Jakarta."

"What's happening in Jakarta?"

"Riots, chaos, hundreds killed."

"Where is Jakarta?"

Exaggerated exhale. "See that's the problem," she said, as if to someone else.

I paused. "Sinatra died," I said meekly.

"Oh for fuck's sake, Frank Sinatra. Never mind Bosnia. Never mind Jakarta."

"He was the Elvis before Elvis."

"He was Boney M. before Boney M."

"Who the hell is Boney M?"

"More a what. Ask any European in their twenties or thirties about Boney M. Boney M was major. Just because you don't know about something doesn't mean it doesn't exist."

"But if I don't know about someone, I can't be expected to appreciate them. Boney M? Give me a break."

"You're responsible for your own ignorance. And if you're going to be ignorant, then you shouldn't vote or pay taxes."

"Well I don't do either of those things."

"That's fine. But you might, things change. People grow up. You can't sit around in your underwear all the time, watching broadcasts you don't understand and eating crisps."

"How'd you know what I was eating?"

"You crunch right into the phone. It sounds like a building collapsing for fuck's sake."

"My underwear?"

"Men always do that. A lucky guess."

"Do you want to come over?"

"No, not really."

Squid Rings con Chorizo

> Fool with knobs on oven until oven is hot. Put DIA squid rings on one of Paz's greasy baking sheets. Stare off balcony and eat DIA chorizo; when you have finished the package of chorizo, the DIA squid rings will probably not be cooked thoroughly, so you'll have to find some other way to entertain yourself. Warning: do not eat DIA squid rings from the oven if they are still partially frozen; this will induce severe vomiting. Serve with chilled or unchilled DIABRÄU.

CHAPTER 7

Bar Kentucky was an after-hours lounge in the Raval, just a few blocks from the municipal clinic. The Quiet Man had closed, and my friends had left long before anyway. I found Bar Kentucky as I was walking home, staring up at the stone geometry of the apartment buildings. I stumbled into the bar, bouncing off both sides of the doorway, as if I was falling, as if someone was shaking me down into a hole at the bottom of the world. I looked around Bar Kentucky and saw a place that I could one day reflect on as the lowest point of my existence.

It was almost 5 AM and an unbroken wall of human backs still lined the bar. In a dim corner near the toilets, a girl was hovering around a small man quietly playing the clarinet. He blew no distinguishable tune, but a rhythmic hum found the niches in the bass music that was thumping from the boom box behind the bar. As I approached, the girl had her eyes closed and rolled her head and shoulders back and forth in an attempt to synchronize herself with the clarinet sounds. On one particularly shrill note, her breast bounced out and then back into her low-cut blouse. I drifted closer. The distorted notes from the clarinet were ascending to another crescendo, and as it broke down completely, the girl went spastic. She more or less threw some kind of red beverage that she had been holding onto my shirt.

"Ooh, I'm sorry," she said, "I put my drink on you." Only later did I consider that she probably did that on purpose, that she was too drunk to just gush at me in English.

"It's OK, don't worry about it," I said. She began pawing at my wet shirt with a cocktail napkin.

"Oh, I'm sorry," she persisted, "so sorry. I put water on your shirt to clean."

"No, don't worry, really. But I'm afraid you lost your drink."

"What?" She turned her head to the side so her pink ear was directly in front of my mouth.

"I said you need a drink."

"No, isss OK. I buy you a drink, please," she pleaded.

The clarinet player continued blowing, aloof to us. He was at least seventy. Where was his family? Where were his grandkids?

She grabbed my hand and pulled me to the bar and asked me what I wanted. "A beer," I said. I got the feeling that he knew this girl, but they didn't speak to each other.

"What you do in Bar Kentucky?" she asked.

"Drink," I said, and tilted the Damms into my face.

"You are American?"

"How'd you know?"

"You have the sad soft face of all American men. I was in America one time. Texas. The long star state."

"What were you doing in Texas?"

"I went to Dallas to study English. A very big school—The College of English Speaking."

I thought about the Dallas I had seen from the Greyhound Bus window: the twisting freeway ramps, the desolate sidewalks, the dust and glass. "How was it?"

She was peering over her new red drink in the thin cylindrical glass. She shook her head in disapproval. "It was terrible. Everything is money and what looks good," she said nervously waving her left hand. "I returned unhappy with my breast."

"Your breast is just fine. But I know what you mean—everyone stays cooped up in their cars," I said. "But there are some nice places too. Like where I live. San Diego. It's nice." Whenever I talked to a foreigner, my speech became stunted, my attitude apologetic.

"I would like to sometime visit San Francisco. I hear it is the most beautiful city in America. That is why the gays enjoy it."

I lit cigarettes for us. I noticed two characters sitting at the bar, one holding a cat and the other lighting a joint. This is one of the rooms, I thought, where I could hide if things didn't quite work out. This defeat will always be waiting for me, I imagined. Here were the details of my consolation: black-light beer posters, tinny rock music squeaking from blown-out speakers, and the smell of wine and puke.

"Why do you come for Barcelona?" she asked.

"I'm a teacher," I said in a cavalier tone. "I have students all over the city." I gestured towards the heavy, pockmarked door of Bar Kentucky.

"Maybe you will be my teacher?"

She leaned over, touched her fingertips to my neck, and kissed me on the cheek. I thrust my head forward and kissed her on the lips, a little too hard. She veered back, surprised. She looked at me and seemed to calculate something in which my desperation was one of the variables. We stayed for another fifteen minutes and then walked through the garbage scattered on Carrer de Ferran to my apartment.

I woke up around noon with my head lying just in front of her legs. Her white thighs were covered in tiny moles and thin blue veins. It reminded me of a road map of the United States: her top thigh Nebraska, the bottom one Kansas. I thought about my trip to my father's funeral, those long days on the Greyhound Buses—the grumbling diesels, the pancake houses at 1 AM, the forty year-old cowboys calling their mothers from pay phones.

The girl woke up suddenly and immediately began pulling on her pants, socks and shoes. She said some things in Catalan. I could hardly understand a word, but I believe it was a kind of blanket apology about drinking so much, though it seemed directed more to herself than to me. She turned away from me to fasten her bra.

The night before she was so relaxed, as she stroked my arms and stomach. She said that I had a nice skin—a nice skin, as if it was a singular, individual thing, which I suppose was more-or-less correct. But "a nice skin" still indicated the inappropriate use of the indefinite article—a usage problem not uncommon for ESL students. I thought it was funny, that when I taught, I was preoccupied with sex, and the first time in months that I had sex, I thought about teaching.

She sat on the edge of the lumpy couch and politely waited for me to make coffee, though I could tell that she just wanted to leave. The only clean thing I could find to heat the milk was a large frying pan, and even that was a little greasy. My only wish was that neither Paz nor Enrique would tumble from one of the rooms in their underwear, their pale and pimply bodies wrapped in dirty sheets.

We sipped coffee, uncomfortably rehashing the insipid dialogue from the night before. All of her gestures and words implied that I was keeping her, that I had somehow tricked her. I was wearing jeans that pinched and a t-shirt that was a size too small—not my most flattering outfit. As she stood up, I expressed my resolve to call her, though that hardly put her at ease. She scribbled her number on a matchbook and left it on the table, next to a saucer full of crushed butts.

The sun crept over the top of the neighboring building and began to light up the dingy apartment walls, the nicotine-yellowed curtains. A moped whined on a nearby street. I looked out the window and waited to catch my final glimpse of her, walking down Portal Nou.

EL ANGEL GRANADAS.

Paz called Enrique her little *Duende*. *Duende* I learned was a kind of demon that wasn't evil, and so it never really fit Enrique. It was just her way of glossing over all of his deliberate shortcomings—his overnight absences, his delinquency with the rent, the piles of laundry he left next to the washing machine.

I walked in from one of my lessons and found Enrique watching a soccer game.

"Soccer is the most boring sport imaginable." I said.

"Oh, that's brilliant. Your analysis is scintillating me."

"They just kick the ball back and forth. No one scores for Christ's sake."

"You have no original ideas Ferry. Everything you say has been said before. You are the weak intellect that makes the world so dangerous and poor."

"What's with offside? If they let the guys go offside, then you'd have something."

"Then you'd have someone standing in front of the goal for the whole game. You'd have two or three guys there. The whole field would be wasted. You're an idiot."

"Offside is OK, but you can't go into the goalie's little area."

"Stick to basketball. That is a sport with plenty of sweetness for you."

"At least they score."

"And 99% of that scoring is without meaning. A foul shot in the second quarter is nothing more than a numerical abstraction."

"But you can't beat a tight game decided by a buzzer-beater."

"Yes you can, it's silliness. They should eliminate the game clock in that sport. Play each game to one hundred. No more buzzer beaters, no more circus shots,"

"Then everyone would just dribble around and wait for the perfect shot."

"Not the shot clock, but the game clock. Listen to what people say."

"That's street ball. It would never fly."

"There would be, or course, tremendous resistance from the corporations. But think of it. Game winning shots every night. No intentional fouling."

"How do you know so much about basketball?"

"Argentina has an excellent basketball league. But your government doesn't want you to know that. You are like the perfect citizen for your country. And if you are smart enough to at least leave for a little while, I can only imagine what kind of people are left behind. It frightens me."

CHAPTER 8

The long-term strategy of surviving in Barcelona required finding *alumnos privados.* A teacher could earn two or even three times what a school paid, while the student would still only pay half. The best part, from the teacher's standpoint, was that these lessons were always more casual, and there was less pressure, less expectation.

My first private student was Marta. A Catalan divorcee pushing fifty, she owned an elegant boutique in the upscale neighborhood of Sarria. I had to take the *Ferrocarrils* from Plaça Catalunya. Her apartment was also in Sarria, near a little cemetery. She lived there with Javi, her grown son who had posted the notice for her at the University. I suspected that Javi's father had been from Madrid or South America, because Javi spoke to his mother in Spanish and not Catalan, though I know both spoke that language fluently. The two lived almost like husband and wife, with Marta serving her petulant son. "Mama" he would interrupt our session in the clean, lightly-used office, "you know I am going with Eva to the coast. I need those shirts washed, Mama!"

Marta was attractive and high strung, with an air of inconsolable sadness. I mentioned this observation to my friends one night, and Gordon said all Catalan women were like that, and it was because all of their husbands were unfaithful—all of them, he said, without exception. Kylie suggested that there might be some truth to that, but those women had the chance to leave their husbands, and a lot of them did. "What they're suffering from now is their unlimited freedom. They have no idea how to be fifty and single. It's not in their cultural hardwiring. So it's a burden. They were raised under Franco, the ultimate patriarch. It's going to take a generation for Spanish girls to bloom. The ones who are twenty now, those are the girls that are breaking the mold, those are the ones to keep an eye on, though not in the perv way that you're thinking."

I rang the intercom of Marta's apartment building. Javi answered and told me that his mother was at the doctor, getting her collagen injections. There was something of the exhibitionist in

Javi. He loved being so candid with me, especially in his English, which he spoke very well. I suspected that he may have considered me a rival for his mother's affection, though it was probably unconscious and was, in any case, obscure. It bothered me nevertheless because I in fact had a deep and wild attraction for his mother. Giving Marta a lesson while she sat on my lap was my most enduring fantasy of that time.

Yet I was not too disappointed by her cancellation because I had established with her that she must pay for the scheduled time unless I was given twenty-four hours notice. Still, she was home only about half the time. I think she retained me as if I were a language accessory or consultant rather than a teacher. As a way to recoup some of these losses, she would often call me from her boutique and ask me to explain for a British or American customer her instructions to avoid paying duty on a 45,000-peseta lamp. One time she called me giggly (and not alone) at midnight to ask the full implication of the phrase "lady of the night."

I went into La Granja bar around the corner from Marta's flat. Empty sugar packets, crumpled napkins and squished cigarette butts littered the terrazzo floor. A television leered down from its high, corner mount. The bartender was wiping the inside of beer glasses with usual deliberation. "*¿Cómo estamos tío*?" He said.

"*Bien. Cerveza. Damms.*" There were a few other patrons, all men. Here were the married men that Gordon was telling me about, the men who had all the affairs. Not possible, I thought. They were drunk and morose, paunchy and quarrelsome with each other. Probably they had eaten and drank their way to the point where they had no choice but to be faithful. They traded the mistresses for glasses of sherry, the afternoon liaisons for little plates of little fish in puddles of oil.

Instead of taking the *Ferrocarrils*, I decided to walk to the green line, and spend the hundred pesetas I saved on another drink. I ended up spending that hundred pesetas a dozen times, drinking a beer at every bar that I passed, all of them more or less identical. The same TV was perched near the ceiling, the same dopey men shuffling around with their shirts tucked in, the same sides of ham hanging around like trophies.

I walked up Passeig de la Bonanova, passed the grounds of an old asylum—whole buildings were abandoned, the windows broken. The main building was bright and glowing from within, while a couple of other surrounding structures were closed, garishly-lit on the outside. My final memory of that night is shuffling past the closing gates of the Penitents metro station, hoping to catch the last train down to the Ramblas.

I dreamt of Marta that night. We were in her boutique, after closing. She asked me questions as she rummaged through a pile of English workbooks on her desk. "I'll explain irregular participles," I said, "for a kiss." She listed some phrases in Spanish: "*La Mesa, La Jolla, El Cajon*. Ferry, what do they mean in English?" I patted her buttocks, she pouted and sulked. If only the world were so easy for me, for Marta. Her questions kept coming. "In English," I told her, "it only means *I want*."

I awoke to the sound of trickling fluid, and the pungent smell of raw sewage. In a second I knew where I was, laying on the ground in the Raval, but I didn't move right away. I watched the people's legs march past. There was a girl in tight black slacks, another in dirty jeans, and a tourist in shorts, white socks, and sandals. I saw the blue noon of the sky twisting around the brown buildings, like a river rushing to the sea. Pigeons fluttered across the space—first two, then three, and I wondered if they were friends or relatives, and if they were happy to be flying to the beach, or to the top of Montjuic.

I stood up, brushed myself off as if I had merely fallen, and walked to the Ramblas. The sun had already climbed to the top of the Columbus statue and was warming the pale leaves of the plane trees. There were only a handful of tourists on the Ramblas, though in a few hours they would cover every inch of it. These were like scout ants on the carcass of a fallen bird.

I bought a pack of cigarettes from a short man at the Liceu Metro entrance. The package read Marlboro, but I knew they were contraband. They tasted harsh and burned so quickly that they were only good for a couple of drags. I leaned on the metro railing next to him.

"You like selling cigarettes?" I asked, finishing my smoke.

"*Más o menos*," he replied in a heavy, likely Pakistani, accent. And he was, when I took a long look at him, astoundingly small—maybe under four feet tall. He glanced over his shoulder and nodded furtively. It occurred to me that I was acting like a fool, that I might have crossed a boundary, standing there disheveled and asking questions. I was trying to be normal, to get my bearings. Clarence had once lectured me on the Spanish Mafia, how they had cornered both the petty trades and real estate market in Barcelona. I glimpsed two shadowy, masculine movements from across the street. I looked back at the little peddler but he had vanished. I would have believed he had been just an apparition, but empty cartons of cigarettes were lying on the cobbled pavement.

I quickly went down the stairs of the metro, which were strewn with wisps of newspaper and hundreds of crushed cigarette butts. To my horror, two men in expensive business suits descended from the opposite stairway and walked toward me on the platform. It was too late to go back up, so I decided to play it cool. I sat across from a mobile phone advertisement, the idiotic face of a balding, effeminate man in mock surprise.

The train wooshed into the station, and I boarded like everyone else. But the second before the doors shut, I jumped out and ran up the stairs without looking back. At the top, the little vendor was kneeling down and positioning pastel lighters on a small piece of cardboard.

That night I saw Gordon at Flann O'Brien's. "Catholic and alcoholic are very nearly anagrams," he said.

CHAPTER 9

I woke up a few days later and could tell by the quiet and the stillness around me that no one else was in the apartment. I had a headache—the likes of which I had only felt once before, when I had seawater trapped in my ear and it became infected. Although I wasn't a morning drinker, I had it in my mind that a drink did the trick for a thick hangover.

I scanned the fridge. I pushed around the pots and pans in the cabinets, lifted the blue cloth that hung down over some shelves, where Paz kept cans of tomatoes and jars full of rice. No booze, not even a lousy bottle of beer. I opened the fridge again and rooted around with a little more urgency. The bottom drawers were empty save for some lettuce that looked more like boiled cabbage. There was a drying peach that looked like a pygmy skull, a tomato with bright mold on one side.

But then, among the bottles of ketchup and oil, I spotted an old thin bottle of cooking sherry. It had about two fingers in the bottom. When I wiggled it, debris agitated on the surface like a derelict navy retreating from a terrible battle. I never considered putting it back. I drank it straight from the bottle. The taste was not altogether bad, I thought, something like cough syrup mixed with bacon grease. What struck me was the thickness; it clung to my teeth and coated my tongue. Still, I didn't bring it away from my lips until it was empty. I then ran some tap water into its neck, swished it around, and drank that too.

Only then, with the warm electricity of the sherry pulsing inside, did my day truly take shape. I smoked the nub of cigarette that I found on Enrique's windowsill. I shaved—my month-old razor felt like a hot coal raking across my face. I smoked a half of a cigarette that I found behind the toaster.

The rest of the day was less certain. I wanted to go to some bars—I knew that without thinking it. Seven or eight beers and I could map out the afternoon, though that would require some real money. I searched every pocket of every pair of pants in the house, but only came up with forty-five pesetas—not much, but on the way to a one-hundred peseta carton of DIA wine. I loved Spain if only because I could arrange some drinks without any folding money. American coins were only good for soda machines and gas station vacuum cleaners.

I looked under Paz's couch cushions, but only found a couple of *duros*, five-peseta pieces, and some cigarette butts. The tingle in my head was still there at that point, but fading. There was a promising inch gap between the backrest and seat, but I couldn't fit my hand in there. I tilted the couch on its side and heard the jingle of coins tumbling to the bottom. With just a small slit in the thin fabric along the base, I was able to reach my hand into the guts of the couch and pull out a handful of coins, like a prairie surgeon extracting bullets from the wounded sheriff. *Hold on Jimmy, we got one more slug near the kidney. Quarter inch to either side and you'd be dead. They say Lonesome Lenny was a hair quick, say he had his fingers on the trigger before the call. Reckon he'll go back to his people in San Antonio. Reckon we've seen the last of him and that he won't be long finding his bad end.*

The barkeep brought me the second beer. I sat at the crappy bar in the Santa Caterina Market and sorted out my little pile of lint and money. There were four hundred-peseta coins. Each one so heavy that I thought it might in fact be worth its weight in whatever metal it was cast from. It made a pleasant snap on the stainless steel bar, like the doctor's qualified slap on the newborn's behind. The severed head of King Juan Carlos was suspended on its face, the levelheaded witness to all my indiscretions.

There was a single five-hundred peseta piece, a coin that always made me a little anxious. It was too much money condensed in one coin, too much of a chance that it would tumble out of my pocket, as it probably had done to end up in the couch's entrails.

There was also a two-hundred peseta piece, my secret favorite. It was roughly the same size as the hundred-peseta coin, but packed double the value. It was silver and etched with "Masters of Spanish Art." I liked it because there was something earnest but hopeless about it. As if it was trying to hard to be liked, begging to be taken seriously—not like the gimmicky two-dollar bill back home.

I also had a bunch of single peseta coins and a half dozen Spanish quarters with the hole in the middle—all that extra metal earmarked for some national adventure.

Finally, there were ten or eleven *duros*—the Spanish nickel. I imagined they were called "hard ones" because back in the day, when everything was harder (but better) these little numbers could really get a man somewhere. A drink, at least. Life was probably measured out in hard, five-peseta segments. *A* duro *for a good strong beer after a sixteen hour workday in the mill; a* duro *for a train ticket to the mountain home to bury a friend crushed in an avalanche; a* duro *for an hour with the town's sturdiest whore.*

Now the money gushed every which way, extravagance devoid of meaning. Thousands of zeros, gallons of beer, a lifetime of sex on a single subway car, and a *duro* nothing but a little piece of plankton floating in the vast ocean.

I paid for my beers almost entirely in *duros* and one-peseta pieces, a nod to my forefathers who endured their hard and endless days.

I walked up to the Ramblas, and was surprised to find Clarence sitting at a card table. He was next to an Indian guy who was painting people's names on a grain of rice for a hundred pesetas. Clarence also had a sign, in English only:

Your name on a potato: 100 pesetas.

No one was buying his potatoes, so he was just writing profanity on them in a black magic marker: dickweed, fuckface, asswagon.

"What's 'asswagon' mean?" I asked. Without speaking, he picked up a potato and scribbled on it. He handed it to me: "rotten sot," it said.

"You or me?" He took it back and added an "s."

"I'm going to a bar," I said. He just looked at me sternly, adhering to some new vow of silence that accompanied his potato stunt. I picked up one of his potatoes and wrote BAR on it; on the other side it already said "pussy." Clarence stood up and kicked over the little box that he had been using as a table. The potatoes bounced and skipped on the brick pavement. A woman who was waiting for her rice grain pulled her little boy into the folds of her skirt. "*vés amb compte, fill, vés amb compte*." Careful, son careful.

"So why do we hate Catalans?" I asked Clarence at the bar.

"We hate them because they are everything we left behind, everything we tried to get away from back home." The floor of this particular café, over by the San Anton Market, was littered with cigarette butts and napkins and empty sugar packets. "Their self-satisfaction," he said, "their contentment, their severe domestication. Let me tell you something: any expat who tries to crack his way into Catalan society has basically wasted five years of his life. He may as well have stayed home and integrated. You and me—we're here because we don't want to integrate. You think I want to go have dinner with some Catalans and hear their stupid ideas about current events?"

"Well that sort of domestic bliss is basically the point of this whole society, far as I can tell."

"How many Catalans does it take to screw in a light bulb?"

"Fifty, I don't know."

"I think it's zero. Or maybe one, but he doesn't do it. The point is, is that they're trying to save electricity. Save money is what I mean."

"Yeah, that's funny. So why not just fuck off to some place really far out, like Ethiopia or Sri Lanka?"

"You think I've ruled that out?"

I imagined living somewhere in the desert or the jungle, thousands of miles from any city, a place where people die before their fortieth birthday, where they etch tribal customs onto their skin with ink made from indigenous plants and urine.

A San Diegan says: "power lunch," and I say: "inedible gruel."

A San Diegan says: "homeopathic," and I say: "the healing of fire."

A San Diegan says: "lease to own," and I say: "pillage."

The travel editor of the San Diego Union Tribune interviews me in my adobe hut: *Yes, yes, I have become quite renowned in this nation for my keen ability to procure animal skins from the hostile tribes of nomadic bow hunters. I sometimes bludgeon the animals myself, sometimes I let their guts slop onto the tops of my feet, out here in the jungle or the desert or the steppes, far from home, far from all concern.*

CHAPTER 10

On Saturday mornings, I had my only other *alumno privado*. Marta recommended me to Jordi, a friend of her son's. Twenty-one with a receding hairline, Jordi lived with his parents, who paid for his lessons. Right from the beginning, Mr. and Mrs. Puig suspected—with excellent reason—that their son was not receiving professional instruction. This pressure no longer made me feel nervous, like it did when I started with him. I had come to know a lot of English teachers, and was sure that another one would not only be an irresponsible lush just like me, but might in fact be mean or dangerous. Or some lollipop would arrive at the lesson ten minutes early and bore poor Jordi to the brink of his own alcoholic collapse. At least Jordi and I had a personal rapport. I let Jordi describe in faltering English about the rising and falling performances of the Barcelona football team, in which I had begun to feign an interest (some teachers, I knew for a fact, used their class time to bone up on their Spanish or Catalan). Jordi sometimes asked me about political matters, like the Clinton-Lewinsky scandal. I'm pretty sure that he thought we were transcending the lesson and having an intelligent discussion about things American, which could only be properly discussed in English. The truth was that there was nothing to transcend, because I had nothing prepared, had no pedagogy to employ, and was utterly unfamiliar with the contents of the stodgy language books that Jordi had left over from high school.

I walked out of the Llacuna metro station already fifteen minutes late for Jordi's lesson. I hurried down Carrer de Badajoz to Avinguda d'Icària, through the old industrial sector of Barcelona. I passed a wedding at a corner church just in time to see a large but glamorous bride duck into a Seat coupe. To witness this ceremony next to all the desolate factories, the seemingly vacant apartment buildings, stirred within me a certain melancholy. I had quick beer at a bar next to a print shop. This neighborhood always struck me as apocalyptic, what all of Barcelona would look like after a nuclear detonation—sparse traffic, pedestrians with shopping bags scurrying from shop to car to doorway, leaves and paper garbage blowing in swirls. For some reason, I felt a longing for this future time, as if it would hold some special promise for me. As if finally I would know what to do with myself.

The Puig family lived in one of the recently-built apartments that housed Olympic athletes in 1992. Jordi told me that they purchased the flat while it was still occupied by the South Korean Women's swim team. Mr. Puig buzzed me in and was waiting for me in the doorway. "*Bon dia*," he said grimly and looked at his watch.

"*Bon dia*," I replied, as if confirming a password.

"Ferry, how are you?" Jordi said from the dining room.

"Hello, Jordi. How are you? It's nice to see you. Sorry I'm a little late, but I had to wait for the metro. For some reason I always just miss the one that would get me here on time." I had learned that a flurry of English could wield a bit of magic on Mr. Puig. It not only drove him away, but also reiterated my qualifications. Despite the fact that I was American, I knew that my facility in English impressed Jordi's father. For him, and other Catalans, there was something supernatural about English. It was a language impossible to master—most language books said as much—and yet I had mastered it. "Man oh fucking man, it's hot as a motherfucking crack pipe out there!" I once said to Mr. Puig. Puzzled and disarmed, he shrugged: *the kid's got it, what can you say?*

I liked Jordi. He was so chubby, so domesticated. His parents adored him. I could never imagine being anything other than pleasant to him. But Jordi was going to become an exact replica of his father, I knew it for certain. That's the way life shaped up, I was learning, and besides, Jordi told me outright that he idolized his father. I also knew that I would not be like my own father, that at twenty seven I was already not like my father. At my age he already had his dishonorable discharge from the Navy, Tyrone and I toddling at home. I remembered him from a photograph, standing around drinking with similar-looking men, each one tilting a different way. My father smiled back at me, the impending separation, the years of drifting, the eventual alcoholic oblivion—all darkened the edges of the picture.

I told Jordi about the wedding at the little church. "It was weird," I said, "I don't know why, but it made me think more about a funeral than a wedding."

"Yes of course. This is the church when I marry," he said.

"You're getting married?"

"Yes of course. Everyone must marry. When I finish at University. You know, Eva."

"But you're not finished for at least another three years."

"Yes of course. Maybe we wait, after, for my job. Don't you want to marry? Don't you want to family?"

"I don't know, yeah, I guess I want to marry. But you just seem young. And to put it off for years, it seems strange to me."

"But Eva and me are together for five years. It is—would be?"

"Yes, would be."

"It would be strange not to marry Eva. It would be strange to begin a new girl."

I bought a *pollo a'last* from a shop that only sold *pollo a'last* and only on Sundays, between 11 and 3, though frequently all the broiled chicken was gone by 2:30.

Paz and Enrique were in her bedroom with the door closed. I sat down to eat with an old *El Mundo*, the paper that Enrique read religiously. ETA detonated a car bomb, I discerned, but was not able to understand the details in depth because I lacked the necessary vocabulary. A clerk had been killed, that much was certain. He had a wife and child, who may have been quite young. The government issued a statement full of sophisticated verbs that I didn't feel like searching for in the dictionary. I knew that I'd have another chance the next day, or the one after that, as this story would drag on, and be replaced soon enough by another bomb, another statement, and another tedious aftermath.

I heard what was probably a lamp fall over in the bedroom. My life too, had a way of repeating itself. In San Diego I shared a house with several people, including a girl from Ireland who had a lot of boyfriend visitors. From my bedroom I used to hear work boots hit the floor, the bedsprings squeal. I encountered her lovers in the hall, in the kitchen, in the driveway. They made small talk and joked around with me. One fellow even affected an Irish accent, said to me: "Top o' tha mornin' to ya, Ferry. A pint of plain is yer only man."

Not that Lydia, the Irish girl, had anything in common with Paz. Probably pushing forty-five, Paz shuffled around in a constant gloom over a life that clearly had not unfolded according to plan. She tried to defy this by hamming her Andalusian role: her soft c's and z's, her traditional gazpacho, her unrelenting sloth. She knew Flamenco, watched bullfighting on TV, and kept *The Collected Poems* of Frederico García Lorca handy on the bright tile-top table in the living room. The only Andalusian trait she lacked—and this was conspicuously lacking—was *La Familia*. Enrique told me there had been a violent husband. Paz herself spoke of "el accidente terrible," but would never elaborate. I occasionally found her alone in the kitchen, weepy and eating sweets. "Ferry," she said to me in Spanish, peeling the paper skin off a *magdalena*, "I too am away from my country. I always miss Sevilla." An Andalusian in Catalunya was no doubt a foreigner, and she was perhaps the most pathetic of us all.

Paz came into the kitchen wearing her green and white Betis jersey that hung down to her knees. "*Hola* Ferry," she whispered.

"*¿Qué tal*?" Her liaisons with Enrique always brightened her spirits, though they would plummet when he made appointments on the telephone with other girls. "No lessons today?"

"No," I lied, surprised that I could understand her at all.

"That's lucky," she said absently and moved toward the refrigerator. "I'm just going to have a little something to eat." She arranged a wheel of cheese, a loaf of bread, a package of salami, and a carton of wine between her left arm and breast. "Do you have any cigarettes?" she asked. I put four in her free hand. "*Cariño*," she said, and waddled away.

Legumes con Chorizo

> Open can of DIA beans with black blood sausage, add entire package of DIA sliced chorizo and cook in a medium saucepan. Eat DIA tostadas topped with DIA margarine until the sauce smokes and splatters. Serve with entire carton of DIA red wine, the one with the horse-drawn carriage on it.

I sometimes imagined an indefinite sojourn to an institution—not necessarily a prison, but maybe a minimum security mental ward, a kind of state-sponsored retirement. Robes and slippers, set meal times and evening gin rummy; solid, unflappable authority and peace, at last. My life would be governed by a qualified professional. She would schedule sensible activities to stimulate my motor skills. TV would become the voice of sanity that it longs to be, mounted on the ceiling with a shatter-resistant screen. No longer would I wake up and say, "what now?"

CHAPTER 11

All of the cooking and heating fuel in Barcelona was transported by hand. Men in orange coveralls, the *butaneros,* walked down the alleys and streets, banging their fifty-liter tanks with wrenches, waiting for someone to yell for one from a window. I always wondered if the smack of the wrench on the big orange tank ever caused an explosion. Enrique said if the metal was thin enough to spark on the other side of impact, then it never would have been able to absorb the filling pressure. "The metal must be made thin by some unnatural process," he said. "But I am sure they never check for this. The *butaneros* are what you might call expendable assets." Enrique's sole responsibility in the apartment was to keep the *butano* stocked. He'd call down to a *butanero*, who would then have to haul the heavy tanks up the four flights of stairs. Enrique gave him an extra one hundred pesetas for each tank that he delivered. He would also lecture these guys, who were always from tropical Asia, about the benefits of unions and collective rights. They shuffled out of the apartment, squeezing their wrenches and reading the notes and names of books that Enrique had scribbled for them on the back of an envelope.

I found in my wallet a business card for a club called The Spot. I'm not sure how it got there, but I thought that it might be a sign. The Spot's address was Carrer Nou de Sant Francesc, no doubt somewhere in the Barri Gòtic, where the short and cramped streets were never identified by their names. The back of the card had a black and white picture of a naked woman slouched on a divan, wearing a lot of bracelets,.

I also thought that by finding this bar, by solving this little puzzle, I could achieve a certain competency, I could learn the city, I could "hack my way through the cold shackles of time," and staunch the flow of bad feelings that always awaited in me on the days I had nothing to do. I thought that the bar might be some kind of spiritual counter to the Sagrada Familia, which I was yet to see.

By the evening, I found myself wandering around the odd corners and filthy plazas near Plaça de Sant Jaume. In front of the Generalitat, a few dozen young people were crowded near the front of the parliament building, punching their fists in the air and shouting. As I stood there watching them, Gordon sidled up to me out of nowhere. "They want the government to recognize their earnestness and naivety," he said pointing at the group. "They are feeling the urgency because some of them are beginning to mature, at which point such recognition would be humiliating. Especially since many of them will end up working there."

I explained to Gordon my situation with the business card, and how I imagined this place might be the antithesis to the Sagrada Familia. We started walking toward the Picasso museum.

"The Sagrada Familia is not that bad," he said. "It's like any tourist trap. You see it, you pay a few pounds to climb the stairs to the top, you buy an ashtray. That's life."

"The downside?"

"The staircase is very cramped, and they make you go up like ants. Not a place to go if you can't soldier past someone's gas."

We had descended upon Santa Maria del Mar, a gothic church crowded on either side by apartments and restaurants. "Let's see if The Spot's in there," he said, pointing into a busy café.

We leaned against the stainless steel bar and I ordered some potato pie along with beers. "Something about potatoes and beer that really responds well in my body," I said. "It's food from pre-history. It's genetic coding. It makes me feel that I'm the spearhead of my ancestry, thrusting into a new age. I have taken the spiritual sustenance from the village elders and have ventured over the western knolls in search of our collective destiny."

Gordon wasn't paying attention. He was staring at a gaggle of American girls chatting at a table. A blonde laughed and lit a cigarette. Gordon reached into the inside pocket of his jacket and took out his pack of Marlboros. "Excuse me a moment," he said dryly, stepping over to their table, "could I trouble you for a torch?" They looked at each other with wide eyes and bright grins. Gordon had his unlit cigarette down at his side. He brought it up to his serious face. "Do you have a lighter or some matches?"

They all laughed and scrambled into their purses. There were four of them—all pretty and rosy-cheeked. The girl with blonde hair sparked her lighter and Gordon hovered his cigarette over the flame and inhaled indulgently. "Cheers," he said. I kept my distance at the bar, watching Gordon ham it up and waiting for them to dismiss him in a humiliating way. "You're all Americans?" he said after half-turning away.

Instead, Gordon scraped a chair up to their table. Madison, Brie, Heidi, and Larissa were backpackers from the University of California—the San Diego campus, as luck would have it.

"Ferry's from San Diego," Gordon said, calling me over.

"They all cooed with recognition, all except Larissa, who was also the only one not to shake hands with us when we sat down; instead she just offered an ironic little wave. Larissa wore a plain purple T-shirt and jeans. She refilled her glass with beer every few minutes. She seemed annoyed by Gordon's transparent maneuvers. I was more or less smitten with her.

"What part of San Diego are you from?" Brie said.

"Golden Hill."

"That's downtown, east of downtown—isn't it? That's where all the Mexicans live." Brie said.

"Right, just up the hill. As far as Mexicans go, they pretty much live everywhere in San Diego." I said.

"Right, but in La Jolla they're like, normal. In Golden Hill, they're like, *Mexican*," Heidi said.

I looked over at Gordon, to see what he was making of these fools, but he had carved out a side conversation with Madison. He was leaning over the table explaining something with his hands, but he was looking past them at her breasts.

"So you guys must live in La Jolla then," I said wearily.

"Actually it's PB. Just by Tourmaline," Brie said.

"Our building is sooo freakin' old though," Heidi interjected. "There are like, these weird holes inside the cabinets. I swear you could reach your hand inside and like, pull out something from the neighbors."

"I wouldn't stick my hand in there!"

"And the landlord is like, whatever."

"Totally."

"He's like, *It's the beach. I could totally rent this to someone else.*"

Brie and Heidi proceeded to explain the precise details of each of their living arrangements, including the relative compatibility of their roommates. It was a series of in-jokes and knowing allusions that pushed me further onto the margins. Larissa was ignoring them, and had peeled the labels off six or seven bottles of beer and had turned to dismantling her cigarette pack. The goal seemed to be to make the pack a single sheet of paper without ripping it at all.

"Are you guys traveling too?" Brie finally asked me.

"No, we live here," I shouted. "We're English teachers."

We went to some nearby Basque tapas bars, Gordon narrating the whole way, like a tour guide on his first tour. We met two other girls, from San Sebastian, both named Oihana. "It means forest in Euskera," one said. "We are the forest."

Gordon lent me two thousand pesetas. I ordered a round of drinks and a plate of miniature salami sandwiches. I recognized it as a moment that I had been longing for, though I mistakenly thought that I'd be feeling that way from then on, forever. There was a clear sweet liquor and fried calamari so superior to the stuff I heated at home, to even the stuff I made back at the restaurant in

San Diego, that I looked at the bartender and couldn't help but regard him as a mystical figure. Living in Barcelona, growing up around the old buildings and strange parades, allowed him to fry the calamari to such a succulent state, that I could only sip my beer and relish the awe that I felt.

One of the Oihanas explained to me the origins of the Basque music that we were listening to, but it was too loud and drowned out her explanation, even though she was shouting. Every light in the place was on, every machine was whirling and grinding—microwaves, fryers and even espresso. I felt like there was some kind of raw energy pouring in from the ceiling.

By the time we arrived at Penúltimo, a bar with a crowded basement for dancing, my limbs were feeling heavy, and my vision was cloudy. I was determined to drink my way out of it.

The basement was so smoky, I thought it may be on fire. People were very thin and composed, dressed in designer clothes. Techno music thumped and screamed like the approach of an angry and wronged jungle people. Gordon danced with Brie; Madison and Heidi danced with each other. The Oihanas had vanished, perhaps hours ago. I was left with Larissa, whom I suspected had warmed up to me just so she could witness my final disintegration. "What if I told you were we lesbians," she said to me.

"I'd say you're right on the money. If I were a woman, I'd be a lesbian too."

I went to the toilet, drinking drinks left on the tables along the way. When I got back to where I left Larissa, she was gone. I drank more, though I'm certain that I never actually ordered a drink. A man in a velvet suit accosted me, and I responded with a litany of Spanish profanity that I learned from Clarence—*puta madre, joder, coño*— though I added, inexplicably, some of the Barça players—*Figo, Rivaldo, Luis Enrique.*

The last thing I remember was being carried through the parting crowd by people I didn't know—these strangers gripping my limbs. I saw the faces flush with disapproval, as if I was being led from the courtroom to prison, a criminal beyond forgiveness.

I woke at dawn, trapped inside the Antic Mercat del Born. The old place hadn't been used as a market for years, but there were rumors that it would be a new flea market, a concert venue, or an art space. Yet it sat empty and forlorn, surrounded by a cyclone fence stretching from the pavement to the roof. It struck me that this was the kind of thing that happened to homeless people, and I wondered if I was beginning to finally become one of them. I could easily picture myself mastering the circuit of San Francisco soup kitchens, sleeping on a soiled cot in a Florida tent city, or shaking the clammy hand of some sympathetic clergy outside the Tulsa Y.

The old market was like a cavernous fortress. I looked through the bars and metal mesh, the thick concrete, and wondered how I would get out. A fat man was hosing down the terrace in front of the corner restaurant. I remembered eating lunch there soon after I arrived in Spain, some kind of casserole that had bits of bone in it. Calling out to that guy would have been too pathetic—I couldn't bear to do it. Besides, if the police were called I'd certainly have to explain myself. I couldn't imagine what nonsense I would say to them, what kind of explanation I would have for being stuck in the Antic Mercat del Born, for being in

Barcelona, for wasting my life by stringing together these meaningless episodes.

My pockets were empty save for a pack of crushed Ducados. I began walking around the perimeter, nudging with my foot places in the fence that might be vulnerable. It was an absolute prison. I had the first pang of panic. There were sheets of newspaper scattered all over the floor; one of them was dated: *Dilluns*, 2 *Juli*. 1995, a full three years ago. I sat on the floor. Sunshine beamed through the opaque roof windows; the drone of traffic echoed on the trusses. I heard the whistle of a train departing the not-too-distant Estació de França. I closed my eyes and tried to imagine the market during its prime: *the shrill women haggling for pears; the sweet smell of rotting lettuce; the sight of Ernesto the mute carrying a sack of dates across the wet dirt, his life but a procession of chores and meals.*

From behind a partly demolished wall, just a few feet from where I was sitting, a voice called out. "Psssst *sorti, sorti.*" Exit, exit. A man peaked over the wall, his face was bright red and unevenly bearded. I stood up and walked over to what I soon realized was his little sleeping area—newspapers were spread for a mattress. When I was just a few feet away, I noticed his dark eyes were so dilated that he looked like a doll: a huge, homeless, unlovable doll. He was also wearing a U.S. Navy jacket, soiled so heavily that it appeared soaking wet. I'd seen lots of military garb in the thrift stores here, even stuff like this from home. Still, the jacket reminded me of my father. It was theoretically possible that it could have been his jacket, that he could have worn it all the way to skid row, where he traded it for a pint of Four Roses. From there, the jacket could have been bartered and traded, stolen and swapped, all the way to this living wreck.

He waved me over and pointed to a dark nook where the iron was twisted and bent. "*Sorti,*" he said again. "*La salida.*" His exit was like a crab trap—the metal bent inward, so entering was more or less easy, as long as you didn't try and reverse. Getting out, without the benefit of having your nerves dissipated by alcohol, would be difficult and painful. I hit the pavement and began to inch beneath the fence. The wire edges were like teeth—clamping down on my stomach; for a moment it looked as though I would be stuck in a painful embrace of metal and concrete. But then the old hobo bent over and pulled up the wire mesh the crucial inch to let me through. He stood red-faced on the opposite end of the fence, like a pitiful ferryman. I rolled my pack of crumpled cigarettes under the fence to him. "Thanks *tio*," I said.

The imitation Levis that I had just bought at Humana were ripped at the waist and I had to hold them up as I walked down the damp Passieg del Born. The Santa Maria del Mar loomed in front of me, like an offshore storm ready to crash onto land.

That night, I was drinking beers with Clarence on a smelly dock across from Barcelona's waterfront amusement mall, Maremagnum. "Hard drinking is like the cat fucking the skunk," he said. "The cat doesn't get all he wants—just what he can stand."

CHAPTER 12

For some reason, I told Kylie about my episode with Gordon. I tried to make it sound cavalier and adventurous, but instead my story seemed desperate and confessional. She was quick to suggest that I might be an alcoholic, or at least a pathetic lush, and she recommended that I visit her friend Sabine. A palm reader/psychic from Los Angeles, Sabine helped people overcome their destructive vices. Her successes included separating a Canadian and his compulsion to play the slot machines found in every Spanish bar, relieving an English girl of her kleptomania; and Sabine even helped Kylie herself overcome her teeth grinding. "I don't know how much I can afford," I said.

"She works on a sliding scale," Kylie said.

"For me it will have to be all the way slidden."

Her building was on Aribau, in the heart of the Eixample. The balconies were full of bicycles, large orange butane containers, and folded furniture. Wisteria and other vines hung from the wrought-iron railings and swayed to the roar of traffic.

The apartment itself was a disappointment. I had expected lots of new-age paraphernalia—hand-carved figurines, photos of gurus in cheap frames, voices chanting from a small CD player. Instead, shopping bags stuffed with recyclables crowded the foyer along with a pile of shoes. The hall leading back to the sitting room was painted sea green and so dirty and faded that it looked like a weather-beaten fresco. There were a few votive candles along the far wall of the back room, but that was about it.

"Why did Kylie ask you to visit?"

"I'm having some problems in the lady department," I said.

"Your problem is not love. Or at least not the kind of love that you think. Have a seat, Lester." Sabine motioned to a sheet-covered armchair.

"Do you want to look at my palm?" Sitting in the musty chair I saw the colorful spines of new-age books lining the wall adjacent to the door. Beneath the sheet, I felt the springs poking through the foam and ripped upholstery. Sabine sat in a chair next to mine, a table with a huge pack of tarot cards between us.

"Yes, I'll look at your palm if you want me to. But first things first. Your energy is overwhelming, sorrowful. You're a very sad person." I creased my face into a smile, trying to convey mild amusement and patronizing understanding. In fact, she caught me flat-footed. My mind scrambled to offer a defense.

"I'm not sad. If anything, I'm a little heartbroken. But not sad. I feel pretty good."

"Maybe you feel good with a stomach full of wine. But not now you don't, not usually. You say you're heartbroken? Is it Kylie?"

I chortled, guffawed and fluttered my hands in a very overdone way. "Kylie? Are you kidding? We're friends. We work together. Besides, she's Australian." Sabine just stared at me. I felt sick, heavy and sweaty, as if my skin was peeling off my face.

"It's not so important," she said dismissively. "You must compromise with yourself first, and with it the universe, before you could hope to achieve that type of love."

"OK, that sounds fine. That's what I'll do."

"Look Lester, if you're OK, if you insist you're happy and you can manage on your own then fine, though I wonder why you came here at all." She leaned back in her chair and crossed her legs—invisible to me beneath her purple sarong

"Well I'm not wildly happy, no. Most people aren't all that happy. The people I work with, the people I work for—they're not happy. They're glum. People on the street. Do you really see people smiling all the time? I think relative to most of the population, I'm right there. I have my moments both ways."

"You're free to go. No charge."

I could stand up, I thought, collect enough composure and dignity to offer a polite handshake, and march to the door where I could turn and remark cordially about Kylie, our mutual friend. I rubbed the big five-hundred peseta piece in my pocket and remembered that just outside Sabine's flat, I had passed an eatery with aluminum furniture scattered on the sidewalk. I thought how relieved I would feel sitting in one of those chairs, listening to the traffic rush, tilting a beer down my throat, the hundreds of anonymous bodies walking by.

In the same moment, I remembered waking up in parked cars with unaccountable cuts and bruises, the swaths of unrecorded time, the everlasting dread. My drinking, I knew, had accelerated and was generating its own momentum. Maybe Sabine knew some trick that could help me prevent the inevitable mudslide. It felt like either way, I was giving up; either way the end was near.

"Thanks for your help," I said and got up to leave. Sabine looked stunned, which pleased me.

"If you need a drink, I have some wine," she said. "It's nothing fancy. In fact it's from DIA."

She had certain charm, that Sabine. I allowed her that. Her brown eyes shone with sympathy. Light freckles highlighted her pale skin, except for her shoulders and chest above her sarong, where they were darker and recklessly spread. I noticed for the first time that she was wearing enormous turquoise earrings, the kind you might buy at a gas station in rural Arizona.

"I see your aura of sorrow mostly with alcoholics," she said.

I finished the wine from the large coffee cup. I refilled it from the carton, which was also now empty. I held the carton at some height, the last drips squeaked when they hit the surface. "Let's just say, for the sake of argument," I said, "that I am an alcoholic. That I am deeply, irrevocably disturbed. That I live in fear and resentment—let's just say that I feel these things every day. What then? Shall we chant? Burn sandal wood incense?"

"Do you know Dmitri?"

"Acupuncture? Aromatherapy? Frappuccino?"

"Don't be a twit."

"No, I don't know him, I know he's sick. I took over his classes at English Time."

"Instead of any kind of payment, I want you to go visit. I helped him a few years ago with a similar problem. But he smoked hash. Maybe you could be of some help to him, maybe you could get out of your own vortex for a while."

"No rubbing the Buddha's belly?"

"No, you can go home and rub your own belly if you want. Besides, I'm out of wine."

*Down at the Municipal Clinic of Barcelona, tucked in a dirty pocket of the Raval, a Catalan nurse was telling Clarence how to apply the satiny cream every four hours to his genitals. He had stood before her with his pants pulled down to the middle of his thighs while she inspected his aching and itching groin. The nurse treated him disrespectfully, and who could blame her? She said "*como ladillas,*" (like crabs) but did not offer a precise diagnosis, or an English translation of his apparent venereal disease, his miserable rash. He was hoping at least for a cognate on the medicine. Instead the metal tube had a peculiar, Slavic-looking word on it.*

The stern, middle-aged nurse in the STD annex of Barcelona's municipal clinic warned Clarence about the dangers of unprotected sex. He thought about her daily witness to the parade of infected genitals, the pained faces of lovers broken by love. When she handed him the metallic tube of ointment, she told him not to have sexual contact while the rash was present. But if he must, then a condom would be essential, and she nodded toward a wicker basket of prophylactics. She said this with unmistakable resignation, as if Clarence was a rapacious sexual deviant. He was so humiliated that he obediently grabbed four condoms. They were on a table next to an issue of HOLA! *that featured Julio Iglesias and his thin blonde wife walking on an Aegean beach. Clarence felt a pulse of longing. He caught himself imagining that things would be different there, in Greece. He once felt the same about Spain. Now of course he knew this longing was all a folly, a ruse. He understood it was all so commonplace, so banal and squalid. The banality is what is so squalid, he thought. He smirked as he put the condoms in his top pocket; the nurse averted her eyes.*

PART TWO

DIGUI DIGUI

CHAPTER 13

Dmitri's apartment was on Carrer de Cadena, in the heart of the Raval. The first day I visited, a dozen or so kids were playing soccer in the plaza in front of his building. One kid in particular stuck in my memory. He looked about thirteen, at least two or three years older than the others. He was a big kid too, broad faced and chubby. As I rang the buzzer of Dmitri's apartment, this kid was yelling for the ball in front of a makeshift goal. Goal hanging, we used to call that. But the ball was stuck in a scrum down at the other end. The kids down there were booting the ball as hard as they could, but they were so packed together that the ball never traveled more than two or three feet. Children no older than five or six were drawn to the action and danced around the pack, flailing their arms and mimicking the kicks of their older brothers. "*Miraaaaaaaa!*" The big kid shouted in vain. He yelled the word again and jumped, but could barely lift himself off the concrete.

I went over to Dmitri's quite a bit after that first day, and I never saw the plaza empty, no matter the hour. There were no trees or monuments, benches or structure of any kind, so the center was always more or less vacant. Occasionally Muslim men in white robes strolled across the open space in twos and threes, their capped heads leaning toward each other in conversation. Boys on bikes too small for them darted around the middle, doing modest wheelies and unremarkable jumps. Even the odd soccer fields were parceled from the edge, and never right in the middle. On the perimeter however, pockets of people were always hanging around—mostly grown men and teenage boys, a few sisters and girlfriends (but never a group of girls on their own). The men leaned against cars, the boys sat on mopeds, all of them smoking cigarette after cigarette. The plaza was a plodding, aimless episode that never ended, but simply cycled back to the first frame, day after day after day.

And it wasn't really even a plaza. "There used to be a building there, not more than twenty feet away from my window," Dmitri said on the first day. "They knocked it down. They're knocking a whole row of buildings down. They say it'll be another pedestrian street, another Ramblas. I say it'll be another hash-infested boulevard of whores." I leaned off Dmitri's balcony. A crane and a bulldozer that I somehow failed to see earlier were parked in a pile of rubble just to the north. Three sides of a building were already demolished, leaving the interior of the remaining one exposed to the whole neighborhood. The soiled wallpaper and fading paint of the former rooms created a checkerboard of yellow and green, sadness and loss.

"Got any cigarettes?" Dmitri asked.

"The rolling kind."

"The rolling kind? Where did you come here from, a soup kitchen, jail? Hand me that pack over there on the TV. You're making me smoke one from my last pack." He shook his head in disgust. "The rolling kind."

Everyone at the language school told me that Dmitri was in bad shape. He had some kind of cancer, Darnell said, though he was vague about exactly where. Considering I was the new teacher—Dmitri's replacement actually—I was shy about asking direct questions. Later I realized that information shifted and changed, that in fact everyone had their own collection of data and theories. At one point Clarence suggested Dmitri's sickness might be AIDS. "After all," he said, "since when do guys in their 20's get cancer like that?" Whatever his illness, he looked horrible. His black hair seemed unnaturally thin and he was pale and damp like a squid.

"What kind of name is Ferry?" he asked.

"It's a last name. My first name is Lester, but everyone calls me Ferry."

"I don't blame them."

The sun shone sideways in the window. I heard a diesel engine crank. "Who sent you over here anyway?" Dmitri asked.

"Sabine."

"Sabine? How do you know Sabine?"

"Through Kylie. She did some holistic healing for me. You know, heavy drinking. I have a penchant for waking up in strange places."

"With strange people?"

"Usually not. Usually I am the strangest person I wake up with."

"So you blackout."

"I suppose."

"Are you in a blackout now?"

"No, I haven't drank anything since this morning. Besides, Sabine said drinking was not really the problem. My problem is that I'm too self-centered and I'm getting sucked into some kind of vortex."

"A fucking vortex?"

"She said that if I didn't do anything, the vortex would get more and more intense, like a hurricane sweeping across a warm sea."

"So what does this have to do with me?"

"She said that maybe I could help you out."

"Help me out? You? You look like a corpse that fell down a flight of stairs. She sent you over because you look like shit and she thought that might cheer me up. And she's right, it does." He smiled facetiously. I could see the outline of his collarbone through a T-shirt that read, "*Esport català.*"

"How do you know Sabine?" I said.

"I know Sabine because I banged her. I banged her a couple of dozen times. She might not look like she'd be good to bang, but she is. She's pretty good." He took a long drink from a bottle of water. "I banged her right in this room. Once over there on the balcony. Half in the room, half on the balcony. That was before they tore down the building next door. The lady one floor up looked down at us humping like we just invented humping halfway on a balcony. She was afraid to keep looking, afraid to turn away. We just kept humping." Dmitri tapped a cigarette out of his pack and leaned over to let me light it. I got a whiff of sickness, half human, half chemical.

"Why'd you guys split up?"

"Split up? Let me tell you something Ferry, it wasn't like that. There was never anything to split up. You don't know anything about me. I might look a little sick right now, but let me tell you, I've had my share and then some. I've had hundreds and hundreds of women, maybe a thousand. I don't think that I could give a reasonable estimate. My margin of error would be bigger than most men's whole *oeuvre*. My mother's Greek, my dad's Presbyterian. I lived on a Greek island for about two years. I banged more women in those two years than some men would in a dozen lives. I used to sit on the beach and watch the cruise ships sailing in, knowing that there were two or three girls on that boat that I'd be banging." Dmitri pushed himself up on his bed, excited by his own bragging. "That's a pretty good feeling, you know, sitting on a Greek beach, watching the ship roll in, knowing there's some girl on board that you're going to be banging."

"That does sound nice," I said.

"I banged more women than entire genealogies. I've banged more women than you, your father, your grandfather, your son, his son—everyone, and all their brothers. Combined. And you know what I want do? I want to do it again. Even sick, it hasn't gone away. I feel like a sailor on shore leave."

"Well you know what they say. Desire breeds more desire," I said.

"What? What are you, aphorism boy? Nobody says shit like that. Listen, don't come over to my flat and patronize me. Indulge me. You want to help, tell me what I'm missing." He put up his hand, palm facing me. "On second thought, don't. I know what I'm missing. You'd just pull me around the yard with some sentimental bullshit. I can tell just by looking at you and your little notebook. You're probably a poet." He chortled knowingly to himself. "Tell me. Tell me you came to Barcelona to write poems. When you're not passed out behind a dumpster, you probably go to cafes and write down little lines about all the girls you see. 'Her velvet hair, her Iberian eyes…' Jesus Ferry, that's really, really boring and cliché, you know that? How about a little originality?"

I didn't see how I was helping him, or how this was supposed to make me feel any better about myself. He was getting worked up, which probably wasn't a good idea. I wondered if it was medication that was making him act like that. "You need anything from the store?" I said.

Dmitri didn't respond right away. He had gone quiet. He looked sad and brooding. "No, I'm sorry. I'm sorry, Ferry. Sometimes I just get down and frustrated being sick, you know? It's the cancer talking sometimes." He winced and put his hand on his stomach.

"Don't worry about it. I don't give a shit. Say whatever you want. Call me an asshole, that's fine."

He squirmed a little, and adjusted himself in the bed, the top half of which was tilted at about a seventy-five degree angle. "I don't need anything from the store, Ferry, but did Sabine say anything to you about the bedpan?"

"No, she didn't really tell me anything. She said just stop by."

Dmitri lowered his eyes. "Well, the bedpan. I need it," he said grimly.

"No problem," I almost shouted. "Where is it?"

"In the bathroom, Ferry. I'm sorry. You might have to clean it first."

I walked into the bathroom, trying to seem nonchalant, though I felt a strange nervousness tingling in my stomach. What the hell was I doing? I'm no nurse.

The bedpan was tucked behind the toilet, mercifully clean. "Hurry Ferry," Dmitri called softly. I trotted out of the bathroom with the contoured basin stretched out before me, as if a turd might fall from the ceiling and I'd have to catch it. "Hurry," he said desperately. Just as I had steeled myself to lift the sheet, Dmitri brought his hands to his face and howled with laughter. For a moment I was confused, and held the bedpan solicitously in front of me. He looked at me holding it and literally turned purple with hilarity. I put the bedpan on the floor and sat down in a chair. His laughing turned to coughing, then back to laughing, before petering out into prolonged wheezing. He dropped his cigarette into a soda can and hopped onto the floor. "That was genius," he said walking to the bathroom "Maybe someday I'll need that, but not today."

When I left his apartment and turned down Carrer de l'Hospital, it was like jumping into a fast-moving stream. Old people leaned on aluminum walkers, delivery trucks bumped onto the sidewalks, hydraulic jackhammers rattled sporadically like machine guns. All at once I smelled wet plaster, carbon monoxide, and rotting onions.

I entered the flow of people, directly behind a bare-legged Catalan woman, who I followed all the way down to the Ramblas, and even into the Cafè de l'Òpera. The whole way, her buttocks pumped like pistons in her tight short skirt. She kissed an oily-haired man on both cheeks, as I sat at the only vacant table. I figured I'd have a beer to see what other adventure might unfold. But I had a hard time getting a waiter to take my order, because like all Barcelona waiters, these guys seemed to lack peripheral vision. They treated customers like awkward acquaintances that they were trying to ignore. I sat there alone, and opened my journal.

I took note of a lanky character by the front window, and I immediately pegged him as American, though I couldn't point to any telltale sign. Maybe it was because he was sketching the Opera House façade, even though it was mostly blocked in scaffolding. This American may have come all this way to see that famous place—a place that for all I knew was some fantastic, architectural feat. But when he arrived, he found it covered with green nets and surrounded by dumpsters and workmen who shuffled around with dust masks dangling around their necks, accosting the women passing by.

I remembered how Dmitri ridiculed me for sitting around in cafes writing poems, even though I just wrote random sentences in my journal, and not poems at all. But I realized all at once, sitting in that stupid café, how clichéd and pathetic my story was, how I had left home to forget a girl. I was going to be sitting in this café for a long time, waiting for a beer, waiting for some act of providence to give me a purpose; and that I was likely to fall on some mistake or another, some wretched life would squeak open like a cellar door, and I would tumble in.

CHAPTER 14

The fact that I was yet to visit the Sagrada Familia became a source of celebrity for me. Gordon joked that I might be some kind of anti-Christ, and that I would sizzle and wither if ever I beheld the landmark. Kylie just thought I was being cheeky, trying to win attention with some overdone apathy.

Only Clarence seemed to take it seriously. "Do you avoid all churches?" he asked me when we met outside of the Urquinaona Metro Station. We had plans to meet Kylie in front of the church, the side with the Nativity, at 5 PM.

Clarence suggested that we have a beer at a bar just one block away from the metro. The Dow Jones Bar was a gimmicky place where the prices of various beers were indexed like the stock market on an expensive-looking electric chart above the bar. It was empty when we walked in, as the Chemical Brothers thumped and hummed from unseen speakers.

I had with me *The Collected Works of John Keats*—a book I happened to find at the Now Super Time Book Store. I had started carrying it around to hold my attention on the metro, thinking that one day I would be able to crack its sophisticated irony. But I could only stomach a few of the pathetic and remote poems. I combed through the Odes, searching in vain for a punch line.

When she brought our beers, the bartender nudged the book on the bar and said in a breathless accent: "Dutch is the only major literature never to have gone through a period of romanticism." I had heard so much of my student's crude, English sentences that her casual command of the present perfect tense aroused me.

"That's nice," Clarence said, "but Dutch isn't really a major literature."

"And what do you know about Dutch Literature?" she said crossly.

"I don't know anything. That's the point."

"You must be Americans. Satisfied with your stereotypes. I suppose you think we all wear wooden shoes." Her blonde hair was cut short, and was so smooth and clean it seemed a single unit.

"Yes, behind closed doors, wooden shoes. It's likely," Clarence said. "Though who would care? Who cares what Dutch people wear? The Dutch, that's all."

The girl looked at Clarence incredulously, as if he had just peeled off a mask to reveal that he was some long-forgotten nemesis.

"You are such an asshole," she said.

"I'm just being direct. I thought that was a prevailing trait of people from your region."

"My region? What is wrong with you? You don't know anything about my country."

"Picturesque canals, Rembrandt, weed."

"You are a motherfucker, a prick, and a shithead."

"Tulips, Anne Frank, liberal attitude towards social deviance."

"McDonalds, Monica Lewinsky, *The Simpsons*."

The Simpsons were in fact playing on the television propped up on a counter behind the bar. She turned abruptly, grabbed the remote and turned up the volume—her way of sealing the argument. Homer was delivering a soliloquy in Catalan. I couldn't understand a word of his speech, but the desperate, pleating tone was all too familiar.

The beer index updated itself and the price of our Voll Damms, predictably, increased.

Somehow we ended up on the Ramblas, which was in the opposite direction of the Sagrada Familia. We had stopped at a few more bars, and I had run out of money. Clarence was paying, paying without mentioning it as a favor or a loan. It seemed like he was luring me away from the famous church, baiting me with beers like someone would coax a donkey to the slaughterhouse with sugar cubes and peanuts. By the time we got to the bar in La Boqueria, I was drunk. The market was closing, but there was still a lot of activity. Wheelbarrows full of meat careened down the aisles covered with crushed ice. Leaves of lettuce were strewn about like the pages of a ruined book. Someone yelled in Catalan, and it echoed in the hall like the cry of a sailor trapped in the hull of a sinking ship.

I apologized to Kylie the next day for missing our appointment. "What I like about Barcelona," she said, "is that the days just go on and on and never arrange themselves into any kind of narrative. It's all just one big endless day."

I called home. I had been trying to get a hold of my mother. She had threatened to visit me a month or so ago. Reese told me they were considering a three-week vacation to France, Italy, and Spain.

As usual, Tyrone answered. "Question: how much would it cost to ship a Mercedes E320 to France?" I know Tyrone meant Spain when he said France. France was just the catch-all word for anything foreign.

"It depends on whether you'd ship it by the air or the sea."

"Whatever's cheaper."

"Well it would be pretty expensive either way. You'd have not only the shipping costs, but then you'd probably have some kind of tariff. And a Mercedes would be at the high end area."

"Couple thou?"

"At least."

"But if the E320 was free, and had the deluxe trim package?"

"Then it wouldn't be too bad, I suppose."

"What are you driving over there?" he said. I heard him open a can.

"I don't have a car. That's one of the great things about living here is that I don't need a car."

"What's so great about that? What do you do, take the bus?"

"And the metro, and I walk. Barcelona's a big city, it's like Manhattan. A car would just be a pain in the ass."

He chortled. "What do you do with a date? Wait at the bus stop?"

"It's totally acceptable. Everyone takes public transportation. It's great."

"Sounds like it sucks."

"Well it doesn't matter anyway. I haven't had a lot of dates."

"I see why. Get a car. Just get an old Duster or Dart or something."

"They don't have Dusters or Darts here."

"Well get a French Duster, you know what I mean." For a moment I thought that Tyrone could be right. I tried to imagine how my life would be different with an automobile. I pictured myself in a leathery Duster/Renault driving toward Plaça Catalunya on Passeig de Gràcia. Listening to The Chemical Brothers, smoking a brand name cigarette. Catalans in the crosswalk shuffled in front of my car and peered at me through the windshield. Tough and foreign, my exhaust leaked a menacing rumble.

"Listen, speaking of dates, you seen Svetlana?"

"Yeah bro, I see her all the time. She works at the Italian coffee place at the bottom of Washington Street."

"The one with the ice cream?"

"Yeah," Tyrone sounded distracted, and I thought I might have heard the turning pages of a magazine.

"Have you talked to her?"

"Couple of times," he said casually. He knew that I was desperate about her.

"Well asshole what does she say?"

"God, cool your jets. I just say hi. I told her you're in France."

"She knows where I am, I emailed her. She didn't email me back, at least not the second time. Does she have a boyfriend?"

"I don't know. If you're so worried about that, why are you in France?"

"What, you think she'd go back with me?"

"What are we, on Oprah? Get a grip on yourself man. How the hell would I know?"

"How does she look?"

"Pretty hot."

"Shit."

"You blew it bro. You were in the big leagues for a few months." I heard him take a couple of swallows from the can. "Now you have to play ball overseas." He chuckled at his accidentally extended metaphor. "With no wheels."

"Is anyone else around?"

"Reese," he burped.

"Where's mom?"

"She's helping the blind or the deaf. One of them, maybe both." I heard Reese in the background. "Hold on, Reese wants to talk with you." Tyrone's voice was giddy because he knew I'd be loath to talk to my stepfather.

"*Buenos dias Lessimo*. How are you?"

"Fine Reese, how are you?"

"Fine, fine. Tell me, have you been to any bullfights yet?"

"No, I haven't. I don't think they're so popular in Barcelona."

"It's Spain, Les. They're around. What about the Tango?"

"No, I don't care for dancing much. But I did see some Flamenco dancers performing on the street the other day."

"That's great Les. Once in a lifetime opportunity you've got. It'd be nice if Tyrone could do something like that," he said. I could practically see Reese's sidelong glance at my brother. "What about Hemingway?"

"Haven't seen him."

"He's dead Les. I'm talking about his novels. He wrote something about Spain you know. You really should read something like that to get the whole experience. I have some of his books lying around. *Old Man in the Sea, Farewell to the Farm, The Incredible Feast*. They're all in one, Reader's Digest Edition. I think it might be a trilogy. I'll send them to you."

"No, don't do that. They'll get stolen. Packages from overseas get opened and they take anything valuable."

"No they don't, Les. That's the post office you're talking about. They're international. They're accountable. Everything is going to be fine."

When I hung up the phone, I imagined the words of my stepfather—"Everything is going to be fine"—crackling above it. They drifted over the smoldering ashtray, the miscellaneous tarot cards that Paz read while she talked on the phone. In a second, they were gone, and I was alone again. I stared at the wooden end table, nicked and chewed on the edges, light rings from dozens of drinks spinning randomly across the top.

CHAPTER 15

I entered the stairwell of my apartment building, a place both ragged and elegant. The first flight of stairs was wider than the rest and made of marble, which was so worn that it looked like melting ice. The rest of the stairs were dirty terrazzo. An ornate iron banister twisted all the way to the attic, where a window on the ceiling let in a rectangle of sunlight. Enrique called the stairwell "the womb."

"I haven't been to the Sagrada Familia," I told Enrique when he came into the TV room. "I'm not sure if I should finally go, or I should stay away as long as possible and try and be the person who has been in Barcelona the longest without seeing it. In five years I could get interviewed by the newspaper and there could be some kind of ceremony when I finally go."

"You think about yourself very much, don't you? In very strange circumstances. You realize that you will eventually force such a thing to happen."

"That doesn't answer my question."

"Stay away from it if it's the same to you. It's just a big Catalan teddy bear."

Enrique and I watched the Catalan news coverage of the violent outbreaks in the south of France. Drunken British soccer fans had gone on a rampage and indiscriminately beat up some Tunisians, who seemed to be regular citizens. When the commercials came on, I waited for Enrique to offer his interpretation. "They are mad that they are not an empire," he said. "With each blow, they are saying where is the empire?"

"These freaks are only in their twenties. You'd be lucky if their father's even have any direct memory of those days."

"They are drunk because of a fear they are not even conscious of, the fear and humiliation that comes with being born in the era of post-empire. They lash out at foreigners because they feel weak. It is better for them if they never were an empire. It would be better for everyone. Imagine England if it were never an empire, if it were just a shit little country with a lot of rain. It would be a nice little place to go for vacation, for a honeymoon, to do some kind of anthropological research. These hooligans wouldn't be drunk at soccer matches, they'd be mending their seining nets, roasting scones or making cheese. As it is, they're lost. It will one day be the same for your unlucky descendants."

The British papers later reported that many of the hooligans were postal workers, a fact that I found pretty surprising. When that postal person went on a killing rampage in Tennessee a few years before, I remembered having the same feeling of surprise, though at that time I was sure that it was nothing more than a crazy fluke. Postal workers should be the most passive citizens, I thought. To say, "he got a job at the post office," is practically the same as saying "his days are mapped out, the future for him is a certainty, the world will offer him no unjust surprises." The more I thought about it, the more I understood why they became unglued.

In some ways I envied people who never questioned the form of their lives. They get their girlfriend pregnant in high school, or at college, or at the factory—and the next thing you know they're in a rocking chair on the porch sipping iced tea and doing a crossword puzzle, waiting for the social security check to arrive. They're spared the tortured trajectory of the aimless life, the thorough reading of newspapers in public parks, the thought of things they should have said to girls they once knew, the little plans and designs that involve no one but themselves.

"What about the beaten-up Tunisians?" Kylie said when I saw her at work the next day and tried to impress her with some of Enrique's analysis. "Leave it to a couple of white men to see this as an occasion to sit around and analyze themselves for a few hours. Those were women and children that they beat up for fuck's sake."

Perennial favorite Brazil pounded Morocco in the opening round of the World Cup. A lot of Catalans were on the Brazilian bandwagon, not only because they were loath to identify with the Spanish team, but also because Brazil's best player, Rivaldo, played for their beloved Barça team. When he scored on a header ten minutes into the game, the bars on both sides of my street erupted into shouts and cries. Still, the mood was a lot mellower than an actual Barça match, and the game and response seemed boring, somehow scripted. The outcome was never in doubt.

That night, at about 3 AM, a Moroccan man stood in the damp alley down the street from our apartment, and began yelling. "You think you are better than we are, but we have families just like you. We work a lot. You are not better and worse than the Moroccans." He spoke in Spanish so broken and rudimentary even I could understand some of it, and Enrique translated the rest. He and I stood on the balcony, smoking. The Moroccan's voice was high-pitched and strident—it seemed like he was stoned or maybe even drunk. Our neighbors began shouting back at him, mostly just to shut up. "They're pissed because he's speaking Spanish," Enrique said, "and not Catalan. If he was yelling in Catalan, they'd eat out of his hand. Throw money to him. They'd remember his face and tell him *bon dia* whenever they saw him again." The guy then started airing vague and general complaints, saying it's "difficult to live," and, "my country is warm, Morocco is warm." He even cried, and then kept repeating, "mint tea, mint tea." The chorus of neighbors continued, though their shouts were growing listless.

Enrique yelled: "shut up you motherfucker," in English, and went to bed.

I found myself going to Dmitri's two or three times a week, encouraged that finally I had something to feel good about. Unfortunately, it did nothing to curb my drinking—in fact I found myself drinking *more* than before. But at least going to Dmitri's gave me a chance to stop thinking about myself for a while. He enjoyed my company, if only because I let him mock me, and I listened to his weird rants. There was a certain desperation to his peevishness. I think it was a way for him to ward off the specter of death. If he could remain cruel and impenitent, then the universe would let him live until he repented. He didn't respond very well when I offered to help him, as much as he needed it. I came to believe that the best way to help him was to let him try and help me. This made it seem like he was earning the small favors that I did do for him—like going to the store, wiring a VCR to his TV, and later by reading him the papers. He "helped" me by entertaining me with his stories, or doling out random advice. It was my fourth or fifth visit when he finally asked about any of his former students, all of whom I had begun teaching.

"How's that slob Guimerá?"

"I think he's getting ready to fire me," I said. "He suspects I'm unqualified and not really interested in helping him learn English."

"Sounds like he's right on the money."

I laughed. "It's easy for you, for the rest of you guys. You've all been trained."

"Trained? What are you talking about trained? Nobody's trained, Ferry. You don't have to go to school to teach your own language. Nobody goes to school."

"Kylie did. Kylie did the whole shebang at the International House."

"That's a dog and pony show. They teach you how to play language bingo. Besides, Kylie's Australian. You can't ever discount that."

"C'mon Dmitri, you must have gone to school at some point."

"I didn't even graduate *high school*. I got kicked out when I was sixteen. I fell asleep in the coatroom because I ate a couple of downers. They pumped my stomach, which was totally unnecessary. I was failing anyway."

"Well tell me: how do you teach when you haven't been trained? What the hell do you do for ninety minutes? Tell me how to teach, because I suck at it."

"You're not using a book, are you?"

"I have to. If it wasn't for that goddamned book, Guimerá and I would have nothing to talk about."

"Jesus, Ferry, you really are dumb, aren't you? Those books will fucking ruin you. Just talk to him. Talk to him about anything besides what's in the books. Ask him about his hot-ass secretary. Is she still there?"

"The one with cake-icing eye shadow?"

"God just give me fifteen minutes with her in a disabled elevator." Dmitri creased his mouth and slapped the side of the bed, as if he had minutes before missed his opportunity with her.

"Better yet, ask him about his stupid cars. Get him to talk about his cars and you'll be fine. He's got an SUV. Jesus does he have an SUV. It's his screensaver. Look at the new models of his SUV on the Internet. Guimerá is a fucking monkey for the Internet. Think of your job as making small talk while the website is loading, period. That's all you have to do."

"My talk is already too small. I think he wishes something bad will happen to me and that I won't be able to show up anymore." I was trying to be funny, but I realized my blunder the second it came out of my mouth. But Dmitri didn't notice—he was already thinking about what he was going to say next.

"Here's an example Ferry. One day we we're talking about SUVs and I told him how soccer moms in the U.S. love SUVs. Then I explained 'soccer moms' to him, you know how they've become this whole political demographic, blah blah blah. Soccer moms love Clinton, I said, and Clinton sure loves those soccer moms. So one minute we're talking about SUV gas mileage, and the next we're talking about voting mothers giving pleasure to the President. Soccer moms would line up to give Clinton a handy, I told him. They'd do it under the bleachers, or behind the concession stand. When I said that to Guimerá, he nearly died laughing. He didn't even understand half of it. I was just saying words—Clinton, soccer, SUV—and going like this," Dmitri motioned with his hand. "From then on, I couldn't do anything wrong."

"Sounds like you already covered everything."

"'Sounds like you already covered everything,'" Dmitri mimicked me in a nasal voice. "Don't be such a noodle, Ferry, you're so pathetic. Talk about *anything*. Talk about what we already talked about. He'll like it. He doesn't want to learn. The company makes him take the classes. He wants to be there less than you want to be there. And you know what? By the sounds of it, I can't blame him. Be a man, Ferry, be an amigo. Don't go in there like a pussy with a book and a lesson. I'm bored just imagining it."

Gemma came in while Dmitri was in the toilet. Gemma was Dmitri's upstairs neighbor and had assumed the responsibility of feeding him. She carried a hunk of tortilla española and a plate of salad. "I used a lot of oil for this," she said to me. "He needs the oil to be fatter." Although she was Catalan, her British English was crisp and polished—I couldn't imagine she learned it from fools like us. She set the plates down in the dining room and went straight to the kitchen and started to wash the dishes. Dmitri told me later that she was divorced and recently abandoned by her grown son who went to live with his girlfriend in Belgium; according to Dmitri, Gemma still had plenty of nurturing to dispose of.

"You want me to help?" I asked.

"No, that's all right. I can manage."

"Leave her be," Dmitri said shuffling back to his bed. "She has to do this stuff or else she'll fall apart. I'm just glad that I'm here to help her. If it wasn't for me, she'd have no one to cook for."

"If you don't eat the salad, then I'm not going to give you the flan," Gemma called from the kitchen. I was a little embarrassed for Dmitri, because she spoke to him as if he were a schoolboy.

"Yes you will, Gemma. You always say you won't give me the flan, and then you always give me the flan."

"This time I'm serious. No salad, no flan."

"And you say that too. But in the end, you always just give me the flan. Flan. I love flan. You should try not bringing the flan and then once I've eaten the salad, then break out the flan."

She walked over to the table where Dmitri was seated, drying her hands on a dishtowel. She felt his forehead. "How are you feeling?"

"I feel better now. Can I just have my flan?" Dmitri was talking baby-talk to her. Now I was really embarrassed. I cleared my throat and stood up to leave. Neither one of them even glanced in my direction. Gemma was sitting next to him at the table, stroking his arm. Her hair was pulled back into a ponytail, making her look young, though she couldn't have been much older than forty-five anyway. She crossed her legs and the hem of her dress caressed her knee—she was sexy, no doubt about it. Dmitri had parlayed his generous neighbor and poor health into an Oedipal fantasy. It seemed to me a tremendous act of cunning. I couldn't believe I felt a pang of envy as I let myself out of the apartment.

In the plaza, the big kid that I had seen on the first day was surrounded by a dozen other kids, some a little older, some his own age. They were kicking the soccer ball at him. Whenever he tried to break free, they pushed him down and the circle adjusted around him. He was almost in tears, not from the pain of the ball bouncing off his shoulders and his legs, but from the humiliation. I stood and watched, the same as everybody, the same as the other grown men, smirking with their arms folded. My first impulse was to run out there and put a stop to it, though I had no idea how exactly I'd do that. But I stopped myself because I realized that it would only make it worse for that kid, to be saved by some goofy foreigner. He was probably going to spend his entire life on this street, I wasn't. Who knew how long I'd be coming back here? Once or twice, maybe ten times. Who knew how long Dmitri would live? He was getting worse. The kid just had to take it. I didn't know how things were supposed to work out. I didn't know what was best for everybody, least of all this weepy kid. Given the chance, this kid would probably love to be on the perimeter of the circle, booting the ball at some other sap. He'd probably love to kick it at me.

The beginning intermediate class that I had inherited from Dmitri met every Tuesday at 6 PM in the basement office of Schusselbauer y Puig, a small consulting firm that specialized in international business. There were nine students, and I taught them together even though they were a mix of levels. Manolo, who handled all of the firm's advertising, was more of an advanced student, and he tried to demonstrate at every turn that the intermediate work was beneath him. On the other hand, Caterina, in charge of all the French accounts, was closer to a beginner. Everyone else's level was somewhere in between. The class formed a haphazard crescent that arced around my table and dry-erase board. I always just improvised, and they were unafraid to ask random questions. I sometimes felt like a scandal-ridden politician cornered by a hostile press.

“If when you use ‘been,’ before and after ‘have’?” Caterina asked. It was our third or fourth class, and I was just beginning to realize that I would be of little help to any of them. I creased my lips into a grim smile. Manolo, leaning slightly forward in his chair, looked at me skeptically. For his sake, I tried to give the appearance that I understood her question while I was cataloguing her other mistakes, which I would address in due time.

“You use it after,” I said finally. “You always use the participle after the helping verb,” though I instantly doubted whether it was true.

“He have been early yesterday, yes?” she said slowly.

“Yes, but has. He *has* been early yesterday.”

Manolo looked at me reproachfully. “I mean,” I said flustered, “you use it in the present moment. He has been early today.” Manolo let out an exaggerated sigh. What was I saying?

“You use it to talk about things usually,” I said. “He has been early a lot, frequently. He has been on time all the time.”

Caterina’s face sagged, her eyes drooped. The rest of the class stared at me blankly, their opaque faces connected into a mosaic of unknowing.

“You know, we can talk about this stuff all day,” I said quickly. “English this, participle that. Honk the horn, back up the truck, fill it with all kinds of things, random things, things of a random and uncertain nature.” Gordon taught me to ramble on aimlessly if I ever felt trapped by my students. “When push comes to shove, you’re all a bunch of illiterate mutants.” I sauntered behind my table and picked up the textbook. “But the only real way to *learn* English,” now more slowly, “is to *write* English.” I put my hands in the pockets of my second hand pants. I conveyed the impression that I was deliberating about something.

“Get out a piece of paper,” I said decisively. Manolo dutifully drew a ready sheet from his binder, and I wondered momentarily how much he understood. The other students followed his lead, though they surely didn’t grasp even the gist of what I said.

“I want you to write down sentences using each of the participles on page ninety-one,” I said. “Let’s do the first one together.” I wrote “page 91” and “arisen” on the dry erase board.

"This means to get up." I scribbled, "I have arisen at nine o'clock." I turned and read the sentence aloud. To my surprise, they murmured the sentence in quasi-unison. Their groping voices gave me the creeps, but also a sensation of power. I could control these people, I thought, and make them say whatever I wanted. Perhaps I could send them on sinister errands, or make them produce some profitable contraband.

"Good. Now you start with 'been,'" I said, "and go down the list. I'll come around and help you."

Manolo began scribbling immediately, as if it were a race. Caterina also started writing eagerly, though her book was still closed. Luisa, the creative director, squinted at the dry-erase board as if trying to decipher the arrangement and code. She, not Manolo, would ultimately be the one to lead the revolt against me, I decided. I went over to her first. "Can you think of a sentence for the participle 'been'?" I asked.

"*Si, si si.* Yes yes yes." Exceptionally well-dressed, she wielded a quiet but certain power over the other consultants. They never interrupted her or tried to wedge their own questions around hers, as they did with each other. "Yes I been in English now six month," she said.

"Close," I said, "but I want you to write it." I tapped the blank sheet of graph paper on her desk.

"Ahh! OK," she said, realizing for the first time what I wanted her to do.

I turned and crouched next to Carmen, the secretary, who was staring blankly at her list. "Do you need help?"

"Yes. No. I'm thinking." I moved behind her, so we shared the same perspective. I pointed at the participle 'been,' and asked "What word goes first?"

"I. Has. No, have. Yes." I studied the back of her bronze neck. She wore a blouse cut low in the back and the front. Her bra was satiny silver and so rigid that I wondered if it had metal in it.

"Good. I have…what?"

"I have been early all the time."

"Terrific! Now write down the others."

I looked over Manolo's shoulder. As soon as he saw me, he leaned back arrogantly. He had scribbled quite a list:

I have arisen at seven o'clock.
I have been in English class for one years.
He has beaten the man.
He has become an intelligent student.
He has begun the assignment.
He has bitten a sandwich.

I pointed to his list. "How many years?"

"One. Ahhh!" and he fell on his mistake. For all of his conceit, Manolo was easily humbled.

I sauntered over to Caterina, who had opened her book and was cherry-picking from the list:

I have been in class long time.
I bought a book.
I have dreamt a man.
I have felt his face.
I have blown Eva.

"Mmmm, I don't know about this one," I said pointing to "I have blown Eva."

"Yes, like "golpe," she said defensively. "I look in the dictionary."

"Oh, you mean hit. Blow as in hit. But blow is also the wind. The wind has blown." I puffed my cheeks and blew out a stream of air. She gave me a dumb look. "You have blown out the candle."

"Candle? What is candle?"

"It's a thing with..." I put my fist forward, holding a phantom candle, shaking it for emphasis, "with this thing on top." I swirled the index finger of my other hand above my fist. The word fire escaped me momentarily. Caterina beamed.

"Yes, I blow this thing Professor Ferry. Candle."

S. PERE FOHCS.

I saw Clarence that night at Kitty O'Shea's. He was calling the beer lager that night, and he repeated it a few dozen times before offering an explanation. "The root word may be associated with gulag, as in the Russian Gulag. Welcome to the gulag," he said. "Or it's etymologically linked to lagan, as in something left in the sea. It's like we survived a shipwreck and it's our goddamned buoy."

CHAPTER 16

Clarence gripped the handle of his black briefcase so tightly that his knuckles turned white. He clenched his teeth and felt the familiar pain of a long-neglected cavity. As he approached the Hello Its English Time School, he thought of the possible discrepancies in his pay. Rounding down, for instance, was something he had to watch out for. Unlike the Europeans who were part of the great bureaucratic system of the EU, Clarence knew he had no legal recourse if he felt cheated—there was no authority to which he could plea. For that reason, he thought he might be too submissive. A lot of Americans were that way, he thought, though some of those fools imagined that they might actually get deported if they caused a stir.

Clarence calculated his salary in his head: 1900 pesetas per hour times twenty-four and a half hours equaled 46,550 pesetas. Isabelle would likely put into play Óscar's cancellation on Monday. But Clarence went all the way to Winterthur before being turned away. The school would no doubt be paid the same. He suspected Isabelle would try and shave his pay and keep the extra money for herself. She had quite a racket, he imagined.

By the time he walked up the two flights of stairs and into the office, he was rehearsing his speech in his head. Hay siempre una problema, *he thought.* Estoy siempre jodido. *He relished translating his rage into another language; it offered him the chance to refine it, crystallize it, make it new. There is always a problem, I am always fucked.*

Clarence watched Isabelle tally up the hours. She did it by hand, even though there was an adding machine on the desk in front of her. Typical incompetence, he thought. Turning from calendar to writing pad, she looked like a child copying a classmate's homework. Her brown hair was held up in a tangle by three or four plastic contraptions. She wore a white dress covered with images of people, each the size of a dollar bill. These images were people of some particular vocation: a baker, a policeman, a lady surgeon. How, Clarence thought, is this woman in charge of me? With a rigid jaw, he watched her count his bills and coins.

"Vamos a ver," *she said. "You worked 24 and one half hours, yes? That is then 46,550." She gave him 46,600 pesetas even. She turned away, without so much as a passing glance at his reaction. She had had her arguments with Clarence, and was happy enough to give him his pay and nothing more—not a word, not a smile, not even the simplest of gestures. She, in fact, hated him.*

On the street, Clarence walked slowly away from the building. The bitch, he thought. What an absolute bitch. Why couldn't she just pay him exactly what he was owed? Rounding his pay up 50 pesetas was the ultimate insult. It would have been better if she short-changed him. Then they could at least argue as equals. And she couldn't round it up all the way to 47. But 50 pesetas was too meager to be construed as a kind of bonus. 450 would be enough to have a couple of beers, maybe a sandwich, certainly would convey gratitude for a job well done. Isabelle deliberately insulted him with the 50 pesetas, no doubt about it. With 50 pesetas you could buy a box of matches, or a lollipop—not even a regular candy bar. Here is 50 pesetas—this is the amount I am willing to spend to dismiss you. He should have given her back 50 pesetas. Damn, that was surely what he should have done. If only he had thought of it then! Instead he meekly accepted it—did he say thank you? He stopped in his tracks. God, oh god, he thought, I hope I didn't say thank you.

But he did. He said thank you. She was still laughing about it now, he was sure. She probably designed to give him the small coins beforehand. She was just goading him into making a fool of himself. She gave him small coins like this before, from time to time. Had he always fallen for it? Had he been her clown like this since—

"What are you doing standing there, Clarence? You look mental." Kylie was at the bar adjacent to the school, sitting in an aluminum chair on the sidewalk. She knotted her brow a little, trying to appear concerned. She sipped her beer through a straw. He walked over and sat down. "Did Isabelle tear off her dress and throw herself at you again?" she said.

"The dress, exactly. What's up with that dress? Did it have cartoon characters on it?"

"I think so. It's French. If I wore that dress they'd run me out of the country. But if you're French, you can get away with anything."

"She is the most unattractive woman I have ever seen."

"Someone loves her. She's dating a Catalan, far as I know."

"I'd prefer sex with a jar of wet sand."

Gordon came, then Ferry. Every Friday, and sometimes during the week, the English teachers drank at this nameless café, like so many others, the outdoor tables scattered beneath the plane trees. Gordon began telling some long-winded story about getting lost over in the Clot neighborhood. He made it sound like he was running for his life in a Moroccan medina. Clarence was hardly paying attention. He drained his second beer straight from the bottle. "The markets are closing," he said. "You can smell it in the wind. And I need dinner."

"We'll see you at The Quiet Man?" Kyie asked.

"Friday night. As usual."

Clarence walked up to Diagonal and turned left. The traffic was heavy, and he could literally taste the burnt petrol. He walked up Aribau, passed the shops of expensive clothes. He glanced at the price of a suit—74,000 pesetas, almost twice the amount he had in his pocket. You'd need a car for a suit like that, he thought. You'd need more than one of those suits too, you'd need a whole closet full. If you wore a suit like that once, then everyone would look carefully at what you wore the next time. It's a suit, but not really a suit; it's part of a network of suits, he thought.

He turned again on Travessera de Gràcia. The line of cars was unbroken as far as he could see. He liked this part of the city—the heavy traffic, the bustle, the swirls of noise—and not the gothic quarter like all the other expats. He felt a sense of belonging and anonymity. Faces streamed by on his left. Woman woman man woman. The perfumes, the honking, the occasional brush of shoulders, the ache of sexual longing.

Caprabo was busy. The security guard was over by the bakery counter, helping a woman collect some magdalenas *she had dropped. Clarence remembered that shoppers were supposed to put bags and cases in a locker. He patted his pockets, but had given his coins, his six 600 pesetas, to the waiter at the bar. He tucked his briefcase under his arm and pushed through the turnstile.*

In his plastic cart, Clarence piled a carton of milk, two six packs of beer, and spaghetti next to his case. He wandered around, taking some vague comfort in the aisles of colorful packages. He began perusing the meat. It had been a long time since he enjoyed a steak. Steak cooked on a grill, he thought, is on the top of the list of things I miss. He thumbed over the miscellaneous cuts left out by the butcher, nothing recognizable and probably nothing more than stewing meat. These fools probably have to send the prime cuts to a more developed country, he mused. The French have likely arranged a favorable exchange for prime rib, telling these simpletons that the fatty racks are worth only a crate of second hand boots. And then suddenly, among the strips and lumps, Clarence saw a huge porterhouse steak. It was too big for the Styrofoam plate, as it bulged against the plastic wrap. How could the butcher let it escape his precious case? Clarence picked it up and appraised its heft—over a kilo easily. An old woman reached into the case in front of him and grabbed a package of pale ground beef. "That's meat for a king," she said in slow Spanish, gesturing to the steak in Clarence's hand.

He pushed his cart away from the case and passed the bottled water. Clarence leaned on the front of the cart and looked at the price of the steak for the first time—3,630 pesetas. People shuffled by oblivious to him, even though he had slowed to almost a complete stop. They could all afford a steak like this, he thought, but would never buy it. They're too cheap to treat themselves right once in a while.

He unzipped the side pocket of his leather briefcase. He turned a corner and started up the next aisle. A few people were scanning the shelves, reading labels. In one smooth motion, Clarence shoved the meat into the pocket of his briefcase. It was a tight fit, but he managed to get it zipped. Still, the case was noticeably swollen. He turned it over, meat side down. He grabbed a few more cheap things he vaguely needed—dried garbanzo beans, ketchup, potato chips—and headed for the checkout.

The line moved slowly. The woman with the pale ground beef was in front of him, piling item after item on the black conveyer belt. "Ah, the king," she said and looked in his cart. "Pase, pase," *she said, gesticulating dramatically for Clarence to go ahead of her.*

"No, that's OK," he said in English.

"Pase!" *she implored, tugging the front of his cart toward the cashier, who was now looking wearily at them both. A layer of sweat tingled his back. Over the cashier's shoulder, he saw the security guard firmly directing a young woman to put her oversized purse into a locker. Clarence positioned the cart next to the cashier and handed her the items to be scanned. When he was finished, she looked at his bag in the cart and clicked her tongue. She said something quickly in Spanish and pointed to the lockers. With the meat side facing away from her, Clarence lifted the briefcase to show her that he wasn't hiding anything beneath it.* "Oye," *she said to the security guard. Clarence went cold. He thought of grabbing his bag and running for the exit. Surely he could outrun the guard, but did he really want to run down the street with his briefcase? That would be too absurd a scene, he thought. The security guard sauntered over to the cashier, who was already talking to him, pointing at Clarence's bag. She was reprimanding the guard, and not accusing Clarence at all. This will pass, Clarence thought. But then, the security guard beckoned him with a curling index finger. The cashier stretched her hand out to the guard. "Wait," she said to Clarence. "1,150 pesetas."*

No one as yet was watching him. This was a routine procedure. The security guard had to give Clarence some attention to atone for the lapse of letting him through with a big case. Sweat dripped down Clarence's temples. A bribe, he thought. I could probably buy this cretin off with two-thousand pesetas. "Open it," the guard said. Clarence bent into the cart and unzipped the large middle section of the case.

"Look," Clarence said in Spanish, "only books and papers." The guard showed some interest in the materials. He had a large bulbous nose covered in blackheads. He looked at the front of the book, written entirely in English, and turned it over. He acted like he was a customs inspector scrutinizing the belongings of a mysterious foreigner. "I'm an English teacher," Clarence said in Spanish, gaining confidence. "Headstrong—es la fuerza de la

cabeza." *Clarence tapped his index finger on his sweaty temple.* "Headstrong," *he said winking, instantly loathing himself. The guard looked at him with new suspicion. He put the books back in the cart and not in Clarence's bag, a bad sign. Clarence's heart was in this throat. He could see that the guard had not yet decided whether to go through the rest of the bag or just let him go. A few shoppers straggled around now, watching the goofy guard harass the nervous foreigner.*

The guard turned the case over and prodded the swollen pocket with his chubby index finger—indeed as if he were testing the doneness of a steak. He knew that he had something. He yanked the zipper open and roughly pulled out the package of meat. For a second he held it slightly aloft, as if he were a magician who had once again foiled the laws of nature. But he collected himself in an instant, and turned his attention to Clarence, whose face had turned the color of wet cement. More than a dozen customers had stopped by this point and looked on with a mixture of curiosity and glee. They are a shameless people, Clarence thought. The idea of running helter-skelter out the door once again crossed his mind, but with the contents of his bag spilled inside the cart, it would just lead to more trouble. He had business cards from school in the bag. His new objective, now that he realized he was merely at the beginning of an ordeal with this guard, was to prevent this information from spilling over into his personal life.

The backroom of Caprabo was what Clarence expected: drifts of paper, folding chairs, and a wall hung with rain slickers. "We are going to call the police," the guard said. He was joined by the store manager, a man not much older than Clarence.

"Wait a minute," the manager said. "I have some more questions." He bent one leg onto a stool and leaned forward. They are playing good cop/bad cop, Clarence thought, but to what end he did not know. The meat in the bag was obviously the extent of the crime—there was no syndicate, no accomplice, only that singular, pathetic act. They are going to drag this out to relish their feeling of power and superiority, he thought.

"Why steal a steak when you have almost fifty thousand pesetas in your pocket?" The manager asked. It was a good question, one that had not occurred to Clarence.

"I don't know," Clarence mumbled. "That money is for my apartment. For my children," he said reflexively.

"You have children?" the manager asked surprised. Even the security guard turned to him with the faintest sympathy.

"Yes, I have three children," Clarence said.

"Where is your ring? A married man must wear a ring. My wife wouldn't stand for me not wearing my ring." The manager joked condescendingly, as if he considered Clarence's story a little suspect. Still, the guard laughed along and pointed to his own ringed finger. He then made a motion of cutting his own throat, implying the same grave consequences if he were to take off his ring.

"My wife is dead," Clarence said. He did not know how to say widower in Spanish. Besides, the blunt statement had a sobering effect. The guard turned away and thrust his hands into his pockets, ashamed at himself for making such a foolish gesture. The manager, perhaps not completely convinced by Clarence's claim, nevertheless nodded knowingly and told him that he was sorry about his loss. There followed an awkward silence, as the manager, having relinquished his advantage, could not bridge the gap back from a dead wife and hungry children back to the business of shoplifting. Clarence sat before him, trying to seem a man hardened by tragedy, no stranger to despair, dutifully awaiting his punishment.

The manager let him go with a warning, and a vague suggestion to seek help for his problems. The moment Clarence was gone, and the guard was sent back to his post, which had been left unattended, the manager sat alone in his small office and knew that he'd been duped; he knew it when he was letting him go. But he did not feel resentful or cheated. He knew that an intelligent man like that, forced to tell the most embarrassing lie, would suffer in his mind more than he would a day or two in jail.

CHAPTER 17

I'd fallen into the routine of going to Dmitri's every Saturday. I usually stopped at The Quiet Man for an afternoon ale. On the reading table, mixed up with a bunch of old Irish newspapers and slick magazines, I found a single sheet of paper that was crudely designed to look like a newspaper/language book example. In fact, I recognized the drawings from the *Headstrong Beginners Workbook*. The word "*Sic*" was printed in bold across the top:

Lesson 50: Making Friends

Person 1: My name is Gyula. I am from Hungary.
Person 2: Your face reminds me of a desecrated grave.

Person 1: The primary exports of Hungary are coal, wheat, and the famous paprika.
Person 2: I have killed small animals using only my hands.

Person 1: Our country has no ocean but rather tremendous plains.
Person 2: Your mother sends her regards. From our love nest, high atop Montserrat.

The back of the sheet had a large headline of my employer, "Hello Its [sic] English Time School," along with this text:

> **Too Stupid To Read This?**
> **Enroll Today!**
>
> We'll begin to explain this sentence to you over the course of thirty-six weeks. You will pay us, up front, no less than 500,000 pesetas for this service, which could be provided with equal or surpassing effectiveness by a quality textbook-CD combination at roughly 1% of our cost. By paying one hundred times more than necessary, you will have the opportunity to pose random and useless questions that will detract from the overall efficacy of the lesson. You will also have the dubious privilege of welcoming an "English teacher" into your home or office. This "English teacher," who earns somewhere in the neighborhood of 10% of your fee, will likely show up slightly drunk or a little stoned; this is not helpful, despite what the teacher thinks; he/she believes that they are thus "loosened up," though of course their senses are simply blunted. He/she is merely justifying his or her irresponsible behavior. If you are exceedingly lucky, you will have an attractive teacher who you can try to have sex with; if you are a woman and the teacher is a man, consider it done; if you are a man and the teacher is a man, give it a whirl; if you are a woman and the teacher is a woman, please give it an enthusiastic whirl, videotape all proceedings, and send it to the offices of Sic; if you are a man and the teacher is a woman, you will likely have to settle for fantasizing about such an occurrence, though this is probably to your benefit, as female "English teachers" have more baggage than a 747 flying Paris to Dallas on Christmas Eve. More than likely, you will have a roguish male teacher who will try, in all sorts of embarrassing and distasteful ways, to have sex with you (if you are a female) or any other female who enters

the realm of the "lesson." This includes, but is not limited to, secretaries, wives, daughters, mothers, nieces, passersby, associates, postal workers, friends of the family, janitorial staff, as well as all acquaintances of unknown origin.

Your "tuition" also entitles you to "administration." This will come in handy if your regular "teacher" is too hung over to attend your lesson. In this instance, the "administration" will find a substitute "teacher," often fresh off the barstool himself/herself. The "administration" will also issue receipts and research discrepancies on your bill with a listlessness that will make other kinds of Catalan bureaucracy look like a Swiss watch factory by comparison.

The remainder of your fee, a cool 70%, is pure profit for the Hello Its [sic] English Time School, school's proprietor, Joan Cirlot. Mr. Cirlot, a man with many unhappy traits, exchanges your fee for any number of high-ticket items, such as sailboats, Mallorcan villas, and first-class flights to London, Miami, and New York, on which he is served a chilled alcoholic beverage immediately upon entering the cabin. All this of course requires that your "tuition" be combined with other people's "tuition," which in turn is invested or simply dumped in a bank and compounded with interest.

But don't worry, some of your "tuition" is utilized directly. For instance: teak polish on that sailboat; a Turkish carpet for the villa in Pollença; a porterhouse steak in an upscale New York restaurant; or perhaps simply a nineteen-year-old Brazilian escort in Miami. These are all things you can hang your hat on.

So, English lessons: because your life might be on the long side, and you've got to fill it with something.

When I went over to Dmitri's apartment with the paper, he was watching a soccer match, smoking a bowl of hash. "That's a teaching supplement," he said. "Clarence cooked it up. Gordon and

I helped him from time to time. I did it to humor him. I am surprised there are any still around."

"How come no one told me?"

"Get a hold of yourself. You sound like we left you in a public toilet while we went to Disneyland. That was months ago, before you got here."

"Still, this seems like the kind of thing that I should know about."

"Have you always been an imbecile? While we were publishing this, you still had your head up that girl's ass. You were still frying oysters and microwaving clams."

"No one actually used these in classes, did they?"

"Besides Clarence? No, I know I didn't. My students couldn't understand the original drivel."

"When was the last one?"

"It's been a while. You'd be better off asking Kylie, who believe it or not helped Clarence with the layout. I backed off when I started getting sick. Forget about talking with Clarence. He was here the other day. He's either becoming a wet brain or some kind of dangerous sociopath, in case you haven't noticed."

"Oh I've noticed. He's a sot. I go out with him to witness what my future might have in store."

"Should I cry now, or wait? Are you going to say something even more pathetic?"

"I'd wait."

"You need to turn it around, Ferry. You have to make your mark on this world, or at least let it make its mark on you. If you've got nothing to lose, so much the better."

"Listen to you. Every time I come over, you're looking cross-eyed at that hash pipe."

"I'm convalescing you dipshit. I'm in pain. You are what the Spanish call a *super-idiota*. Besides, I've done it. Eight or nine years I'm gone. I've watched the sun rise at the blue mosque in Istanbul. I've eaten fish caught right on the beach in Crete. I had sex with Ursula Andress's niece. What have you done?"

"Well, I microwaved that clam. And I'm here, I mean, that's why I'm here. I want to eat fresh seafood too. I want to see the sunrise. I want to have sex with the niece of someone who used to be sexy."

"Well you're going to have to get busy."

Sunday was always the loneliest day of the week. All the shops were closed. The streets were quiet except for the hum of the odd car. The pointless wandering of foreigners was cast into stark relief. There we were, newspaper tucked under our arm, crossing the street, checking our cheap watches. We fooled no one—we had nowhere to go.

Soon after I arrived, I thought that Sunday would be a nice day to eat out, but it turned out to be the worst. The restaurants were always crowded with families, and the menu was ratcheted up a few hundred pesetas, probably to keep out the foreigners and the neighborhood alcoholics in greasy sports coats.

I tried avoiding them even for a drink, though sometimes I had no choice. I was walking home one morning after sleeping next to a church at Plaça Lesseps. I stopped for a quick beer at the "clock-tower" restaurant in Gràcia.

The place was jammed—waiters darted through bands of smoke, children writhed in their stiff church outfits. I saw a man pause from his plate of broiled chicken to make a polite point with an old, but elegant woman who (I would have bet my life) was his mother-in-law. It was a timeless scene, and I could find nothing to tie it specifically to this century—not a cell phone on the table, not a TV above the bar, not even a gambling machine whirring in the corner. I got the feeling that over the years a lot of writers tried to capture the essence of these Sunday family meals at neighborhood restaurants. They likely named these stories after the restaurants themselves: *El Marisco, El Salmonete, La Cuchara de Oro.*

CHAPTER 18

"There were a lot of cooks in that kitchen," Kylie said. We were sitting in the office, and she was sticking glossy stars on her students' papers. "Dmitri was behind it as much as anyone. They were sick of using the dialogue from *Headstrong*, you know that nonsense, riddled with all the exceptions that need explaining. Believe it or not, they wanted to make it easier. They wanted to eliminate all of the irregularities. Well, that lasted about five minutes. Gordon pitched in and within an hour, they had this." She slapped the newsletter with the back of her fingers. "They must have done a dozen issues. And they got far more bizarre. I think the last few they did away with the cartoons altogether and just filled it with lots of rambling jokes. Obviously it was just a place for them to unconsciously air their regrets, articulate their fears, reveal their sexual longing—that sort of thingy."

The two of us rummaged through the cabinets near the copy machine. We found spent ink cartridges, empty beer bottles, a pencil case filled with clipped cigarettes, but no more issues of *Sic*. None of us had anything like a private office or even a desk, but everyone reserved a little shelf space below the window facing the street. Kylie went over to Clarence's pile, and began thumbing through the stack, careful not to disturb the integrity of the arrangement.

Lesson 9: At the Hotel

Moustached Patron:	I have reserved a room.
Moustached Clerk:	My brother is in prison in Lagos.
Moustached Patron:	I need a wake up call at 6.
Moustached Clerk:	My nights are spent with hashish, regret, and whores.
Moustached Patron:	What time is breakfast?
Moustached Clerk:	Death will make us equal one day.

In the street outside the office, I bumped into Martin, the French and Dutch teacher. From Belgium, Martin spoke five languages, not including his quickly improving Catalan. His style was European flair tempered with casual American. He tucked expensive Italian shirts into faded Levis. His black leather shoes had just enough scuff to belie their high quality. He was known at the office as a sort of ladies man, though he seemed neither romantic nor tough—handsome perhaps in a chubby, boyish way. Clarence called him a "milksop."

Martin rarely socialized with anyone else in the office, though he never failed to elicit shrill, somewhat unconvincing laughs from Isabelle. He remained aloof and indifferent to everyone, which was somewhat easy, as he only worked part time. He had a better paying job with his uncle promoting concerts.

I had been waiting to ask him for advice about improving my luck with women. "I can't get females to talk to me," I said, "unless they are my students. Shop girls talk to me, and sometimes civil servants. But getting them to have sex with me would be like engineering my own personal moon landing."

"Of course this is your problem. The reason we travel is for sexual intrigue," he said, gesturing down Enric Granados with an open palm. "It is why we are here, you and me." We shuffled over to a bench and sat down, like a couple of old Catalan men stealing hours away from their wives.

"So what's your secret with the ladies?" I asked.

"I date only English, American, or Australian girls."

"Students?"

"No, that would be impossible. My clients are all Catalan. These are women I find on the beach."

"How do you know where they're from?"

"Because they are alone and read books," he said. "Sometimes Dutch or Belgian girls are reading, but they never are so friendly to me, so I always go away if they are these kinds of girls. To you, perhaps, they are friendly."

"Why would they be friendly to me? I'm a slob."

"Well, not to you precisely. But to an American. It's about being something different. If you can be different, you can be sexy. For American girls, I am very different and sexy. It is like they come to Europe just for a romantic time. I am happy to help them with their little adventure."

"I'm different to Catalans. Why can't I have sex with a Catalan?"

"Spanish and Catalan girls don't read," he said quickly, "and also they are never alone. They require a different approach. It is more difficult, and usually not worth the trouble. The idea of sexy and loose Spanish girls is a myth. Try English girls. They have sex with everyone."

"So how do you begin the adventure?"

"I ask them the time, anything, what they are reading." Martin spoke in an eager yet condescending tone, like he was a woodshop teacher explaining how to operate a lathe. "I believe I could ask them anything, and they would answer. I tell them many things about myself."

"How about lying? Do you lie? I hear lying works."

"It's possible, but I never lie, it's not necessary. Lying is like a crime, as if what you're doing is wrong. My way is the best way—I have nothing to hide. I am a nice Belgian boy, that's what they say to me."

"So you use that as a kind of tool, the niceness."

"It is not a tool, it is the reality. Your problem is that you think the world is wrong, that it has somehow cheated you, and that you must cheat it in return. That is not something I can help you with."

"OK, so what do you say to them?"

"I explain my job working for my uncle's music production company. I complain about working around famous musicians—they are always impressed with my complaining about this. And it's true—the more famous someone is, the more of an asshole he is, too. But it seems for them something special to complain about. I ask them questions about themselves, their jobs in America or England, or even their boyfriends there. For some reason that is a very good thing to ask. Then I give them a ride on my moped to their hotel. I pick them up later, we have dinner, usually in the Born, and I drive them by the Sagrada Familia, you know with the lights. And then I have sex with them until the morning."

The next day, I went to the beach. It was late afternoon and the sun was already dropping towards the gray and brown buildings of Barceloneta, though there were still plenty of people on the beach. The sand was dirty, and left an ash-like powder on my feet. I chose a spot some ten feet from two girls lying on their backs, oily and topless. I stretched out one of Paz's bath towels and sat down, resting my arms on my knees. An old, heavy woman with a cooler strapped to her back labored by shouting, "Cerveza, Fanta, Coca-Cola." Her foreign accent and the repetition of the words made it sound like an incantation.

I leaned back on my elbows. I was afraid to take off my large button-down shirt and expose my pale, pudgy body. I was wearing a pair of large cargo shorts, white socks and sneakers. I looked ready for a hike in the mountains.

I untied my shoes and pulled off my socks. I thought the smell might damage the mood, but the wind was already carrying a slightly putrid smell, like a rotting crab. I stood up and inhaled deeply, looking out at the murky, vast sea. I sauntered down to the water's edge. An old woman in a bathing cap was swimming parallel to the shore. There weren't any shells on the ground, just muddy sand and odd pieces of plastic.

When I walked back to the towel, a few more people were leaving, but the girls were still there. I sat down again and unbuttoned my shirt down to my stomach. I leaned toward the girls. "*Que hora es*?" I asked—almost shouted. Their four oily breasts heaved forward in a moment that I was not at all prepared for. My heart thrashed like a fish in the bottom of a boat. My movements lost consequence. I fantasized about fantasizing about this moment. *I'm a lurid man,* I thought.

The sun seemed to shoot back to noon, drawing the sweat from the back of my neck. The girls ignored my question, and were clearly embarrassed. A fat man nearby peered over an aluminum-covered triptych. Trying to recover my dignity, I asked the man for the time, tapping my wrist—which I was stunned to find had a watch on it. "Wait, it's broken. *Roto*," I pleaded. The girls were stuffing their wicker bags with their walkmans and water bottles and jars of lotion. They quickly climbed into their sundresses like actresses changing costumes between scenes. The man put down his sun reflector and just stared at me, like a cop waiting for his suspect to make one more foolish, criminal move.

I lay on my back and sweated through my shirt. I had ignored all of Martin's rules: only approach girls on their own; only talk to girls who are reading; avoid girls that I suspect are Catalan. I hated that crummy beach, hated Spanish people, hated all the Catalans. Why were they so uptight, so impenetrable?

I stayed on my back but turned my head toward the sea. Italy was out there somewhere, just across the water. I should have gone there—after all, that was the place Svetlana had gone on about. What was I doing in Spain? The Italians were probably a lot warmer and more friendly. They'd give me the time, let their breasts bounce around, even if I had a watch on. If I asked them the time, they'd give me an aperitif and some prosciutto. At the very least, a big Italian guy wouldn't just stare at me. He'd commiserate, offer some blunt, time-worn advice on the folly of men chasing women, give me the number of a lady who'd love me for a fee.

Clarence and I drank gin and Fanta that night on Montjuic. "The broken places are what makes us stronger," I told him. "That's what Hemingway says."

"Was that before or after he shot himself in the face?"

CHAPTER 19

In Barcelona, I had no family, no history, no commitments beyond the lessons that recurred like a chronic headache. My days did not accelerate toward anything—there was no accumulation, no point at which I could say, "this is built, this is finished," or "I have arrived at this attractive destination after executing a gritty but effective plan." In fact, it was as if my activities dissipated whatever significance might reside in the day.

I walked to the Hello Its English Time office to pick up my paycheck. Some of my colleagues had finished the week's work and were drinking at the bar below the school. When I walked up, Kylie was in the middle of an animated tirade. "Our whole existence is an illusion," she said. "Look at us for Christ's sake, we're so stupid that we can only teach our own language."

"English is the language of the world," Gordon said unconvincingly, "by 2020 it will overtake Mandarin Chinese. We are performing a global service."

"You sound like a brochure for International House. It's like teaching people to walk, to breathe. We're nothing. I've got friends in Sydney making fifty times my salary and they sit around doing nothing"

"Right. They're doing nothing. At least we're doing something," Gordon said. "At least we're professional."

"Oh, aren't we fucking professional. Look at Clarence's pants for Christ's sake. Look how worn they are. What off-shop did you buy them in?"

"I bought these pants at Sears last time I was in Baltimore," Clarence said.

"Which was like five years ago. They're too big besides."

"I've lost weight."

"More like self esteem. You'd have to work five or six hours here to buy a new pair."

"What does it matter what my pants look like?"

"Matter, what does it matter? They look like circus pants. All you need are some bowling pins to juggle. Which would be perfectly fitting—we're like entertainers, not educators. Make the dimwits laugh. As for materialistic, you twit, I'm the only one saying it, asking what's so important about teaching skilled professionals a new skill? Why bother helping the upper middle class achieve anything? It's because they're the only ones who can pay us. And we get paid shit besides."

In addition to a bunch of business students, Kylie taught an intermediate class of mixed adults in the office classroom. A few days before, I tried striking up a conversation with one of her sultry students by asking about Kylie's class. "She is a saint," she said, the Catholic metaphor arousing in her a fawning glow. "She is tolerant and always giving care to us."

Along with Gordon, Clarence and Kylie at the aluminum table, there was a new guy who looked to be around sixty. "Tom, Wichita," he said to me when Kylie finally fell silent. "Call me Wichitom, they all do. Irish kid named me that in Zurich. That was his thing, giving people little names. Peach-Pit Paul, Colleen from Aberdeen, Bicycle-Michael." In the space of a few minutes, I learned that Wichitom had lived in Europe for the last ten years—the first few in Brussels, and then stints in Berlin, Zurich, Milan and finally Paris, where his most recent marriage to a Swiss woman was still smoldering. Everywhere, he worked for Berlitz.

"Came in last Saturday," he said. "Blitz posted an immediate opening. Kid from L.A. got dysentery. Went home. Probably looking for an excuse. He'll come back, they usually do."

"Where is Berlitz?" I asked.

"Near one of the stadiums. No metro, but a bus. The usual pain in my ass."

"Darnell hired him for the summer test prep class," Clarence said. "Those silver-spoon-up-their-ass teenagers that no one likes."

"You don't like anyone," Gordon said.

"True. But these kids don't even like themselves."

"That's fine," Wichitom said, "they're fine. It's just side work, we all need it. Blitz pays shit. No secret there. But they're franchised, easy to change cities with them. European cities, they're all the same. Millions of these schools. Always need help, all the time. Kid from London gets a sick mom, flies out the next day. Girl from Boston breaks a nail, goes home." He patted Kylie on the forearm. "Better watch your purse sweetheart." Clarence and I made eye contact, expecting Kylie to rip into the old geezer for the patronizing endearment.

"Oh right. For fuck's sake," she said. Two guys that I hadn't noticed were talking behind Kylie's chair, and her bag was lying on the ground next to her.

"I was robbed soon after I arrived in Brussels," Wichitom said. "In the park. A fellow with a soccer ball asked me if I liked European football. 'Sure,' I said, what's the harm in that? Well, he dribbled behind me, mentioned some business about tackling, and put his forearm on my back. Homosexuality came to my mind, rather than larceny." Wichitom poured a beer into his tilted glass. "His hand went in and out of my sports jacket so fast, I didn't realize what was happening until he was five steps gone. I would have given him a good run, but my wallet was empty save for a hundred francs and my ex wife's expired MasterCard."

After our beers, the five of us disbanded—Kylie and Clarence walked toward Gràcia to see a film, Gordon alleged he had a date, and Wichitom was going downtown, more or less in the same direction I was headed.

We strolled down Rambla Catalunya. The sidewalk cafes were full of tourists, sunburned and eating dinner four hours earlier than the Catalans.

"I'm interested why people come to Europe, or go to Thailand or wherever." I said to him. "That was the most surprising thing when I got here. I thought I'd be the only one. But there are thousands of people from America. Some people say there's fifty thousand native English speakers here."

"They say a hundred thousand in Paris. Sometimes two, depending who you ask. Always big even numbers."

"Fifty thousand people. That's a small city itself."

"A city of exceptions."

We crossed Carrer d'Aragó. All six lanes were deep with pulsing, anxious cars.

"Why do so many people move away? I mean, why did you come to Europe in the first place? Heartbreak?" I said.

"No, too cliché. Anyone who says that they are here to forget a girl is lying to themselves. For me it was a dangerous accumulation. I had a lifetime of reasons. Small things. It got so you couldn't smoke in public places. They demolished my favorite restaurant and built a Hardees. Computers called me at 11 PM and asked me if I wanted my carpets cleaned. It wasn't the bears that chased me from the forest, it was the mosquitoes."

I pointed at the brick building two hundred yards on our left. "There's the Tàpies' museum." It was more or less indistinguishable from those surrounding it, except the roof was strewn with barbed wire, a chair tangled in the middle.

"Oh, I had my share of wives. Three, not counting Josephine," he said. "Worked for Hewlett Packard. The warehouse, then the mailroom, then sales. Moved to Chicago, Kansas City, Little Rock. Three kids, I'm still on terms with two. Went to the track a lot. Just a sort of vague, gnawing discontent. Got fired after twelve years for padding my expense account. Hooker, Atlanta. Took a traveling sales job. Always had a hundred pounds of cleaning powder samples in my trunk. Drove to restaurants from St. Louis to Fort Worth, Harrisburg to Memphis. It's those hours that I regret, those hours I'll never get back, those hours on the interstates," he said wistfully.

The most seductive thing about living abroad is the detachment from previous experience. Talking with Wichitom, I had the sensation that we were already dead. Living abroad is exactly what we want death to be like. Our previous mistakes, no matter how spectacular, are rendered anecdotal. Gone are the credit card bills, the telemarketers, and all responsibility. But our pleasures are made new, refined. "I remember sitting in a café in Brussels," Wichitom said, "about a month into my life there. I was waiting for a woman, I can't remember her name. The produce delivery man and the bartender were having a small argument, in French of course, which I was listening to, trying to piece together. Then the song 'Everything Happens to Me' came on the radio. Frank Sinatra. I thought that I felt good because of the argument, you know, the whole business of having your expectations fulfilled, the whole Latin temperament, the postcard of it all. But what it really was, was that I realized all at once that my life as I knew it was slipping away. It was a matter of volition after all, putting all that behind me. I had just turned fifty-two."

English Teacher 1: I'm going drinking tonight at the Quiet Man. Possibly I'll vomit, and for sure I'll black out. Falling asleep at the back of the NitBus is not out of the question.

English Teacher 2: There is nothing like a series of pints to release you from care and worry, from boredom and distress, from loneliness and endless fear. I'll meet you there in five minutes.

Paz was in her bedroom—which she kept, with a couch and an easy chair, as an alternative sitting room—with Solangel, a Columbian woman and fellow volunteer at the Sisters of Mercy church on Carrer de Ferran. The two of them gave a few hours on Wednesdays and Saturdays to the Sister's hard-luck soup kitchen and clothing giveaway center. They washed the donated clothing and served big steaming dishes of pasta tossed with tuna fish and boiled eggs to Barcelona's legion of homeless.

I was lying on the couch watching an unbroken sequence of soccer goals on the TV. There were goals from every league, from Cape Town to Japan, Lisbon to Monterrey. Headers, bicycle kicks, impossible corners. There were goals from the seventies and eighties. The whole program was looped with cheesy computer music.

The two women emerged from Paz's little room, and Solangel took a tentative step toward my lair. "We have no man," she said.

I looked at the tan slope connecting Solangel's neck and shoulder.

"We need man in the kitchen," she said to me in rehearsed English. "In the kitchen. It is nice to have a man to lift." She bent down and mimed a person lifting a box.

"I have to teach," I said, and patted the only reading material in arm's reach—a stack of *Hola* magazines on the table. "*Yo soy profesor de inglés. Esta noche*." Solangel looked at Paz for confirmation. I wasn't teaching, but was going to visit Dmitri, which in my mind qualified as charity. Besides, I didn't want to tag along with these women to the soup kitchen, only to be greeted with images of my father, toothless and haggard, urine-soaked and eating a week-old muffin. Paz shrugged her shoulders, and Solangel clucked her tongue.

Paz could afford to volunteer her time because she owned her apartment and, according to Enrique, also received some government-sponsored income that was further supplemented by our rent. Where this Solangel character got her money, I had no idea, but I noticed as they were leaving that she cut a nice figure from behind.

When they were gone, I settled onto the couch with a plate of squid rings and a pool of ketchup. My favorite show, *Impacto TV,* was just beginning. I took comfort from the opening montage: a guy falling from a balcony on a home video, another careening down an embankment during a police chase, and some poor janitor catching fire on a power-plant security camera.

The episode itself started with a helicopter rescue during a flood—only a large dog was left wallowing on the roof. The tops of trees poked through a sea of brown water. The announcer said, "yada yada yada, Oklahoma." A man swung on a rope ladder, looking back at the yelping hound. Maybe the dog would last until a boat could come, or the water ebbed, though maybe he'd slip into the gloom, along with the couch, the TV, the wife's bric-a-brac.

The man may have felt a certain peace, I imagined. There would be redemption in such a flood. All the years washed away, the photographs floating toward the woods like so many leaves, the days and nights churned into the murk, the new life beginning at the Red Cross shelter far from the broken levee.

The next segment of the show was a garden-variety car chase. It ended in a less-than-thrilling crash into a guardrail and a subsequent pursuit on foot; a large, white cop lumbered after a chubby black guy in a sweat-suit. Eventually the guy climbed over a fence only to find another large white cop approaching from the other side. Familiar with the routine, the fellow got down on his knees and put his hands on his head. The panting cop tackled him anyway, and wrestled him into handcuffs. Filmed with a night vision camera, the whole thing seemed archaic and conceptual, as if it was Civil-Rights-Era footage that I had seen time and time again. The only saving grace was at the end of the tape, when one of the cops breathed heavily into his clip-on microphone and said, "take it easy son, we've got you." Four or five other uniforms converged on the scene, ready with their guns and batons. "It's over," the first cop said. "Son, son, it's all over."

CHAPTER 20

You must move to another city. Why? Because that is what you do, you move to other cities. You continue to search for what you've been searching for for years, what you've searched for in vain, knowingly searched for in vain for all these years: a place untainted by you, by Tom, or Wichitom, or whatever name you call yourself these days. You've settled for the novelty of new places temporarily diminishing your acute self-awareness. You've settled for the intensity of a foreign environment temporarily reducing your ego. Though of course, in time, you've sullied these places all the same. You've grown as restless in these strange cities as you were in the one-traffic-light town of your Missouri youth. The singular traffic light of Dredgemore blinks on the edge of every city you quietly leave, blinks to remind you that you are still arriving. You know you will see that traffic light blink at the hour of your dying, if only because you've imagined that you would all these years.

You decide on the Mediterranean. You love the sea, not the way some people love the sea, the way these people say, "I could never live away from the sea," yet you love it in your way. You love the sea because it represents to you a vast strangeness, the setting of so many epics and dramas—even one of your own. You vacationed with Bridgette in San Remo and played tennis on a clay court. You later made love to her in a seaside pension; you made love to her despite your jealousy. At dinner, she had showed off her rudimentary Italian with the waiter, who looked at you with a mix of condescension and contempt, as if you were an unwanted chaperone. At fifty-four, you were only twelve years her senior. Still, his look made you aware of your graying temples, the loosening skin around your neck. The handsome waiter followed Bridgette with his eyes, out of the restaurant and into drizzle and yellow streetlights. You made love to her that night despite the jealousy, despite her refusal to put you at ease by claiming she felt nothing for that waiter. She lay, her face turned to one side, submitting to you out of habit, a remnant of her devotion to you. She went to the bathroom, showered, dressed, and lay on the bed with her back to you and fell asleep. Still, you think back to that time by the sea with nostalgia; at least you and she were still together, at least you had her sweetness beneath you.

Barcelona. You arrive at night. You disembark at Estació Sants and take the metro into the Barri Gòtic. You've studied the guidebooks and maps for weeks—you pride yourself on your ability to find your way through these strange terrains. Stepping onto the train, standing next to the door with your coat folded over your arm, you think of the strange present participle: belonging.

The famous string of connecting streets known as Las Ramblas is exactly what you expected. Even at midnight, these streets are teeming with people. You ask directions to your pension from a man working at a kiosk. The streets off the Ramblas are not easy to navigate. They twist and change names. They lead to other streets, the names of which utterly surprise you, as they don't appear on your map. But you are finding your way. The streets are damp; the putrid smell of garbage and open sewers reaches your nostrils with a sting. Just a block off Barcelona's signature street, you are astonished by the abject seediness. A huge, gorgeous plaza swarms with punks and criminals. The central fountain gurgles water that must, by the appearance of those sitting around it, be absolutely filthy. Tall and broad-shouldered kids juggle and smoke, one of their dirty dogs barks and approaches you as you try and cut across the plaza. "Pssssss. Hash?" A shadow of a man, suddenly within inches, asks you. And yet, amidst all of this squalor, you see silver-haired tourists sipping drinks at outdoor cafes. The perimeter of the plaza is in fact lined with such places. Walking down a side street away from the plaza, you pass a spit of roasting chickens, so close that you could reach into the fire and grab one. Ten meters away you pass a sleazy bar, an assortment of hookers standing in front, their thick limbs ensconced in blue and pink spandex. Where is your pension?

You decide to ask for directions at a restaurant with white curtains in the window. But before you can open the door, it opens from the inside, violently, and a man comes barreling out. He sprawls on the cobblestone street. A man in white kitchen garb follows him, shouting the whole time. He ignores you. He begins to kick the man on the ground, who has assumed the fetal position and who shrieks with every blow of the boot. You take some steps toward the men, unsure what you intend to do. You say, in English, leave him alone. And then you say it in French. The man stops kicking, looks at you, balls up his filthy apron and throws it at you. He's shouting in Catalan, so you don't really understand. Something about a thief, the man is a thief, he seems to be saying. You look down at the man. He looks like a thief. What can you say?

Your hotel: clean, cheap, a bathroom and shower shared by everyone on that floor. The San Louis Pension, it's called, and you lie on the damp bedding and savor the irony, just like you savored it when you booked the reservation three days earlier. Tomorrow you will awake and make the rounds to some flats. You will try and find a place to live—maybe with a widow, or a divorcee, someone who might not mind preparing a meal for you, who might not mind ironing your shirts or washing your socks. You are the kind of boarder who doesn't mind paying a little extra. You may get lucky and have an entire life come together before the sun sets. You know from experience that this happens, that an afternoon can be a mold into which you cast your desires and needs, your logic and memory, and a whole new existence takes shape with ease and then repeats, day after day. And you also know that there will be some day in the future—six months, a year, five years—one single day, that this mold will be smashed, and your days will once again be aimless and without form. You and your bags will once again be huddled together at a train station cafe, waiting to fall on another unfamiliar city, on another broken person, and you will proceed to piece together a new collection of days. In this way you are constructing a life.

You secure a room in the apartment of a neurotic divorcee who smokes two packs of cigarettes a day. "I want to stay at least six months, or maybe a year," you say in French.

"Yes, good, it's a relief," Nuria says, though vexes her brow. "It's trouble to always have people moving in and out." You give Nuria one month's rent. You would rather give her more, but you know that it would put you at a disadvantage in your future affairs

with her, as she would tag you as rich, or at least an easy source of cash.

You easily find a second job at the Hello Its English Time School. You work with a collection of misfits who are rather bizarre, even for expatriates. You meet them on a Friday afternoon at the bar below the school. One guy, Lester Ferry, reminds you of yourself at thirty. He's slovenly, but well intentioned, polite even when steaming drunk, as he became the afternoon you first met him. You live in the same part of the city, so walked home from the bar together. After he was thoroughly drunk, he wouldn't shut up. "I'm thinking of starting a bus service for English teachers. We work in the same areas, at the same times, so it makes sense. It could also be a source of supplies, like chalk and booze. We could keep booze in it. And cots. Chalk, booze and cots, except for the chalk. No one really needs chalk. It could be like an ice-cream truck or a bloodmobile. We'd cruise through neighborhoods, broadcast detective music that would herald our presence. We'd keep lager packed in ice, name brand smokes, sandwiches, lists of false-friend cognates, deodorant."

While Ferry puts you somewhat at ease, Clarence is so cynical that he may in fact be a sociopath. He seems extraordinarily spiteful and bitter. You must manage your affairs with him deliberately; he is the type who will capitalize on your sentimentality. You must be careful with what you say, because to give him a resentment would be disastrous. You must also be careful to not be sycophantic with him, for that would be equally bad. He looks for excuses to tear people down.

And Kylie, the Australian girl—there is no need to apologize for liking her. She has created a tough exterior of righteousness, assertiveness, and independence. In this way she reminds you of Bridgette, but voluptuous and of course younger. She would make a fine lover for you, you think. You would be smart enough not to engage her in political arguments; you would assume her sympathies because you've realized that such things are only conversation pieces anyway. She would tacitly admire your deference and reward you with spirited, uninhibited sex. You know the routine. And she likes you. You're not yet sure if it is in strictly a fatherly way, though you doubt it. You must play the part of patriarch—it's almost a necessity at your age, and then set about transcending that role. You will listen. You will measure out advice. You will draw on your vast experience. But then you must just as deliberately subvert your position. You have already sent out shock troops in this regard, by relating self-effacing anecdotes of your romantic escapades. You told the whole motley group about the time you were dating a Polish girl in Paris, a girl, you said, not much older than Kylie. Kylie not only did not look disgusted, but rather appeared somewhat interested, or at least her countenance belied a benign acceptance of your half-invented affair. You might work at cultivating that acceptance into an approval, and then that approval into curiosity, and finally sousing that curiosity with a few liters of Blanquette de Limoux and see if that gets you into her pants.

Your schedule is simple. Your students are eager and attentive. They shower you with respect and admiration. They assume that you are some language master, that your life has been built and designed for this pinnacle, this remarkable realization of your skills and dreams. They see you as a man who has achieved a lifelong ambition. When you give them a list of participles they think they divine your affection for these words; you and participles, they think, have a long and studied history. You didn't know what a participle was until you were well into your forties, you want to tell them. You want to share with them the irony that you only mastered English grammar by living in a foreign world and teaching it to foreigners. But you don't, you can't. Instead you examine the list with them, noting with feigned glee the inexplicable irregularities. You wax romantically about the quirky English language, making a wistful, seemingly off-the-cuff comparison between Shakespeare and Rap music. You suggest a strong affinity between the two, but you try and dismiss your own digression. You quell their questions and insist on getting back to tasks. The gambit works, as the students become flush with attention. It's the kind of comment that hints at a broad, analytical knowledge of language, though you have absolutely no idea what you're talking about.

The following Friday, you again meet your colleagues at the bar below the school. The Englishman named Gordon drinks a concoction of lemonade and beer. "A Shandy," he calls it. "An English tradition." You can't tell whether he is drinking it because he likes it, or if it is strictly an ironical gesture. Ferry—no one, you learn, calls him Lester—is already half drunk. He says, "I've fallen in love with one of my students. She paralyzes me. I can't stand it, I don't know what I'm going to do."

"The only honorable thing to do is to teach her the nouns of the human body," Gordon says.

"Crotch," Clarence says, "that's a word I've never taught. Crotch. What kind of word is that?"

"Sounds German," Kylie says.

"Or Canadian," Ferry adds.

"Just begin with phallic symbols," Gordon says. "Begin talking about phallic symbols and see where that takes you."

"I was never so clear on those," Ferry says. "What exactly would you consider a phallic symbol?"

"My cock," Clarence loudly announces, half standing up, "and everything that resembles my cock." People glance over from adjacent tables. You're a little embarrassed, but reassure yourself that they don't understand English.

"More like cigars, guns. Look at the obelisk on Diagonal," Kylie says. "That's an African fertility thingy. Talk about that. They don't get more obvious than that." Suddenly you realize that your colleagues might be offering serious advice to Ferry.

When your group has left their suds at the bottom of their glasses, you again walk with Ferry down Rambla Catalunya toward the Raval. The hour is not yet ten and the southwestern sky is still pale from the day. You have begun to feel almost fatherly toward this young man. People veer slightly out of his path, sensing his inebriation. What does he do when you're not around? You don't lament the time you're spending with him, as it saves you the mild embarrassment of exploring the nightlife on your own. You stop at another bar, even though Ferry seems increasingly drunk. It's called Montparnasse, the only place in the world, he says, where you can still drink absinthe. To tell him that you could easily find it in France would only result in a tedious argument. You are instinctively agreeable with him. You feel that in some obscure way you are destined to help him.

"It's quite an old bar," you say.

He leans his head on the bar. His speech is unintelligible. You try to cajole him with remarks about the odd assortment of characters who surround the two of you. One girl, for instance, is wearing only jeans and a bra.

Ferry stares at you quizzically, as if he never met you. Should you help him home? You get the chilling feeling that Ferry could one day arrive at a bad end. You'll walk him all the way home tonight.

The bartender comes over with your beer. You stroke your salt and pepper beard. She seems to be taking a certain pride in not acknowledging the hapless Ferry; she's seen her share of alcoholic collapses. The quicksilver drool spilling out the corner of Ferry's mouth hardly gets her attention. She has fire tattooed on her neck.

Job Prospects: An Interview with the Hello Its [sic] English Time! Proprietor, Joan Cirlot!

Sic: What do you look for in a teacher?

Joan Cirlot: First, they must be human. And I mean really human, and not just primates. We had some monkeys teaching the Beginning Business classes last year and it backfired. The monkeys actually performed better than the TOEFL graduates, but they caused other problems. The monkeys threw the books at the students and urinated on the desks. The TOEFL graduates, on the other hand, would urinate on the desks and fall asleep. We prefer this latter, more benign approach, if only for liability reasons.

The second thing we look for is...no, wait, that's it. We only ask that they be non-monkey primates.

Sic: What is the average length of time for a teacher to remain employed at your school? Do you offer them contracts?

Joan Cirlot: Well, that depends. Some of our teachers stay on for weeks, though usually it's much shorter than that. If I had to give an average, I'd say twenty-five minutes.

However, our average contract is for forty-five minutes with an employee option to stay for the full hour. We've learned it's best to give them the choice. You see, some teachers walk into the classroom for the first time—stoned or drunk—and soon realize that they don't like teaching, or that they in fact thought they were entering a DIA, a brothel, or a rehabilitation center. In those cases it's best to let them finish the lesson and then part ways, respectfully.

CHAPTER 21

"You know I've still never been to the Sagrada Familia." I was talking to Kylie one afternoon at The Quiet Man. It was Saturday, and she had just come from Dmitri's, and I was on my way to see him—it was what we started to call our shift pint, even though I pretty much stuck to the metrics of the cheap domestic brand.

It was the time of day when the bar was full of teachers who had just finished their private lessons, their little leather bags zipped up beside them, their pens and pencils tucked into their shabby sports coats, their sips and their coins measured across the hours.

"They've opened an Irish bar over there," she said. Let's go tonight. Clarence and Gordon and Wichiwho are coming here later."

"Another Irish bar? Pretty soon you'll be able to walk the length of this city without ever leaving an Irish bar."

"That's cute, but really, let's go. The church is lovely at night."

"Enrique says it's too sentimental."

"That guy's a wanker from everything you tell me."

"You want to know what he says about Catalan?" I patted the Catalan textbook, *Digui Digui,* through the semi-transparent Caprabo bag that she had resting on the bar.

"Let me guess, it's sentimental."

"It's got the perfect tone for making money. Just the right amount of tongue on the roof of the mouth to exploit the Andalucians."

"Well, we're still learning taxis from the airport."

"Why not just take the train? You've already got Spanish down anyway. Why go to the bother of learning Catalan? It's useless the moment you travel more than a hundred miles."

"For fuck's sake, you've got to do something here. Your mind needs something to do. Or you'll end up like Clarence."

"I'm afraid that learning Catalan would be a ticket to the same tedium that I left behind in San Diego."

"And that sounds like your little flat mate."

"No, that one is mine. But he might agree without admitting it. He'd probably just call me a curse word."

"Well, lovie, you might have to punch that ticket eventually. Besides, there's a difference between learning and studying."

"Which are you doing?"

"Studying. That's the one that's detached, like a scientist who dissects a corpse. Learning is becoming, and I came to Barcelona to be gone and not to become."

"I am a human *drinking*, not a human *being*."

"So do you want to go *drinking* at the Sagrada Familia?"

"I think I'll just crash on Dmitri's couch if he's not too abusive."

ESL Teacher Gripped by Self-Centered Fear

Barcelona—A local ESL Teacher today was feeling more than a little down. He was, in fact, despondent. Those close to the ESL teacher claim that the source of his sadness was self-centered fear.

The fear originated in the ESL teacher's belief that he is underachieving. He should, he thinks, be farther along in life—more money, a stable relationship, or at the very least some kind of noble cause that he feels strongly about, is associated with, like Doctors without Borders or the Salvation Army. Even a compelling hobby would do. He'd like to proclaim that his poor station in life is a necessary result of his love of...of...music. You see, he'd like to say, he has dedicated himself to...the cello. The ESL teacher and the cello. He practices sometime twelve hours a day. Small wonder other areas of his life seem flat.

But no, the ESL teacher does not play the cello. He played the bass drum for two years in school, but never bothered to take lessons or get himself a proper kit. He doesn't even listen to music. The truth is that the ESL teacher is a lazy man, a lazy man who hopes against hope that some providential event will take place and provide him with the accouterments of a decent life. Not necessarily winning the lottery, but perhaps discovering an entrepreneurial cousin who needs a trustworthy man with rudimentary knowledge of Spanish to oversee a large office of indeterminate function. The ESL teacher would feel quite comfortable delegating authority, having his own parking space, providing his underlings with a well-dressed and witty administrator to admire.

Of course, nothing of this sort seems to be materializing for the ESL teacher. He in fact is a strange man, awkward when not drinking, humorous in an annoying way, and increasingly given to these desperate moments of puerile fantasizing. When he returns to England, for instance, he lies to his acquaintances about his life in Spain. He alludes to Catalan girlfriends, though he has never so much as kissed a Catalan girl. He tries to give the impression that his job teaching ESL is a vital cog in the Catalan economy. He makes it seem that he is part of a multinational corporation, and is called into service in order to brief his colleagues about impending negotiations with English-speaking clients. In fact, he plays little games with his business students, whom he suspects actually regard him as something of a jester.

Naturally, his acquaintances in London could care less. They are wrapped in their own fear and self-loathing. Luckily, he was able to extinguish these fears with several pints of ale.

Lesson 17: At the Ballroom

Man:	I am enjoying this dance!
Woman:	Being with you makes me feel like I'm floating on air.
Man:	I'm afraid that I've discovered a large wart on your back.
Woman:	That is my inflation nipple.
Man:	Talk like that makes me want to take you directly up to my deluxe suite equipped with a homemade wet bar.
Woman:	I may not be a star, but I've loved enough of them to know how it feels.

Clarence drank some imitation whiskey and walked down the Ramblas. He pushed through some tourists to a couple of Catalans dressed like Homer and Bart Simpson. They were among the usual street performers on the Ramblas.

The cocktail was starting to sting Clarence around the eyebrows. A guy in cargo shorts took pictures of Clarence giving a six foot Bart Simpson the finger. Then he got a shot of Bart Simpson stepping off his wooden box and pushing Clarence backwards. Clarence saw the sandals of the photographer and heard his camera clicking like crazy once he and Bart started swinging wildly at each other. By the time the two were on the ground, wrestling around, the guy was changing his film. Other people picked up the slack. Another guy wearing sandals and socks had his video camera cranking. He stepped in front of everyone else when Bart's head came off. The head underneath was like a red balloon and looked more scared than angry. Clarence was pretty much having his way with Bart, even though Marge and Homer were trying to pull Clarence by the shoulders. Clarence punched Bart three times—whack whack whack—in the face. Bart just sort of capitulated at that point and assumed a defeated supine position. Clarence stood up, nodded to the cameras, and made for Carrer del Tallers, where he remembered there was a crappy Irish Bar frequented by Mike McGowan who owed him five thousand pesetas. Clarence was in the mood to collect.

It might have been days later. Clarence woke up in a pension room that smelled of ammonia and wet rags. He heard the patter of feet descending for the complimentary breakfast. He heard the

sad, forlorn voices of travelers echoing in the hall. "We're hopping down to Malaga," a girl was saying, "I hear they've got really good"—and then she was interrupted by a vacuum cleaner.

Clarence waited until the sounds died down to leave his room. He went down the hall, took a card from the check-in counter and discovered he was in Valencia. All the doors were swung open for the maids. The cotton mattresses arranged in pools of sunlight, wooden chairs nicked up around the legs. The hem of a skirt trailing the maid up the stairs. He walked through the smell of coffee and out onto the street. There were buildings blocking every horizon.

CHAPTER 22

Clarence gave me a copy of the first issue. The headline was "Viva Cataloonya!," with a black and white picture of the Catalan flag in the background. Beneath it was a list of "Jokes for Catalans."

> How many Catalans does it take to screw in a light bulb?
>
> Two. One to screw in the light bulb, and one to rub a tomato on a piece of bread.

> Knock knock. Who's there? A Catalan. A Catalan who? That Catalan sure can *catalan* of money.

> A Frenchman, a Catalan and a Spaniard are in a canoe on a lake in the Pyrenees. The Catalan turns to the Spaniard and says, "*Molt de Gust.*" Then the Spaniard whacks the Catalan with an oar and he falls in the lake where he is mauled by man-eating cuttlefish. The Frenchman then captures some of those cuttlefish, squeezes out their tiny hearts and braises them in browned butter, and serves them on a bed of endive with a rosemary-béarnaise sauce. The Spaniard scoops up several braised cuttlefish hearts on his fork, and then puts a piece of ham on top of them. The Frenchman hits him in the chin with a chilled bottle of an 80's Bourdeaux. The entire scene is then obliterated by a German bomb.

Calendar Catalunya!

May 7. Feast of the Holy Urn. All shops closed in observance of the Holy Urn.

May 8. Commemoration of The Furious Resistance. All shops closed. Commemorates the furious and protracted resistance of the Catalans from the 14th to 19th century.

May 11. National Holiday observing FC Barcelona's 5 to 0 victory over Real Madrid in 1974. Everything will be closed, random dumpsters set aflame.

May 20. Day of Enormous Feasting. Feasting will commence at dawn and will not abate until the afternoon of the 21st. Everything will be closed except restaurants facilitating the enormous feasting.

On the back was a picture of Clarence wearing a ski mask with a piece of paper held in front of him, as if he were reading.

ETA World Open to All

The Basque separatist organization ETA, *Euskadi ta Askatasuna*, has announced the opening of a new terrorist-themed amusement park. ETA WORLD will differ from most other amusement parks in that it will be largely pre-modern. There will be a mere half dozen rides. One of them, "The Fishing Boat," allows park-goers to embark on an actual fourteen-day expedition for cod. They will sleep on planks, smoke homemade cigarettes, and spend nights singing Euskera folk songs to the accompaniment of a crude string or wind instrument.

Those who want to experience Basque life in the modern age will also have something to do. There will be an ongoing clinic on how to make bombs, take hostages, and cultivate political resentment.

For a supplemental fee of 290,000 pesetas, park-goers can take an ETA WORLD flight to the Canary Islands to visit their imprisoned brethren, who were unjustly removed from their native land. They will receive a quick primer in the composition of coded letters.

There will also be concessionaires in the park, including peddlers of cod in tomato sauce, cod in some kind of cream sauce, plain cod, cod cured with salt, squid in its own ink, and those expensive little eels.

Sic has learned that Disney originally wanted to partner in this enterprise, but ETA was unwilling to make certain compromises—for instance they scoffed at the idea of having Disney characters like Goofy and Mickey Mouse replace their ski-masked attendants. ETA summarily killed the Disney representatives in cold blood, and promised further reprisals if the entire Disney envoy did not leave their beloved motherland within forty-eight hours.

"I never cared about making a supplement for my classes," Clarence said. He and I were sharing a carton of wine on the metro. We were riding the blue line back and forth across the city. "I could use anything in those classes. I used to just bring in a bunch of stuff I found in the garbage can at American Express. Candy wrappers, camera instructions, condom boxes."

"So why did you make it?" I asked.

"I can't speak for anyone else, but for me it was a way to look at the world, a way to get perspective. I think I might have gone crazy without it. It was a way to get some kind of control."

"So why'd you stop?"

"I lost control of it."

I called my mother again, but the phone just rang and rang. No machine, no voicemail, no operator telling me to try again later. It must have rang fifty times, that phone. I let it keep ringing just to see how long it would ring, and it just kept on ringing. I suspected there might have been a wire crossed somewhere and the ring that I heard signified nothing, and that there was no ringing in my mother's home. At the most my call might have caused a slight vibration on the end of a wing, creaking on the edge of a lost and distant satellite, one of a million vibrations from the millions of lost and distant sons, calling home, with nothing to say.

My mother changed over the course of the last decade. She began listening to AM radio programs that featured elaborate horoscopes, random dream interpretations, and sure-fire predictions of catastrophe. They seemed to sample both the bible and Nostradamus, giving each one the same grave authority.

Aside from her divorce, my mother appeared to have a pretty good life, though she always kept a hard-luck attitude. Whenever she laughed, she did so with reserve that belied a kind of guilt. I could picture her chastising herself later in the evening for laughing at something that wasn't funny, or that was funny but should not have been laughed at so openly, if at all.

My mother was thin, wore long skirts, and smoked about a dozen Parliament cigarettes a day. She was always admired, always sought after by men, mostly older, mostly divorced and rich.

She dated Clyde "the Glide" Jefferson, a former cornerback for the Chargers. He was in the league before the players made piles of money, though after retirement he wielded his limited celebrity to his advantage by endorsing a Hyundai dealership in El Cajon. Clyde took Tyrone and me to a Chargers game once, in an obvious but sincere attempt to secure a role in our family. Tyrone overdid it on the complimentary booze in the luxury box, and he embarrassed us all by heckling the home team. No one heckled in those boxes, much less the Chargers. It was the kind of misplaced rebellion that had become Tyrone's signature.

Still, Clyde would have stayed in the picture if my mother hadn't dumped him. Her most attractive quality was her air of tragedy, and I think Clyde, along with all the other suitors, misinterpreted that tragedy as unrequited longing for a strong male figure. They thought she was melancholy because of her life of divorce and loneliness, though it was the other way around.

CHAPTER 23

I sat in the office, leafing through *Headstrong*, waiting for Isabelle to finish with the copier. I overheard Kylie and Gordon talking in the next room.

"It's in the genetic coding," Gordon said. "You can't fight against genetic coding."

"That's drivel. Who says promiscuity is part of the genetic coding?"

"This is biology, or anthropology, or geography. Male primates are genetically coded to distribute their seed to ensure the continuation of their bloodline."

"Male primates? For fuck's sake, you can operate a fax machine."

"It's the *coding*. Once you're coded, you're coded."

"So women must be coded too. So by your logic, we must be coded to accommodate all of these seeds. We must be coded to be promiscuous too."

"I'm afraid not. That would be terribly messy. No, women are encoded to nurture, build the nest. You know, make soup."

I heard the whiz and crash of a book, followed by a slap.

"How is the teaching going?" Martin asked me at the copy machine. He was the only one in the office that still asked me about my teaching.

"Well they don't look like trapped game anymore."

"That's a good sign."

"I'm learning how to burn the hours too. Ever play language bingo?

"Weeks at a time. With kids you're a fool to do anything else."

Darnell walked into the office and handed a folder to Isabelle. I hadn't really talked to him since I was hired. "Hey Leonard," he said to me.

"You should call him by his last name, Ferry," Martin said. "Everyone does. Besides, his first name is Lester." Darnell winced like he had just lost a small wager before walking into his office.

"Correcting the boss, nice job."

"He's not really a boss. He's just a teacher with incredible endurance. He's been in Barcelona nine years."

"I never talked to him. You guys friends?"

"We used to play tennis. So did Isabelle, and then there was Karen, Herb, a lot of people who don't work here anymore."

"What happened to all of them?"

"What happens to any of us? We disappear one day and don't leave a trace." There was a hint of forlornness in Martin's voice.

"Why not hang out with us?" I said. "How come you don't hang out with us? We're going to The Quiet Man tonight."

"I do sometimes. But I don't really get along with Clarence, if you want to know the truth."

"You think he's an asshole, huh?"

"That is accepted by everyone as a fact. But we had a falling out a few months ago, before you were here."

"Did you steal his stash of beers hidden behind the dictionaries?"

"I asked him to substitute a class, my only English one. I had to go to Antwerp for a funeral. My uncle was stabbed in a park by a junkie."

"Sorry to hear that."

"No, it's OK. My uncle was a junkie too. But still, there was this funeral. So I asked Clarence to take my class with Albert for only one day, a Friday. I paid him the money in advance."

"And he didn't show?"

"No, he did, that's the problem. I wish he didn't."

"Did he murder him?"

"No, but they fought."

"Fistfight?"

"Almost. Clarence told Albert to meet him in front of Drassanes that night at ten to finish the argument."

"What did they argue about?"

"Albert said that Clarence dishonored all Catalan women."

"How?"

"We can only imagine. Albert would not say anything else. He sounded more somber on the telephone than anyone at my uncle's funeral. There we had beer, roasted meats, a kind of smoked-salmon spread. I didn't meet with Albert again. He fired me on the telephone."

"Why? You didn't do anything."

"Lack of judgment, is what he said."

"What did Clarence say?"

"He said that Albert needed a complete education, not just English. He never apologized or anything."

"Do you think Clarence went down to Drassanes just in case?"

"I'd bet my salary on it."

Lesson 8: At the Jobsite

Teacher One:

I called my boss and told him that I wouldn't be working today, told him I had to arrange some documents for my visa, which I haven't even applied for.

Teacher Two:

I told my class that I'd be right back, that I had to make some photocopies.

Steins clank.

Teacher Two:

I once showed my beginning intermediate students *Blade Runner*.

Teacher One:

I once showed my students an unmarked VCR tape. I found it behind the fridge. I hoped it wasn't porn, hoped it was *Cheers* or something. Turns out it was blank. We watched for about ten minutes, and then I passed out.

I saw Darnell getting into a sharp-looking Peugeot outside the school. I walked over and leaned into the passenger side window. "Nice wheels," I said.

"Got a class?"

"Two o'clock at Anderson."

"Jump in."

I had been in Barcelona for almost four months, and had never traveled by car, not even a taxi.

"Four on the floor," I said.

"Five. Five on the floor. Five on a phrase that ends in drive."

"Three on the tree."

"Righty tighty."

"Lefty loosy."

The seats were soft blue leather. I heard the Chemical Brothers pulsing softly from the rear speakers, and I saw the equalizer bars brighten on the dash.

We stopped at a red light before Frances Macia, El Corte Inglés tucked neatly to our left. The light turned yellow before it turned green. "Why don't we have that yellow light before the green in America?" I said.

"The danger. We couldn't handle that kind of information."

"We should start a grass roots movement to get the lights to turn yellow before they turn green."

"I'm saying that little yellow light probably kills people. Not a lot, but once in a while. That would be an uphill movement. It's hard to make grassroots climb hills to kill people."

"But it's the people moving through the red light going the other way."

"Still."

"How many people do you think would die each year?"

"A dozen."

"But think of all the seconds that would be saved."

"I'm not saying I don't personally like the yellow light."

"Worker productivity would increase exponentially. The post office alone would save billions.'

"Think of the twisted, smoldering metal. All that broken glass. Think of the orphans. One of those orphans would find out who changed those lights and maybe come after you."

"Tyrone says I should get a car," I said. "Says it would help me meet women."

"Tyrone? Who's Tyrone?"

"He's my brother."

"Is he black?"

"No, he's white. How could he be black?"

"Adoption. Different father. Who knows? Black and white guys as brothers wouldn't be the strangest thing in this world. White guy named Tyrone—now that's strange. Tyrone is a black man's name. I've got two cousins and an uncle named Tyrone."

"My mother dated a black guy. But that was recently. Anyway, what I want to know is if you think he's right? That getting a car would make the difference." Darnell looked at me from the corner of his eye and frowned, as if I were his coming-of-age son and had just asked him for some new privilege.

"I suppose you could get to some districts that are not accessible by the metro," he said reluctantly. "You could get to some of those women."

"Like the secret fishing hole."

"Are you a redneck?"

"With a brother named Tyrone?"

"Listen," Darnell said, "having a car in Barcelona is like not having a car at home. It's the same kind of novelty, the same kind of freedom. Sometimes freedom is the thing that you don't have."

"What's it like being a black guy around here anyway? I don't see a lot of black people."

"We stick out. People stare. Old people especially. They just look at you like they're in a museum. I saw a black lady buying a purse in El Corte Inglés awhile back. She sees me walking by and waves. Waves like she knows me."

"What did you do?"

"I waved back. Barcelona can be lonely for a black guy. You take a friendly wave when you can get one."

Darnell let me off in front of Anderson Consulting. The executives were streaming out of the building, hungry for their lunch. I thought again what Svetlana had told me about the Spanish midday. "They take three hours for lunch over there. One for eating, one for fucking, and one for sleeping." During the Spanish lunchtime, I burned roughly a half hour each way commuting to a class, one and a half explaining something as inane as the present progressive tense to Guimerá, and if I was lucky I had thirty minutes to eat a sandwich, standing up, in a crappy nameless bar, among strangers.

Guimerá's desk was covered in paper. His face was red, and his sleeves were rolled up past his white, fat forearms.

"Yes Mr. Ferry," he said, surprised to see me. "I cannot do English today. We have a large client. He wants another company and I am busy to stop."

I was so happy that I just stood there stunned. He continued to rummage through one of his drawers. I looked at the photos on his desk—they were quite familiar to me, my weekly brethren in boredom. His remotely sexy wife in front of what I guessed was a vacation home, a veil of anxiety around her eyes—perhaps she was wondering how they will continue to pay for it all. The husky son with skis, bloated with a sense of vanity and entitlement, smiling with an overdone conviviality that people in business recognize as the mark of the fool. Guimerá's daughter stared back in a stiff pose, dressed in a fancy vest. She alone seemed to divine the gloom that surrounded us, the superficial concerns of the family, the good natured but vacuous guardianship of her father, the monstrous approach of her own family, her own monotony and death.

Guimerá had stopped rummaging through his desk, and was looking at me staring at the photograph of his daughter. "Mr. Ferry," he said, "no English lesson today. Thursday. I call you." And he shooed me away with his hand.

In the elevator I realized that I might never see him or this building again. It seemed like an easy decision for them to make, to permanently cancel the lessons. That this consulting firm would hire me, an unqualified drunk, and pay my company an exorbitant fee to tie up one of their key consultants for three hours a week, indicated the precise lack of business acumen that a consulting firm should possess. I was not surprised that they were losing clients.

Lesson 5: At the Country

Country Host:

Welcome to my sentimental country home! We have authentic cheeses and chunky preserves. We celebrate each change of the season with special décor and sometimes soup! And we engage in backward sexual practices behind the old mill.

City Visitor:

We've brought sandwiches from a delicatessen. We are a different kind of hearty. I'm carrying an STD that I contracted it from a bus terminal toilet. It is resistant to antibiotics and household detergents.

CHAPTER 24

I was lying down, napping, when I heard an announcer scream "goal" from the living room. Enrique was watching a football game with the sound turned up very loud. He yelled to Paz, asking when dinner would be served. She was clattering in the kitchen, making codballs and rice, the dish she made every Friday. For a moment I imagined myself as the son I never was, the son in a nuclear family. I would have been napping not because I was a little drunk, but because I was worn out from my studious week of analyzing chemical compounds, memorizing world capitals, and declining Latin nouns.

I remembered the three of us had been invited to an art show on the second floor of our building. Inga from Berlin lived there in a state of lesbian abandon, according to Enrique. She always rejected his romantic advances, and eventually she threatened to castrate him with an electric sander. Paz told me the whole history as best as she could the night I moved into the apartment.

Inga's exhibit was advertised as "The Vagina Works." Even though I tried to ignore Enrique's comments, I still braced myself for thick red oil paint and penises in trouble. But it turned out that Inga's paintings were mostly just town landscapes. The vaginas were there, a flyer informed me, but encrypted. "There is vagina here, and vagina here," Inga said to a champagne-sipping couple as they shuffled between canvases. She was pointing to a cloud mass, then a doorway. It was the sophisticated version of Where's Waldo.

I approached and asked her to stop; I wanted to see if I could find the vagina myself. I studied a street scene and pointed to a cyclist. "Here's one," I said. "A vagina."

Inga squinted. Then shook her head decisively. "No, this is not vagina. It is a girl on bicycle."

I retired to the kitchen, where I talked with a Serbian girl who came to Barcelona as part of some musical troupe. I immediately took a romantic interest in her. But she then began telling me about her boyfriend. He was a Bosnian Muslim and worked as a waiter near Mostar. Since she was a Christian, their families were unable to accept the relationship. He was trying to save money so he could join her in Spain, but he wasn't saving much; besides, he couldn't get a visa. If by the end of the year he still couldn't come, she said, then she would return to him, return to her life there that sounded pretty miserable. I didn't have the nerve to share with her how I simply fled from a banal litany of days and nights, weeks and months, plump years arriving one after the other in tedious certainty.

At 1 AM, people were still arriving at the exhibition, looking fresh and crisp as if this was the first stop of the night. A gray haze of smoke began to hang above the crowd. I glanced at Paz just as she was folding a humus-covered pita into her mouth. I headed for the door.

Enrique of course hadn't dared to attend. He had left the apartment soon after dinner in his beloved, stonewashed jeans—a clear signal that he would be prowling for females. He had also washed his hair and shaved. Solicitous, clean and thin, he looked like page one of a high school language book: *My name is Pepe. I am from Argentina. The capital is Buenos Aires. I am using my brain to make you naked.*

To my surprise, Enrique was sitting on the edge of the couch, smiling ridiculously at the TV when I walked in. "*Tio*," he said. "It's Friday, the day of your family values." On weekends, Canal Plus, the city's big cable station, broadcast adult films after midnight. Enrique sometimes watched these movies from beginning to end, as if they were dramas or comedies. I walked past him to get to the kitchen, but didn't look at the TV, though I could hear the phony moaning well enough.

I stood in the kitchen, drinking a cup of wine that had been left on the counter. Paz stumbled through the front door, and I heard her say, "*Mierda, mi Cava.*" She straightaway tumbled onto the couch next to Enrique and sounded a long coo, pretending to be thrilled by the hard-core action. I ducked further into the kitchen and became trapped, unable to get to my room without walking past them and their impending passion. Paz probably didn't know I was there, and Enrique certainly didn't care. Every second that I waited brought the two of them closer to their nakedness. Finally I marched past them, staring straight ahead and keeping my jaw rigid and dignified. I was like the new prisoner striding past the inmates for the first time, enduring their taunts and threats, the feverish rattling of the tin cups on the bars. But my roommates were oblivious, their limbs entangled, pulling on each other's clothes. I couldn't help but take a sidelong glance at the TV—a couple of well-tanned Scandinavians executing a carpet mount. I also managed to catch a glimpse of Paz's black satiny bra, gleaming like freshly-laid asphalt.

Burns Attends Lager Gala

Clarence Burns, of the Poble Sec district of Barcelona, recently attended a Lager Gala. Other attendees included a foam couch, a thirty centimeter television, and some chipped dinnerware. Unshowered, Burns attended the event without an escort, though sources close to *Sic* confirm that the eligible bachelor would later employ the services of a prostitute.

I could no longer take any comfort in the fact that I was not as bad as Clarence. I was frightened by my recent string of blackouts and minor scrapes. Waking up outdoors, minor lacerations on my arms and neck, the anxiety if DIA opened half an hour late on Saturday morning—these were all things that I would have liked to one day chuckle away. "Those were interesting times," I would laugh knowingly. "I certainly sowed some oats over there in Spain. But I am now well pleased to be earning this average salary." I felt a growing gulf between the life that I would be living and the life that I *was* living, and was beginning to suspect that those two lives were never going to connect. "Christmas time is my favorite time," I would say. Children and women in clean clothes swirled around me, a smell of eggnog and wood smoke. "Christmas time always makes me feel happy, maybe it's the lights, but I think it's more than that, it has to be more than that." I once found vomit encrusted on the back of my pants. I was not able to remember an entire Saturday. "Now I would like to leave this bright party in my mid-sized sedan. Farewell, my friends, safe home."

PART THREE

TOMORROW I MIGHT BE FAR AWAY

CHAPTER 25

I opened the window and lay down on my bed. The oppressive heat of the day was waning. Television voices drifted into the room. Everyone in the building, everyone in the city had their windows open. I heard what might have been amorous romping coming from the adjacent apartment. I sipped a cold can of beer. Peals of laughter wafted into the space. I looked at my dusty leather shoes by the door. I had recently replaced the worn-out laces with twine, making them look like relics of a bygone age. They could have belonged, I thought, to a French poet from the 19th century. *Full of ideals and smitten with his own folk genius, Pierre traveled from his bucolic country home to the Provincial capital. He moved into an urban boarding house, became hungry, and got a job at the mill. He put aside his literary aspirations, promising himself he would return soon with renewed vigor. He drank the local wine at a ramshackle tavern. He impregnated the daughter of the neighborhood cobbler. Then the years fell on him like blows from a cudgel. One day he realized that the distance between the life he once imagined for himself and the life he was living was unbridgeable. He ended up living a mean existence, indistinguishable from those around him. At fifty, he wondered:*

What happened to the verse I once wrote? Where is that narrative that was inscribed inside me?

"Barcelona is a poor man's Paris," Kylie said.
"Barcelona is more Paris than Paris," Wichitom replied.

I felt more like an American in Spain than I did in America. Blank-faced and chubby, I wore shabby, ill-fitting clothes that I bought at a Barcelona thrift shop. I thought that they might help me fit in—after all, some Catalan had probably been wearing them on the very same streets—but still, I stuck out as a foreigner. I had the sensation of constantly being exposed, that every day was my first day in the city and might well be my last.

When President Clinton's sexual relationship with Monica Lewinsky started dominating the international news, it made that feeling worse. In the eyes of Catalans, I didn't know if I embodied the predatory lecher or the moralizing masses. Everywhere I went the conversation eventually turned to the scandal. This was especially true in my classes.

"Mr. Ferry, perhaps you answer a question to me." Manolo said in my afternoon class of consultants. "Why this sex problem for Clinton? Explain to me the sex problem of Clinton."

"Well, it's politics, not sex. The republicans want to destroy him."

"Yes, but for a woman? All men do this. Men with power have women." Of the six students, Manolo was the only male.

Carmen gripped each side of her desk and shifted it square with Manolo's. "And a woman with power also has men?" she said. I got the feeling that this was just the latest episode in an ongoing argument.

Manolo gave her a patronizing smile. "If you want. But not so much. It is different."

"*¿Ah, sí?*" She said. "How it is different?"

Manolo remained smiling and looked at me as if Carmen were a child who just asked him about Santa Claus. He held out his hand with an upturned palm. "Mr. Ferry, I am not the professor, you are the professor."

"Women with power can have a man," Carmen said impatiently, looking toward me for agreement. I knew it must be true, but for a moment I had a hard time imagining an example. All I could think was Tina, the bartender at the Lucky Suds Saloon back home in Ocean Beach. She sometimes made me uncomfortable with her suggestive remarks. "You gonna go drain the vein?" she'd say. Or, "I haven't got laid since Bike Week."

"Yes, a woman with power can have a man," I said carefully.

"Here, power and sex are like money and politics," Manolo said. "Power is sex and sex is power."

"It is a problem for the women," Mercedes piped in. I was glad to see someone else was following the discussion. "If power is sex, this is a problem for women."

"Why? What do you mean Mercedes?" I said.

"Men use sex to make power, and men use power to make sex. Men always make sex with everyone and always they keep the power." Mercedes' words tumbled among the other students. Silence fell for a moment while they processed the meaning of what she said.

"Does everyone agree?" I asked tentatively.

"Yes, more or less," Manolo said. "But why in the U.S. are other men making a problem for Clinton? They are making sex with power too."

"America is more conservative than Spain," I said, not knowing if it was really true. "Too much sex is a problem. It's bad, something bad, you can make someone look very bad with sex. Here you have sex on the television." I mimed using a remote control, and even put on a lascivious face. They probably thought I was addicted to cable porn. "It would never be like that there."

"But violence. There you have much more violence," Carmen said.

"Yes, true." I began pacing. "Violence is everywhere in America. For me, sex is better than violence," I said in a candid voice. "But violence is for America what sex is for Europe, for Spain, for Catalunya." They nodded knowingly, as if I uncovered a truth they already possessed. Their faces brightened. I was a teacher after all.

CHAPTER 26

Wichitom treated me to a Guinness one night in the Quiet Man. I asked him what it was like to go home. "It had been seven years," he said, "and only for eight days for my daughter Cecilia's wedding. I was there three hours and the regret gripped me like the flu. Have you ever been with someone, and then you break up only to get back together again because you feel bad? When you're back together you realize in five minutes why you broke up in the first place, and all you want to do is run away.

"I drove for the first time in years and I hated it. Driving means you're separated from everyone else. I didn't know how I had grown so fond of incidental touching, to be breathed on, to be noticed. There I felt remote, responsible. Everyone was counting on me to maintain the dignity of my own isolation.

"I went to the mall, alone, to the store where Cecilia and Eduardo, her husband, were registered. There was not one person on foot—not one person on foot anywhere. Crosswalks blinked that little red man and no one was there to see it, except for everyone in their cars, watching it for a clue when the big light would turn green.

"The store itself was obscene. Home Stuffers Inc. Fifteen choices for vegetable peelers. Dozens of plates on display, then a catalog the size of a Vatican bible that had hundreds more. Five, six people asked me if they could help me. I wandered around for over an hour. I got lost in the draperies. I prayed in the linens. I almost bought a cutting board for myself that could have doubled as an emergency raft. It was five dollars. A girl who looked about thirteen finally punched Eduardo's last name—Mendoza—into the computer and began reciting all the things on their list that still had not been purchased. I interrupted her and told that I'll just buy the cheapest item over a hundred dollars. It was a crock-pot. Far as I know, Cecilia got it in the divorce."

Drinking was the prism through which I watched the rest of the world. The time was not 4:17 PM, but 43 minutes until DIA opened from the afternoon siesta. I sat on the dirty bench, trying to seem like a man passing the time, staring at whatever wisp of newspaper that happened to be on the ground nearby. With only eighty pesetas, a carton of DIA wine was my great hope for the afternoon. A woman walked by, looking like she was going back to work herself, and I wondered what sort of booze might be sloshing around in her belly, what sort of buzzing a few glasses of her lunch wine might be making on her brain. I saw another woman toting a Zara bag, on her way home, the wine chilling in the fridge, the hum from the second glass, drank quickly, still just a pleasant anticipation, noticeable in the cavalier swing of this woman's arms, the taut purpose of her calves. Thirty-nine minutes and some birds alighted on the trashcan, looking for something in there to get them stoned.

Lesson 12: In the Doctors

Doctor: All I hear is the swirl of wind, and the cry of a lonesome gull.

Teacher: I see little kids fetching balls and I feel soft inside; or I see a woman push a lock of hair behind her ear, and I can't get the image out of my head for days, weeks. Plus, my liver hurts.

Doctor: All we can do is treat the symptoms.

Teacher: I can't imagine staying in Barcelona, yet I can't imagine going home.

Nurse: I'm ready to administer the concentrated Guinness.

"I don't know where they go in August," Clarence said. "Mallorca, Cadaques, Puigcerda—good riddance."

"The whole month though. It's impossible for every single Catalan to leave. There'd be looting."

"There *is* looting, but it's small scale. Windows are pried open and not broken, bottles are drained halfway, furniture is rearranged—that kind of thing." I met Clarence at the dumpy bar next to my apartment. I only drank there a couple of times, though I walked by it every day.

"As for the people left behind. The only people left behind are us and the derelicts," Clarence said. "If you see a Catalan in Barcelona in August, you can be sure that he's got some kind of mental or emotional problem. He doesn't know how to find his family, doesn't know how to get back to them." There were in fact a couple of neighborhood men in the bar with us, playing cards at a table beneath the television. At first glance, they didn't look like derelicts, but I'd seen them sleeping on benches, urinating on parked cars, and arguing with trees.

Clarence and I left the bar and wandered all the way down to the Universitat Copisteria, the place where Sic was printed.

We hadn't spoken in almost thirty minutes, when I broke the silence. "Did you hear about the American Embassies?"

"Big deal."

"They should really do something about that," I said. "Send in the cavalry or something."

"They won't. Clinton is in the weeds with that intern."

"No one talks about how that intern is exactly the kind of girl who gets banged all the time but is never really given credit."

"What are you talking about, 'banged all the time?' Most women get banged all the time at some point or another."

"But banged by people that don't usually bang them," I said.

"That was her big bang. And she didn't even get banged."

"It's always Kennedy and Marilyn Monroe. That's a tough paradigm."

"Monroe used to look at herself naked in the mirror for hours at a time."

"I don't blame her." We were by the zoo, and could hear the depressing yells of monkeys on the other side of a ten-foot wall.

"How do you know she looked at herself naked in the mirror?" I said.

Clarence just grimaced and gestured with an open palm, as if his claim was so common that it did not need be verified.

The smell of the zoo was overpowering. It was a mix of urine, feces, and garbage. There was something definitely wrong about the smell—it wasn't like a farm, but more like a bus station men's room. "Clinton is damned if he does, damned if he doesn't," Clarence said.

"This whole thing could end in a massive war."

"That would be perfect for me." Clarence said, "I'd be on the first plane back for that. I sometimes think that that's what I'm missing in my life."

"A war?"

"The instincts and purpose. The way a day begins, the way you say, who shall I eliminate today? Who will I rape?"

"Jesus."

"The guys who blew up the embassies forget that. They think they are the only ones with the balls to kill innocent people. They underestimate the American and European capacity to kill innocent people for sport, which is pretty surprising if you've been reading the newspapers for the last hundred years."

The copisteria was closer to the panhandle of the park, and we sat down on a bench a hundred yards from the Arc de Triomf.

"Let the world change," he said. "Tanks on the boulevard, rations of powdered milk, razor wire around the town fountain. I'd adapt just fine."

"You should just move to the Middle East."

"You think if some Ayatollah came to Washington and started calling the shots that all those fat and lazy assholes back home would just sit around and take it? You think if some sultan came to town and corralled a harem of suburban cheerleaders and then flaunted them around the marketplace, that their brothers and fathers wouldn't pack their Chevy's full of ammonia nitrate and drive it into their fucking camels? Is that what you're telling me?"

We watched some old men playing a game with big metal balls. I'd seen old geezers in this routine plenty of times, but I never bothered to find out even the least bit about the game. They tossed the balls onto the dusty field—it looked like a cross between shuffleboard and horseshoes. Some of the players were not so old, maybe not much older than Clarence or me. I figured that maybe these younger guys were anxious to join the old men at their pastime, eager to settle comfortably into their decline, ready to prolong the final stage of their life. Someone's ball clanged against another ball, and a collective groan ascended from their number.

CHAPTER 27

I decided that I'd like to put together another issue of *Sic*, and I asked my colleagues to contribute a personal ad. Dmitri agreed on the condition that he could write mine; Clarence agreed on the condition that he could write Gordon's.

Convalescing Conversationalist. Likes to converse about sex and things that eventually lead to sex. Getting excited just writing this ad. "She leaned over his bed to dry his brow, and her supple breasts stretched her cotton shirt and brushed heavily against his groin."

Drunk and Single. Enough earwax to clog a drain. Softy. Given to random, incoherent and often tedious musing. Does not not look like a penguin. Available immediately for any manner of date, even a gay one.

Misunderstood and Dangerous in the Sexy Way That Seems Inexplicably To Be in Vogue. Loves prolonged silences and refrigerated lager. Willing to maintain most any façade for steady, detached intercourse. Dislikes all animals except dogs.

Lonely Atlanticist. Clean-shaven. Frequent pimples on forehead seem to get a lot of squeezing. Moderately knowledgeable about Spanish Royalty. Gets erections during haircuts. Looking for same.

Australian That Does Not Belong Among These Other Sods. God, just get this over with.

Kylie explained that she was working on something called "The Handy," a semi-serious teaching supplement: part grammar and usage handbook, part cultural almanac. "It's meant to illustrate to ESL students the difference between words derived from German and those derived from French. I start off with the word handbook itself—it's German. Then there's manual, which is French. From there we go to cemetery, and graveyard. Know which is which?"

"That's where your handbook is going," Clarence told her, "straightaway to the goddamned graveyard."

"You see," she turned to Gordon and me, "hardheaded, ignorant people tend to utilize the German words to express themselves, implying that they would merely grunt and point if they could. On the other hand, a more poetic person, a romantic person, would say instead that my *manual* is destined for the *cemetery*. You see the difference? One is romantic, the other is anti-romantic. And Clarence is a prick."

Typical Day in the Life of an Expatriate

Barcelona—The expatriate is up at the crack of noon. The mad noise of Barcelona has been swirling already for hours. The expatriate rubs a sore shoulder and looks off his balcony at the bustling scene: a man pushes a hand truck of milk boxes into the local market; a woman takes off her moped helmet, her hair cascades onto her suit; horns honk. "City Life," by Francisco Ferry.

The expatriate disassembles the coffee maker, still warm. It's 3 AM back in San Diego. That world is dead, asleep. The expatriate's mind hovers above that dark, faraway landscape. He sees the TVs coloring the atmosphere of the dark rooms. He feels the dull rhythms of the 24 hour markets. He hears the unending hum of tires rolling on the freeway. Only by leaning against this Catalan sink and stuffing a stale orange muffin into his stale tobacco mouth does the expatriate discover that scene so thoroughly. A female the expatriate once knew rolls over and lightly punches her pillow. He waits for the coffee to bubble through the stem of the strange coffee maker.

The expatriate tucks a DIA shirt into second-hand pants. The soles on his shoes have become thin as a cracker. The expatriate appraises himself in the full-length mirror: he looks like a man who was reissued his clothes after an extended stay in a psychiatric ward.

When he steps into the street, the expatriate is instantly engulfed in its energy. He is like a paper cup flung into a fast moving stream, desperately bumping atop the tumultuous waves. Every step is a new chaos. He abruptly walks into people heading in the opposite direction, causing both parties to shift and bob around each other. The expatriate doesn't know where he's going.

Not surprisingly, the expatriate ends up on the Ramblas. It is uncanny how he always ends up somewhere on the Ramblas. The kiosks, the caged animals, the fading trees.

And the never-ending packs of tourists: the Scandinavian girls with long tan legs, the British in sandals and socks, the young Americans saddled with backpacks, the Japanese mothers chasing their children.

The expatriate, as always, is buoyed by the prospect of drink.

CHAPTER 28

I realized that I was becoming nostalgic for my future. I thought that feeling bad was just the price you paid for feeling good, and I had it in my mind that someday I would prevail. I would not, for instance, end up penniless in a Chicago boarding house, cadging change for beer and a hoagie. Nor would I sleep in a drainpipe in Palm Springs, selling my blood in order to afford bottom-shelf wine and generic cigarettes. I also did not anticipate dying ignominiously in a Boston soup kitchen, my heart finally seizing under the relentless assault of cigarette smoke and fatty lunchmeat. These are things my father did. If he performed no proper fatherly duties, then at least he showed me how to completely squander a life.

Lesson 62: English Teacher Survey

17%............are currently "not exactly sure" what country they're in.
59%............fear they will die an alcoholic death.
81%............have smoked non-herbal products (like cotton or paper) when out of tobacco.
67%...........think "Presidente Aznar" was a character on Star Trek.
7%...........hang out at the wharf.

46%...........	are paying back a student loan.
45%...........	have sent their student loan bank a picture of self in coffin.
41%...........	brush their teeth at least once a week.
2%...........	were aroused by their surveyor.

I spent the evening wandering around the Gracia street festival with Kylie, Wichitom and Gordon. I thought our crowd seemed detached from the overall celebration, as if we were parading ourselves around—though we represented nothing. I felt like everything we were doing was forced, all the effort to fit in was in vain.

People in costumes marched loosely in line, some had exaggerated feet and hands made out of papier-mâché, others had oversized heads. "What's with the big heads?" I said.

Gordon vexed his brow as if noticing them for the first time. He was trying to think up something witty, but it was too long coming.

"It's tradition," Kylie said. "These parades were a way to protest. Against power, the church, the monarchy."

"So did the kings and popes have big heads?" I asked.

"You have to remember that a hundred years ago, a lot of people were illiterate, so organizers had to make it easy for them. Nowadays you really have to consider the fact that they would look even sillier with normal-sized heads." The figure of a woman danced by with a yellow mop of hair and papier-mâché breasts larger than watermelons.

"Ah, Queen Mammary, I remain your loyal subject," Gordon said.

Some of the papier-mâché faces were so detailed that I imagined they were indeed made with someone specific in mind. One character, with round-rimmed glasses and brown hair parted to the side, looked like Reese. He was jigging around, flailing his arms, full of a carefree nonchalance that bordered on menace. I thought for a moment that he was coming for me, bouncing from leg to leg, preparing to give me an overdone hug, or pull me into the street and make me dance to one of the beats of the discordant music that was blaring from at least three different sources.

Banners written in Catalan stretched between buildings; ribbons twisted down like cartoon moonbeams from every tree, balcony, and seemingly even from the sky itself—looking up I saw only paper and lights, music surrounded us like smoke in a burning building.

Early the next morning I found myself alone in my room. I looked again at its dimensions—roughly the size of a large bathroom. The six-foot length of foam resting on a cheap frame—essentially a beach chair without arm rests. In a small dresser made of particleboard, I kept all of my clothes except the few dress shirts and khakis that I wore to work, which hung from hooks on the door. I craned my neck into the central ventilation shaft and saw the pigeons perched on the edge of the roof. They were cooing and pecking nervously, as if anticipating a terrible storm.

CHAPTER 29

I heard a church bell bong as I made a left onto Carrer Cadena from l'Hospital. The sun, arcing in the southern sky, shone on the broken buildings. Dmitri couldn't be left alone anymore, so we were all making an effort to stop by more often, and stay longer when we did.

I brought with me the sports pages of an American newspaper, which were focused on the home run race between Mark McGuire and Sammy Sosa.

"They're juiced," Dmitri said dismissively. But I knew he liked this story, and I knew that he liked the way that I read the articles with exaggerated inflection, and he liked that I also added details, and even created entire scenes and episodes. I even took to writing some of the stories over, though I never told him that I did.

"Warmth and sun are taken for granted in much of the world," I read. "People spend millions on sun block, sunglasses, sun hats. They tint the windows in their car. They even suggest that the sun will one day do us in, will melt our ice caps and boil our oceans. People have become decidedly anti-sun.

"Not so in Chicago. When the sun shines in this city of nine-month winters, people bask in its rays with peculiar relish. Fat men take off their shirts. Women let their shoulder straps fall down to their elbows. Children pummel each other with water balloons. The elderly lean back and let that faraway ball of yellow steam shine for a moment on their bony legs; it is perhaps they most of all, glancing to the menace of the big northern sky, that appreciate the fleeting moment in the sun. They've been intimate with that sun for a long time, they appreciate the years those rays must travel, and only now do they feel the warmth and the light that they saw when they were young.

"This was the scene yesterday at Chicago's Wrigley Field, where even the ivy seemed relaxed in the bright August warmth. And just as that ivy softens the impact for a leaping outfielder, so too does the pleasant ivy soften the inevitable disappointment of the Cubs fan, who has once again extended his or her hopes this late into the season.

"This year, much of the hope centered not on the pennant, but on a little thing coming to be known as the great home run race of '98. Mark McGwire was in town to try and keep Sammy Sosa in his shadow. As September nears, both men are approaching what is arguably the most storied record in all of sports—Roger Maris's single season home run total of 61.

"When Sosa came to the plate in the fifth inning, the two titans were tied for the major league lead at 47—career numbers for mortals. But it was only August 19th. And only the fifth inning.

"Sosa smashed a hanging fastball into the left field bleachers. The crowd roared; with one swing, they got their money's worth for the afternoon. It gave the Cubs the lead, but more importantly it put Sosa one home run ahead of McGwire. As he trotted—perhaps slower than normal—past first base, the capacity crowd chanted 'Sammy, Sammy.' The slugger grinned but waited until he was descending into the dugout to tip his cap and point upward, maybe to God, maybe to the sun now careening to the west, or maybe in a gesture to the fans in the upper decks, in whose screams Sosa could perhaps discern a note of the forlorn: their lives unfolding with so little flair, so little hope, and so little to distinguish one from the other.

"And then the crowd got some more emotion—perhaps more than they would have liked. McGwire came up in the 8th inning, the Cardinals down by a run. The crowd didn't boo, but they certainly didn't cheer as they shamelessly do in some stadiums that McGwire visits. The noise at Wrigley can only be described as a nervous rumbling. Sosa stood in the outfield, lightly punching the web of his glove. The sun was no longer visible on the grass, having sunk below the buildings. For the first time all afternoon, a breeze blew through the stadium. People who had been half naked moments before, began to pull on jackets. They crossed their bare arms and held their elbows. Maybe it would be an early autumn? That usually means an early winter too. The stadium was gripped in a tentative foreboding. Accustomed to disappointment, Cubs fans were perhaps filled with a sense of relief and security as they watched McGwire's ball sail over the right field wall.

"By the time the tenth inning rolled around, and McGwire once again stepped to the plate, the mood had turned decidedly reckless. A minor scuffle broke out at one of the concession stands. A man and his son were escorted out of their seats for accosting a woman in a Cardinals hat. Someone threw a beer bottle onto the shallow right field grass. Everyone knew what was coming.

"McGwire hit the pitch so hard that the centerfielder just turned and took a few steps toward the wall, not to give chase—the ball was gone from the moment it left McGwire's bat—but to see where it would land. Now the crowd booed, as McGwire jogged quickly around the infield. Not only did he give the Cardinals the lead—a lead they would not relinquish—but he also took the home run lead back from Sosa. Poor Sammy stood in the outfield, his only lead over McGwire this season lasted less than three innings. Maybe he wondered if he'd ever get it back. A few fans turned their back to the field and headed to the exits. Another breeze blew though the park. Winter was coming quick to the Cubs."

Dmitri lay on his back, his face sallow and still, yet somehow not so peaceful. I sat watching him for I don't know how long before Gordon came in to relieve me.

I met Gemma on the landing outside her apartment on my way downstairs. "Gordon came," I said, pointing upward. "I'll come back tomorrow."

Gemma had her arms folded, and was looking at me seriously. "His father's here," she said. "He came in last night."

"Gordon's father? What's he doing here?"

"*Dmitri's* father Ferry. Please try and sometimes think."

"Dmitri told me he was dead. Or that he was living in North Carolina or something."

"He is living in the southern one, but he came here to see his sick son."

She showed me into her apartment. Sure enough, a large man lay asleep on the couch. An overstuffed wallet and plastic glasses rested on the top of a pair of sneakers under the coffee table.

"So what's he doing in the picture?"

"I contacted him. I thought that Dmitri's mother and father should know."

"So where's his mother?"

"Las Vegas. She told me she's in a show and cannot get away at this time."

"Show? What kind of show?"

"Really, I don't think that is something important. But it might be something with Tony Orlando. I think she does something with fire and dancing."

"She'd be too old for that kind of thing."

"Apparently not. Sometimes women can do things when they are fifty that they couldn't do when they were twenty. Dmitri's mother has experienced a lot. Her body has probably been through some very tough ordeals. Tony Orlando is wise to have her dancing for him."

I stayed for dinner. When Dmitri's father woke up, he seemed to be in good spirits, and generally affable. "How long have I slept? What time is it? Seven? At night? This is something. Do I have jet lag? Who's this fella?"

"I'm Ferry. I'm a friend of your son's"

"Bert. Glad to meet you. I sat with him this morning, but he was pretty well conked out. Gemma here tells me that you all have taken good care of him these last few months. I want you to know that I appreciate that. My boy has always done some bizarre things, at least he used to, but he's got a good heart."

"I was just up there," Gemma said. "He's still sleeping. I think if we eat something, when we're done he'll be awake."

"OK. Let's go out and get something. My treat. Might as well have some Spanish food while I'm here."

"I've already prepared tortilla with sausages," Gemma said.

"Burrito, fine," Bert said.

"We're not in Mexico," Gemma said. "Tortilla is like an omelet."

"You're calling the shots. You're the boss around here. I'm still on South Carolina time." He turned to me. "So how long have you known Danny?"

"Who the hell is Danny?"

"Dmitri. You call him Dmitri but his real name is Danny. Daniel Sterling Davis, the Sterling part is after his grandfather, my father."

"I think Dmitri mentioned him, maybe something about his funeral."

"Funeral? No chance. Pops is still alive. Lives in Louisville. Keeps bees. Eats the honey. Says he wants to outlive us all."

Gemma brought in the tortilla and sliced it like apple pie.

"My father worked 25 years for Bethlehem Steel," Bert continued. "Lost an eye and went to work the next day. Say he wanted to go back for the afternoon shift, but the doctor wouldn't let him. That's the kind of cloth he was cut from. Danny's got it too."

"So why'd Dmitri change his name?"

"I thought you might tell me. Before yesterday, I hadn't seen Danny in eight years—no, make that nine because it was 1989 and I remember they had that World Series earthquake."

Dmitri's father spoke with a southern twang, though it seemed inconsistent, like he was just starting to get it, or just starting to get rid of it.

"Danny met a girl at Clemson, and I reckon that was the start of it. He wasn't taking classes, he was just on the grounds crew. She was visiting from Greece, which was a big deal because of his mother, she was from Greece, and he never had a lot of contact with her. None of us did. So I come home one day with a six-pack and some take-out chicken and he tells me that he's fixing to go to Greece. I thought he'd be back in a month or two—maybe half a year. I left his bait in the freezer. Next thing you know it's nine years."

Gemma brought in some wine. I went back to the kitchen with her and got some glasses and a loaf of stale bread.

"I got some letters, a postcard now and then. I never thought of visiting there myself, not that I was invited. I started a drywall business. My family never stays very close, but nine years for a father and son is pushing it. Hell, I see Grandpa Sterling three or four times a year. He says he don't like it, says he'll set the bees on me one of these times."

Dmitri was smoking when we walked into his apartment. Gordon was asleep on the couch, a Spanish Playboy splayed on his lap. I watched Dmitri closely, to see how he'd react to the surprise arrival of his prodigal father.

"Who do you like, Sosa or McGuire?" Dmitri said when he saw him.

"Sosa, no doubt about it. I don't like the shape of McGuire's body. He looks like he should be moving furniture." Bert lifted his son's hand and patted his shoulder. Gordon stirred from the couch and put his feet on the ground. He took one hard look at the Playboy and put it aside.

"How's Greenville?" Dmitri asked.

"Smelly Oscar on Highway Nine added a drive-thru. That Earlson boy you went to school with got put away for exposing himself at a church supper. I built a deck out back."

"You remarry?"

"I've got what you might call a common-law wife. Tamara. She was working the Evinrude booth at the marine expo in Myrtle Beach. Now she fools with fancy crystals and incense."

"I hear the Braves have had a nice little decade."

"Are you telling me that you can't watch baseball here?"

"You can if you have some kind of super cable," Dmitri said, "and don't mind watching TV in the middle of the night."

"What do people do if they don't watch sports?"

"They watch soccer."

"Jesus son," Bert patted Dmitri's forearm, "I had no idea."

"Two to nothing is a blowout."

"I saw some highlights of that World Cup," Bert said. "Guys fall down trying to get penalties and you'd think they got plugged with a shotgun from close range."

"I know, they're pussies."

"Point of parliamentary procedure," Gordon said standing up. "Those are the Spanish leagues. The leagues in the UK employ only the hardiest of men."

Bert looked at Gordon as if he was performing a rudimentary juggling trick. "They keep saying soccer is going to one day be big as baseball," Bert said, looking back at his son. "But I don't count myself a fan yet."

"America is getting their painful education," Gordon said. "The World Cup just finished and the Americans found themselves the worst of the lot. But the question is, can you name one player on the American team?"

"Pele," Bert said. "And Beckenbauer, the German guy."

Later that night, Gordon and I took Bert for the obligatory walk on the Ramblas. "I'm not going to be here long," Bert said, "so take me to the big show-me place."

"Café Zurich would be perfect," Gordon said.

"Fine, let's go there. Sounds fancy," Bert said.

"No, no we can't. It's not there anymore. I said it *would* be perfect. I was deliberately using the conditional. It's been years since Café Zurich was there."

"Why mention a place that doesn't exist anymore? Where's the value in that?" Bert said, aggravated.

"If you had ever been to Café Zurich," Gordon said, "you would be saying the same thing. It is exactly the kind of place that people say these kinds of things about. It is more important and prominent now that it's gone." Bert was becoming clearly annoyed. We had turned left on Carrer de Ferran, avoiding the darker depths of the Ramblas.

"Let's just go in here," I said, pointing to a place called the Florin.

Once inside, Bert adjusted his chair toward mine and away from Gordon who had already tried to chat with the busy waitress. "I see it's nice here," Bert said, "pretty girls, fancy buildings. But why *live* here? I mean, are you going to spend your whole life in this place?"

"I just felt like getting out of San Diego for a while. I felt like I was packed in moth balls there."

"Christ son, San Diego is beautiful. I lived nine months in Camp Pendleton. You can't beat a place like San Diego—the beaches, the weather, that taco food."

"The weather is nice here too, if it's weather you're after."

"I'm not after anything. My mortgage in South Carolina is $288 a month, so I can watch TV in my garage most of the time, don't have to worry about working, don't have to worry much of nothing. The work comes and goes and it's the same to me."

"You live in a garage?" Gordon said, turning toward us. He must have still been smarting about the football discussion.

"I don't live there, I just spend time there. I don't have to worry about my beer sweating on Tamara's 'Tarot Today' magazines. I can fart and snore, smoke cigars."

"Sounds lovely," Gordon said.

Bert's face contorted into such disgust that it was impossible to imagine that any remark could have reviled him more. He then squared his chair directly with mine. "Europe is somewhere for vacation, son," he said, "not somewhere to live. These aren't your people here. Your people are back home." Bert seemed to have associated living abroad with Dmitri's condition, and he was talking to me as if I were in the early stages of the same disease. "Don't you miss the Super Bowl? Don't you want to watch the World Series this year? For Christ's sake son, your Padres might make it there."

"The Padres?" Gordon chimed in, "that sounds rather provincial. All of those team names are silly as far as I'm concerned. The Cowboys and the Eagles—I mean seriously, I thought that football was supposed to be a mock-up of war."

"We're talking about baseball," Bert said. "As far as war goes, just let me know if you need any help on the Falkland Islands. That Argentine Army is a real juggernaut I hear."

"Are the Padres really that good?" I said.

"I'm not sold on their pitching. But look, son, I don't think Dmitri should have stayed away so long. I think he must have gotten into some sort of weirdness over here." I glanced at the Florin crowd over Bert's plaid shoulders and realized it was a little on the gay side, though I wasn't sure if Bert was commenting on that. He continued: "I spent a lot of nights thinking about what I would have said to him if I could."

"What would you have said?" I asked.

"I would have told him that there's no shame in coming home, nothing to apologize for if you just want to work and live and be comfortable. Come home son, I would have told him, come home and relax. The end is gonna come in the sweet by and by."

Bert hit a nerve in me. It wasn't the first time that I thought about going home. It wasn't the first time that I thought about America and Europe in that classic metaphor of shallow and deep. As a boy, I was always content to wade around in the low end. The deep end required too much meaningless courage, the constant treading, the vague sense of peril.

For a moment I pictured my future self—heavy, hairy and wading in waist-high pool water, tossing a beach ball. The water shifting and splashing lightly around me, and I mildly toss the ball to my buxom wife. I scoop chemically-treated water in my cupped hands and splash my armpits and chest. All my little hairs glisten. I pat my beefy neck with my damp palms and wrists.

CHAPTER 30

I received a package from home, from my mother. She sent cookies for my birthday, something she had never done before. For the first time I considered the idea that she might be crazy. She seemed to have adopted the attitude of those mothers who sent their sons care packages during times of war.

She taped a note to the top of the canister:

> Lester,
>
> You're a man now, but I thought you might like a reminder of when you were a boy. Shortbread cookies, though I didn't bake them myself, I wouldn't know how.
>
> Love Mother.

Reese put a book, *Old Man and the Sea*, in the package too. It was a week before I noticed that he had written me a note on the title page:

> Lester,
>
> Hope you can real [sic] in some adventures, like the ones in this book!
>
> Reese

Tyrone, I could tell, helped pack it, because the crumpled up newspapers contained the police blotter of his arrest—four or five copies of it.

Lesson 10: Graduation

Student: I need a teacher who is not going to pee in the bushes before he knocks on my door. Who doesn't leave beer bottles and clipped cigarette butts in the elevator. Who doesn't look at my wife and daughter like he's a sailor on shore leave.

Teacher: Those are the procedures outlined in the International House's six-week training course. It's part of the dialectic.

In the Eixample, "the extension," the streets were laid-out in a sprawling grid with the corners lopped off, creating octagonal intersections. Wichitom told me that when they built this part of the city in the 19th century, they planned on having a little courtyard in the middle of each block, more open spaces and shorter buildings. I stood on the corner of Aribau and Valencia, listening to the hum of the tires, the roar of the motors, and tried to imagine it instead with dozens of trees. *A woman in a sun hat, a man in white slacks, the smell of forsythia wafting about the place. A puppy has meandered to the edge of the grass that's a little overgrown (maybe today is the day the city comes to cut it with their clunky but effective machines). "Here little rascal, here little one. I've got to take you home now. You've had your fun and now it's time to lock you up, and take you home."*

CHAPTER 31

I usually avoided my apartment during the dinner hour because I didn't want to sit with Paz and Enrique, to listen to their various complaints. But the weekend that Enrique went to a conference in Madrid, Paz asked me to take his spot at dinner, and I wondered if there would also be romantic obligations.

She made a tremendous salad with artichoke hearts and sliced tomatoes. I had bought some non-carton wine and poured it into water glasses. It might well have been a romantic dinner, but Paz was wearing a billowy housedress and had some kind of pasty cream smeared all over her neck. She served the chicken right from the pan.

"Have you made any friends since coming to Barcelona?" she asked in Spanish.

"Only friends at the office."

"No Spanish friends? No Catalans?"

"No, no Catalans. My students are friends, but they pay me." I was trying to be funny, but as much as my Spanish had improved, intonation was beyond me. Still, Paz smiled.

"It is difficult to make friends with the Catalans," she said. "I have been here seven years. Hmmmph!" She arched her eyebrows and gestured to either side of the table, as if she had been snubbed that very night by a couple of Catalans.

"Foreigners are more interesting. I don't want Catalan friends. They're not interesting."

"Yes, yes, you're right. You're absolutely correct," she said excitedly. "I too like foreigners. Here the Catalans are like a cult. The cult of the Catalans."

We both laughed. I felt sorry for Paz because she seemed so lonely and Enrique treated her terribly. I knew she would have paid her own way to go with him to the conference in Madrid—it would have been something she could have looked forward to for weeks—but the thought probably never crossed his mind. "I'm going to meet some friends later at a bar. Do you want to go?" I said to her.

"Oh no, I can't go." She tugged on her housedress. "No, no."

"It's right near the Ramblas. For a little while. Have a drink." She paused and glanced at the table of dirty dishes and crumpled napkins. "We'll go in thirty minutes," I said. "I'll clean." She touched her collarbone and looked at the cream on her fingertips as if she had never seen it before. "We'll go in an hour," I said.

With Paz along, I wished that we were meeting at the Quiet Man, but instead we had planned to gather at the sordid Montparnasse Bar. Paz seemed a little miffed as we turned off the Ramblas and into the Raval. When we pushed through the nondescript door, she looked around Montparnasse in amazement, as if I had just untied her blindfold at the edge of the Grand Canyon. "*Que raro*," she said. The one-time parquet floors of the Montparnasse Bar were chipped and filthy and crowded with rickety wooden tables and chairs. Huge chandeliers hung from the water-stained ceiling that looked on the verge of at least a partial collapse. Old posters and cracked mirrors covered nearly every inch of the walls. Above them, just below the ceiling, hundreds of dusty bottles lined shelves around the perimeter of the place, peering down at what would surely be another night of debauchery.

Kylie and Gordon were already sitting at the bar, and I could tell by the gleeful look on Gordon's face when he spotted us that he imagined that I had scared up a date. Paz wore black slacks and a purple pullover shirt and her hair was brushed back and tied in a kind of ponytail.

Kylie met Paz once at my apartment, and she had otherwise tried to protract their discussion whenever she called me on the phone. "*Hola, Paz, como estas*?" Kylie said. We all exchanged stilted greetings. Even Gordon, who I greeted all the time with nothing more than a nod of the head, shook hands with me. All at once the music blared—some kind of techno—and only then did I realize how quiet it had been.

Montparnasse was known for absinthe. Curly, the hefty, bald bartender and proprietor, served the absinthe by placing a small fork across the rim of a glass a quarter full of absinthe, put a sugar cube on top of the fork, and then poured mineral water over the sugar and into the glass. Curly did this only once for the customer, then he or she was on their own. If they failed to remember, then Curly would perform the procedure again, but would comment sarcastically on the patron's general ineptitude, state of intoxication, inferior dress, or whatever else struck him negatively, which invariably was everything.

Curly was himself an American, a native Californian displaced for ten years or more, selling absinthe to the steady stream of travelers and expatriates. He surrounded himself with fit, boyish waiters in tight shirts who lifted heavy crates and kegs like carnival strongmen.

We stayed at least two hours at Montparnasse, and the smoke became dense. Clarence came in drunk, and immediately told Paz a joke about a hooker who gets bludgeoned. He then launched into a profanity-laden diatribe about the Spanish ethos.

"Curly," Clarence shouted across the bar. "Some more neon nectar for me and my brethren." Curly came over, eyeing Clarence warily. Curly knew us well enough, and he knew that Clarence was nearing alcoholic disintegration—absinthe has a way of compounding, like credit card interest. Still, Curly wouldn't consider cutting him off, not because he wanted his money—he seemed to make it hand over fist—but because he maintained an attitude that people should be responsible for themselves, and I also think he took some pleasure in watching people spiral down into misery. "Ferry!" Clarence shouted, as if seeing me for the first time. "I'm buying you an absinthe. But don't drink it like this fuck tells you to drink it, drink it straight without the sissy sugar and without the sissy water." Curly was standing close enough to Clarence to grab him by the neck. But he just stood there, drumming his fingers on the bar. He shot a sideways glance to his first in command—Gran Hector, a pale-faced Catalan who looked like he spent all his free time in the gym. I once saw him lift a man by his belt and shirt collar and toss him into the street like a bale of hay.

"This place is wearing thin," Gordon said nervously. "Let's try Kentucky. It's impossible to get out of line there."

"I've gotta use the head first," I said. Gordon's look begged me to hurry.

The toilet was dank and dim, with puddles of water on the broken-tile floor, and huge holes in the wall. I saw some kind of transaction between two men, one standing in a stall, the other at its door. I saw three legs in another booth. Of the five urinals, I approached the one closest to the door. In the urinal's basin, dozens of cigarette butts surrounded a chunk of soap, like derelict worshippers around their unfeeling god.

Clarence came into the bathroom and went to the farthest urinal. "Look straight ahead," he said to himself. I'm not sure he knew I was there. "Concentrate. Block out all thought. Close left eye, close right eye. Close both eyes. Breathe. Think of a fountain. No, not the one in Plaza Real. It's surrounded by skanks. Think of a fire hydrant with an open valve. Harlem in the summertime." A dapper young man sidled up to the urinal next to Clarence, and I sensed that we were headed for a situation.

"The ocean, the sea," Clarence said. "Waves lapping the hull, there it is, we're swimming now."

"I'm swimming too," the guy next to him said in accented English.

Clarence opened his eyes, zipped up his fly, and punched the character square in the chest. The guy went to his knees in one of the nasty puddles. Clarence shook the sting out of his hand and strode calmly out the door.

I looked at myself in the hazy, broken mirror above the sink. My face was pale and sweaty, and my eyes were a couple of gofer holes.

When I went back to the bar, everyone was gone except Clarence.

I don't actually remember the exact sequence of bars, though we never caught up with the others. I believe we went to Kentucky after Montparnasse and then to Dublin Bar, a place that any expatriate worth his salt avoided. The entire façade was painted dark green, and there was all manner of clovers and other green things to be found inside. I think I insisted on going into the bar because I had never been, and I wanted to have one of the green beers depicted on the sign.

We also went to the Quiet Man, where I hazily remember a confrontation with a Catalan and his jacket that had a fresh cigarette burn on the sleeve. He insisted in mechanical English that I pay him for it, but when Clarence got into the conversation, all the demands were dropped, and we suddenly had a large area to ourselves at the crowded bar. That's the last thing I remember before we were on the street.

We were near Dmitri's apartment, and I suggested we visit, but Clarence said it would be a downer, and besides, he had a class in a few hours and wanted to get home to sleep. I stopped to relieve myself on the side of a building, but Clarence kept walking. It took me a long time to finish, partly because I was straining beneath a light to see if my urine was green. Clarence had walked a good ways ahead of me, though I could still see him up ahead on the otherwise empty street. He looked back but didn't say anything to me before turning onto what I was pretty sure was Carrer de l 'Hospital. I was trying to hurry, but I was also trying to button my fly at the same time.

When Clarence turned the corner, two men were in front of him, blocking his way. One guy was pale and had sores on his neck. The other had long straight hair that looked like it hadn't been washed in years. "Give us your money," the pale one said in English.

The guys didn't have any knives or guns, just a broken bottle each. I turned the corner and without the slightest hesitation, stood next to Clarence and assumed the role of victim along with him. Clarence, I'm sure, was disappointed in that maneuver. The thief chuckled and said "*Quina cara de fill de puta*," which Clarence later told me means "What a face of the whore's son." The other thief repeated the demand for money and stretched out his hand, and I immediately started digging through my pockets. I didn't have much money, so I just gave him all the coins I had, only about six or seven hundred pesetas. When I checked my back pockets I only found a crushed pack of Ducados, but I decided to keep those.

Clarence, he told me later, had a little folding money—two thousand pesetas—but kept it in his pocket. These two derelicts did not press Clarence, as they must have sensed his hostility. So they turned and started to walk away, but the one with sores lobbed a parting insult, something unoriginal about being a foreigner in Catalunya. The pair didn't even run, and Clarence said that that was the final insult.

He had his choice of objects to pick up and throw. Garbage was strewn about, and there were piles of boxes and crates in a nearby entranceway. He chose a sturdy wine bottle, and threw it as hard as he could at the thieves. They were still just fifteen meters away, walking by a dilapidated building that had been cordoned off with a plastic fence. The empty bottle exploded on the back of the head of the guy with long hair. He fell slowly onto his knees and hesitated. It appeared as if he was going to crawl under the plastic fence. The bottle had a heavy base—I learned only later that it splintered and thrust forward simultaneously, piercing his brain. He was killed more or less dead instantly.

Clarence grabbed me by the arm and we hurried back the way we had come. The other thief shouted after us, but didn't leave his friend's side. I looked up and saw the empty balconies, the chipped facades, the dark gray sky twisting around the buildings. We turned down another side street but could still hear the thief's cries, echoing off the buildings like a prisoner's lament in a cell. A moment later we were on the Ramblas.

Two days after the incident, I bought *La Vanguardia* from the kiosk near the Arc de Triomf. I was surprised to find the story on the second page; the kid who was killed turned out to be the estranged son of a wealthy businessman from San Cugat. I asked Enrique to translate it for me, along with a bunch of other articles so he wouldn't get suspicious. Enrique told me that the newspaper was insinuating that the relationship between the father and his estranged son was the parable of the prodigal son, interrupted just before the celebrated reunion.

The other thief gave his account of the story, without mentioning the botched robbery. He was sure that the murderer and his accomplice were foreigners, probably German, English, or American. "But the paper estimates that there could be 100,000 such people in Barcelona at any given time in August," Enrique said. "So they are not so optimistic."

"But," he continued, "you have to understand that this is their way—call it Spanish or Catalan, it makes no difference. By saying the case is impossible to solve, they will be geniuses if they solve it. If they don't, then they are like victims too. If I am not mistaken, in America they always say that they will catch the bad people. Someone is on TV with a large, silver star on their chest, pointing and reassuring everyone. Everybody then relaxes, feels good that someone is in charge, and they go and buy something expensive."

"Do they have a motive?" I asked, trying to sound nonchalant.

"They are not sure," Enrique said, "but they are questioning people at the party where the addicts were beforehand, and they are probably looking over the other guy rather closely. You see, the one who died was the son of someone important and rich, the guy who is living is just another nobody."

"At home it's the same way," I said. "It's all about class."

"In America it's all about race, you need to admit that."

"Did you ever see the Rodney King video?"

"I had a professor who divided it into eighty-one segments, and he wrote a short essay about each one. The compelling thing about that video is you always think they are going to stop hitting him, but they never do, they never stop hitting the man. My professor called that 'The Enchantment of Who Will Hit Him Next.'"

"What did your professor say about O.J. Simpson?"

"It was a victory for White America. It was strictly a statistical analysis. In the weeks and months after that acquittal, blacks were arrested and convicted with an even higher frequency. I don't know why they celebrated."

Enrique would have loved to know about my involvement, and I was sure that he would have kept the secret for a while, but there was no way that I could tell him. Instead, I tried keeping him off the scent by asking him about the front page ETA crisis.

"ETA is not a collection of madmen and extremists," he said. "They are trying to regain something that the modern world has lost. It's not just about independence."

"It's a lifestyle issue?"

"No one likes to have someone or something else control them."

"Madrid crushes everything."

"Washington crushes everything. Modernization has never been painless."

"Sounds like scapegoating."

"Perhaps. Though as a rule, I don't like to agree with you."

The Expatriate Manifesto

We are not morning people. We are not athletic, though rarely are we fat. We have above average intelligence, but are chronic underachievers. We are frequently seen in the company of Australians.

We have our parents back in Michigan or Maryland who fret over our aimless lives. Our mothers often go against solid religious doctrine and pray for specific things to be bestowed upon us: a spouse in a reasonable age range, a job with health insurance, a thirty-year mortgage. We often have a special relationship with alcohol.

We prefer our booze chilled, heated, or at room temperature. We smoke all manner of tobacco. Calamari and salami are two of our favorite snacks, though we maintain a steady diet of noodles.

Sex is often a sore subject, though we engage in it whenever possible. We'd like to say we do so whimsically, but desperation and whimsy do not easily ally themselves. Let's just say we do things we might otherwise not, believing that our actions will not really contribute to our overall development and character.

I saw Clarence at the office the next day. We started walking down the pedestrian center of Diagonal

"That was a necessary murder," he said.

"That seemed like an accident. I thought you were just trying to graze him."

"Necessary in the existential sense. Who did you tell?" he asked me.

"No one. I'm not stupid."

"Gordon?"

"He'd be the last person"

"Kylie?"

"*Penúltimo*."

"How about that Andalusian linebacker you live with?"

"Paz? I don't think I could even explain it in Spanish. I did have Enrique translate the article in the newspaper for me, but along with a bunch of other stuff to wash away any suspicion."

"Does he suspect anything?"

"No, but he'd like me better, probably."

"Well leave your little nancy-boy out of it. You need something translated, ask me. You need someone to like you, then dress up like a woman and hang out in the park."

"The whole thing is already over."

"It's not over until I'm out of here. I'm finally bolting this backwater."

"You're overreacting. That would make people suspicious."

"Don't be a fool. You should leave too. You want to stay to make eighteen-hundred pesetas an hour? You can make that in any city in Europe. You want to stay so you can walk down the Ramblas and watch some idiot stand still for five hours with spackling in his hair? So you can visit the stupid Sagrada Familia at Christmas? "

"I still haven't seen it."

"Life in prison is nothing to fool around with."

"Gordon told me that the prisons here are not so bad. British people come here to commit crimes just to get locked up. It's a country club."

"A country club that you can't leave, and that's full of lazy British people. Imagine living the rest of your life locked in a building with a thousand Gordons. It really wouldn't matter if it was air conditioned or not, now would it?"

Kylie was walking towards us listening to her walkman. Her face brightened when she saw us, and I think she could tell right away that we talking about something secret, something serious. "You boys off to the circle jerk?"

"Yeah," I said. "Except on Tuesdays we form a trapezoid."

She frowned and looked at Clarence. She had been hoping for a better rejoinder from him. "You know you've got snot stains on your cuffs Clarence," she said. He looked at his cuffs, which were in fact a little crusty. He just shrugged, and peered into the distance.

At that, Kylie backed away from us, wary that Clarence might be trying a new, stealth tactic of abuse. She raised her hands slightly, and backed up another few steps toward the office.

CHAPTER 32

I went over to Dmitri's for the five o'clock "shift," as usual. I had a premonition as I approached his door, though I had that feeling all the time, as if at any moment my life was going to change dramatically. Behind every door I imagined some woman might appear, eager for my attentions, or a member of my family might be waiting to tell me about some terrible accident, or a pair of beefy men in light blue uniforms were ready to tackle me at the knees and transport me to Atascadero in an armored van.

I walked in and saw Kylie sitting on the sofa next to Gemma, and the two of them looked pretty sad. Dmitri's bed was stripped to the mattress and pushed to the corner along with a tangle of plastic tubes. Gemma gave me a reluctant glance and put her arm around Kylie.

"He's gone," Kylie said.

"When did it happen?" I said, taking a seat on the couch next to Gemma. I wanted to make a gesture of intimacy, but I didn't know on which part of the body—the knee, the arm, the small of the back—to lay my hand.

"This morning, around six o'clock," Gemma said.

"Why didn't you call me? I would have come right over," I said.

"There was no point. There was nothing you could do. He would have been gone by the time you got here," Gemma said, her hand lifelessly resting on my shoulder.

"Well I guess it's better now. At least he's not in any pain."

"I don't know about that," Kylie said, "flying can be a nightmare on someone in his condition."

"They put enough drugs in him to knock out an elephant," Gemma sighed.

"Why would they give him drugs now? Who are you talking about?"

"His father. His father was here this morning with an American nurse," Gemma explained. "They got him dressed and were at the airport by dawn."

"I thought they'd bury him here."

"Bury him? You twit he isn't *dead*!" Kylie said.

"Ferry," Gemma said, "Dmitri's father came this morning and took him to the airport. They are going back to America. Dmitri's father thought he could get better medical care there. So they're gone."

"Dmitri can't go back there. He'll get arrested. He told me that he robbed some liquor stores."

"They might have been just stories," Gemma said. "Anyway, he was on a gurney. No one will bother them. Bert brought his cousin's passport."

"Did anyone know he was leaving?" I asked.

"When I first talked to his father on the phone, he told me he wanted to take him back but I thought it would be too difficult. I never thought he was serious. I never took that man too serious. He wore little boy underwear, you know. But he had made a lot of special arrangements."

I remembered what Dmitri said to me the last time I saw him. He said, "I want to die here among strangers. It's better to die among strangers, than among family and lifelong friends. Death turns things upside down. It turns strangers into brothers, and family into nobodies. It's better to die among people who you can't imagine grieving."

I began to hate the rooms of my students. Nothing depressed me more than sitting in the same chair, the same book splayed before me, the same blank moment hanging between us like a tasteless joke. Every time I desperately resolved to be better prepared for the lesson, and every time I wasn't.

When I walked into Jordi's apartment for our final lesson, he was working at his desk, a green-shaded lamp was crowded next to his textbook. In a flash I saw him as an old man, older than his father, old in a way that made his younger self seem like an apparition. He'll live forever in this apartment, I thought, or one just like it in every way. He'll scribble and erase at this very same desk—as much as eighty years. *A plump and satisfied old man, he thumps his book closed before going to sleep. Characters labor methodically through his dreams: the butcher, the grocer, the bartender he went to school with as a child. And the wayward English teachers—how many has he known? All so searching and fearful, so lost and confused, tumbling into the rooms, knowing the answers but unable to teach them, knowing the questions but too proud to ask.*

CHAPTER 33

My last night at the Quiet Man (though I never guessed so at the time), Gordon announced that he was dating a Catalan woman. Kylie and I stiffened on our stools, like a couple of drunk drivers spotting the red and blue lights whirling in the rearview mirror. We would have been less surprised had he told us that he was dating a Moroccan, a Macedonian, or a man. "She's Catalan," he said. Wichitom was there too—he was looking at Kylie, who was looking at Gordon with the clear expression of appalled disgust mixed with disbelief. Surely there had to be some variable that Gordon was yet to tell us—that she was really Brazilian, or Canadian, and merely raised by Catalans. Or that she was only half Catalan. Or that she had committed some heinous crime and had been exiled from her Catalan clan.

"Gordon for Christ's sake, don't you know what this means?" Kylie said. "Herb. Remember Herb." I had heard the legend of Herb before. He was an American guy who used to teach at the school. He had married a Catalan woman a couple of years earlier, and now lived with her and their budding family in the dreary, Catalan-heavy suburb of Badalona. Herb was the protagonist in the cautionary tale for those who feared assimilation, for all of us laboring in the strange purgatory of being an expatriate. Herb's in-laws had browbeaten him into submitting to their every ideal, including speaking Catalan and skiing with them in Puigcerda. He allegedly appeared at the Quiet Man on rare occasions, toting El Corte Inglés bags full of small appliances and baby clothes.

We drank silently and with a purpose. An hour later, Alicia herself arrived at the Quiet Man.

"How'd you meet?" Kylie asked her flatly.

"He is my teacher," Alicia said.

CHAPTER 34

"It's like Dmitri died and went to heaven, except he's still alive and in America—Ohio or Pennsylvania," Martin said as he came from behind me. He was wearing a blue satiny shirt and white pants. Gemma had decided to throw a going-away party for Dmitri, even though he was already gone. I came with Enrique and Paz.

"I thought it was South Carolina."

"He never told me where he was from exactly, but he didn't seem like someone from the south."

"What do you know about the south?"

"Plenty. Laziness, corruption, a scapegoat for all your problems. We have a south in Europe too remember."

"Like southern Italy. I saw the Godfather."

"Even in Belgium we have this."

"Belgium is the size of a big mall."

"Even malls have good and bad sections. There is Macy's and there is the Orange Julius in the Food Court. You forget that I was an exchange student in Minnesota. In Belgium, people from Flanders look at the Walloons as backward and lazy. And it's true, the Walloons are total idiots."

Martin was showing off his vocabulary and cultural knowledge for a woman I had never seen before. "*Hola*!" she shouted. "I'm Lizzy, oh Ferry that's a strange one. Is that something Czech? You look a bit Czech." Her voice sounded like breaking dishes. Her bubbly British accent was more than obnoxious, more like a pathological tick. She gushed about the drinks and the music, and how "brilliant" Barcelona was. She switched from her loud, strident voice to a hushed whisper to convey a sort of reverence. She practically yelled "brilliant" when Kylie came over and asked about her impression of Barcelona. But when she looked off the balcony at the glittering rooftops, she practically whispered the word.

"I'm just here on holiday. Barcelona is just brilliant. I had been to France loads of times, my aunt is half French, you see, and took us over to Le Havre for holiday. I speak a bit of French, but Spanish, I'm sorry darling."

Lizzy wore a billowy yellow blouse that hung untucked over a tight blue skirt. Her pale legs shone with some kind of lotion. She wore horn-rimmed glasses that easily weighed a pound. Her hair looked like the nest of a drug-addled bird.

"This flat is brilliant," she said looking down at the quiet street. "It's just like being in Le Havre."

Traveling!

Man: I hope our new city will be less like a toilet, and more like a home.

Woman: Less like a reflection of who we are, and more like who we want to be. Plus, I hope it has a Zara.

Man: And plenty of cheap disgusting Irish bars.

I looked around our little group. Gordon was laughing with his teeth sticking out, which was his unfortunate way. It reminded me of Picasso's horse painting. Kylie was smiling at him and rolling her eyes, the tag of her bra sticking out of her top. Paz was slumped in a chair, pecking at a joint.

"Ferry. C'mere." Wichitom came up next to me and put his arm on my shoulder. "I got two words for you: *land lady*."

"Paz? What do you mean?"

Wichitom closed his eyes and smiled, as if I were toying with him. "Yes, Paz. Is she married?"

"She was, she might still be, but he's not around."

Wichitom looked wistfully in her general direction. "A woman with a dramatic history. That's always the case. If they hit thirty and don't have a story, that's when you have problems."

"You could say the same thing about us."

"You could, but for us it's forty. Forty is the age when you should have done something big, something serious. Even if it's a mistake."

"Paz can be a little sad and mopey—but it's in a cartoon kind of way." I said. Wichitom was nodding sagely. "Don't play games with her," I added, "she's got enough problems."

"I'm not going to play games," he said, offended. "What do I look like, a teenager? I'm a man, I've seen all that can go wrong with a life. And I know what I want. Tell me something else about her."

"She makes a mean Chicken Parmesan."

"She does, does she? What else?"

"Pork chops stuffed with artichoke hearts. Cream of salmon soup with homemade croutons."

"Give me the bedroom picture. Who are the players there?"

"Well, the only other character you've got to deal with is Enrique." I motioned to him just as he was lighting a cigarette for a girl I never saw before.

"He looks like he could be her son. What's he, twenty? Spanish?"

"He's from Argentina. He's pushing thirty."

"What's he doing with her? They're a bad fit."

"I agree. It's a convenience thing. But he might be transferring to Madrid. He hates Barcelona because he thinks the Catalans are assholes."

"Perfect. When's he leaving?"

"Next month, but it's not for sure. I could ask him."

"No, don't worry about it. He's a wimp—I can see that from here. I could shake a newspaper and scare him away."

"He likes the newspaper."

"But sometimes these women go for that," he said thoughtfully. "They like weak men so they can control them."

"Not Paz. She'd like someone strong, at least her equal."

"I'm not saying that a strong woman is bad. There's nothing wrong with getting a little TLC."

I walked over to Kylie, who was smelling her drink.

"Where's Clarence? It's not like him to miss something like this. Free booze." I pointed to the assorted bottles crowded on a nearby table.

"I'm not surprised. He's finally gone off his nut," she said. "Did you know that he was engaged to a Catalan? It was years ago."

"That's impossible. He *loathes* Catalans."

"Apparently she left him for another Catalan. Came to her senses, a cynic might say."

"I can't imagine him dating a Catalan. I really can't imagine him dating anyone."

"That's how he learned to speak Catalan. That's the only way that you can learn to speak Catalan."

"He was always talking about being antisocial. He said that's why we all run away from home."

"You've got it backwards darling. Most everyone here *is* social. We're here because of fear, resentment, unhappiness. We say opportunities, education, experience—but everyone is here because something where we were went broken."

"You make it sound like we're sociopaths."

"All we ever talk about is ourselves—I'm from Sydney, I've read Proust, I'm going to Granada, I speak French. It's really a little pathetic."

"I'd say half of my sentences begin with I."

"The reason we're living here in the first place is because we want to make ourselves more interesting so we can keep on about ourselves. We hope it will last forever."

"I actually thought that I might find a nice place to deposit my old self and then create a new one."

"It's people back home that have the right idea. They have their little kids. Everyone gives them a hard time about making little miniature selves, but it's quite the opposite."

"Sounds like the old biological clock is ticking."

"You useless prat, I'm only thirty-one."

CHAPTER 35

I received a call from Clarence, who was drunk. "I left everything in the room," he said. "I didn't have time to pack it all. You might want to go over there and clean that crap out. Go there tomorrow, it will still be safe. After that, who knows?" I didn't ask him where he was, but the line hummed and I imagined it was far out of the city. "The only reason I'm asking you this is because your name is on some of the new *Sic* drafts. There is enough stuff in that room to incriminate all of us. Plus, there's some booze there that I didn't pack." I heard someone speaking French, and then Clarence said away from the receiver: "Fuck you, OK?" Then there was rustling. I imagined he had snuck behind a bar to use the phone. He would not be long before finding more trouble, I thought. He was on his way to a major reckoning.

His one-bedroom apartment was over in Poble Sec, a neighborhood he called "*pobre* suck." But the area wasn't really poor at all, not like the Raval; all his neighbors seemed like working class Andalusians—I heard a couple of lisping calls on the stairwell as I walked up to the fourth floor.

I pried up the old threshold in front of his door and found the key taped beneath it. The kitchen was tiny and surprisingly clean. Above the sink, blue and white curtains hung on the window that provided a view of the building's central ventilation shaft. Those curtains must have come with the apartment, I thought, because I had a hard time imagining Clarence spending his money on them. The cabinets had no doors, and were full of boxes of pasta, jars of olives, and about a dozen tins of sardines. The idea that serial killers sometimes keep body parts in the freezer occurred to me in a flash as I opened the fridge, though I only found five bottles of Damms and a plate sprinkled with crumbs; the freezer was empty.

In the other two rooms I found the usual detritus of the bachelor boiled down to the essence: a small television equipped with an antenna; a few dozen books piled against the wall; and the couch comprised of stacked foam—the hallmark of the thrifty Spanish living room. In his bedroom I had a premonition worse than finding body parts in the freezer; I was afraid that I might find a cache of porno, perhaps bizarre and spectacular. Instead his desk was covered with notebooks and loose paper sketched with cartoons for *Sic*.

> ## Local Man Flees
>
> A local English teacher has fled the city following an assault on a neighborhood drug addict. The degenerate was pronounced dead at Our Sister of Mercy Hospital, a mildly-ironic touch that was not lost on the murderer, though such an irony seems rather built-in, not to mention played-out, in this absurd world.
>
> The English teacher has been placed on unpaid administrative leave from his employer. He is planning an extended sojourn in an undisclosed country, and just before press time *Sic* reported seeing him board a westbound train from Estaćio Barcelona-Sants, wearing new wrap-around sunglasses and his trademark corduroys.
>
> The miscreant, on the other hand, will reside in the graveyard on Montjuic. He may get one of those little pictures on his headstone, and flowers, because after all someone might have loved him, someone might weep for him, though that could be no consolation to him now.

That evening, I spoke to my mother for the first time since I arrived in Barcelona. "God, Lester, be careful. I heard something on the news about the war. Are you near it?"

"That's Kosovo, and I'm nowhere near it."

"The world is so dangerous. It's not the way it used to be."

"There have always been wars."

"It's not just wars. They attacked those embassies. And crime, even around here. A little Mexican girl went missing here the other day. Her mother was on the news, wailing and shouting, but in Spanish so I couldn't understand her. If you could have seen that sorrow. They found her later, at her grandmother's in Chula Vista. But still. San Diego used to be such a safe place."

My mother's reason for calling was to tell me about Tyrone. He was in rehab. "He's there, finally," she said in a fragile voice, "to find out why he's done all that he's done to himself over the years." My mother always spoke with an air of wistfulness and regret, as if all the world's opportunities had already been lost. Even at that point, when there seemed to be something to be hopeful about, I could imagine her wincing at the thought of all the things Tyrone had done over the years. "Take care son," she said abruptly, "your mother loves you," and hung up without waiting for a response.

She had given me the number of Tyrone's rehab, a place called the Desert Detox and Day Program. A deep baritone answered gruffly and then shouted my brother's name into what sounded like a gymnasium or cafeteria. Then I heard a tap every second or so and I realized that the guy had dropped the receiver and it was knocking against the wall.

I heard the slap of sneakers on tile and someone clearing phlegm from his throat. "Tyrone Ferry," my brother said.

"Lester Ferry," I replied.

"Bro."

"Are you dried out yet?"

"Almost, they say it takes a full thirty days for the system to be totally clean. I might still have some bong hits stuck in my saucepan. Anyway, I'm two-thirds of the way home."

"What's with this 'Tyrone Ferry'?"

"I've floated some applications. Plus you could be my probation officer."

"No, I couldn't."

"You could. Unexpected phone calls and visits are her specialty."

"What happened to the ankle jewelry?"

"They let me take it off when I came in here. They're getting state money."

"What else is going on there?"

"It's hot."

"It's hot here, too."

"No bro, I'm in El Cajon. It's super hot. You know when you look across a blacktop parking lot and far away the air looks wavy because it's hot?"

"Yeah."

"It's like that here, except it's wavy everywhere. Right where you're standing, it's wavy."

"So how's rehab?"

"I've had it worse. Three hots and a cot. More like a danish, a sandwich, a hot and a cot," he laughed. "But they let me smoke. There are a few ladies here, too. They brought one girl in straight from the detox unit. She looked pretty tattered, but you could tell that once she was on solid food and got some naps under her belt she'd be pretty hot. So I'm working on that."

"I don't get it Tyrone, what made you go there in the first place? Don't get me wrong, I think it's great."

"Well, first of all, having that ankle thing on was beat. That thing was really bringing me down. If you're in the hole, you're in the hole. But having a tracking device strapped to your body is just plain wrong. A guy in here says that they can listen in on conversations with that thing, though he also thinks that every motel room in the county has two-way mirrors. And that the Bic lighters they sell in cracktown liquor stores are hooked up with satellites. Like they need satellites to find crackheads."

"So what happens next?"

"Well, that's the other thing. I chill. I'm getting a little tired of the same old, same old, bro, you know what I mean? So I'm listening for once. Stan, the guy in charge of my file, says that my old life isn't going anywhere, so I can always have it back. I have nothing to lose except misery and despair. Besides, Reese is paying for it. Or at least his insurance company. I wonder if he had to adopt me," Tyrone laughed. "Tyrone Crapps. That's sweet. I sound like a gangster."

"Maybe he'll adopt me too," I said weakly.

"Lester Crapps? No bro, that sounds like a principal at some fag school. I'm just kidding anyway. You think I'd want the name Crapps?"

"It's nice that Reese is taking care of it."

"Yeah, we talked. He's all right, I mean, he tries. He's still a moron, still wears that vest with all the pockets, but he's all right. Mom likes him. He's nice to mom. So I've been cutting him some slack. Maybe if I stay clean and do real good he'll give me his old Saab. That's what I've been telling the girl from detox."

"You working?"

"Yeah, we're doing some shit around here. It helps offset some of the cost, so I'm doing that. Spackling, shit like that. I've been spackling. People punch holes in the wall, headbutt them, put their foot in them. So I spackle and the girl from detox goes over it with the sander. Then Dolores and Roy do the painting. Dolores has a broken collarbone and can't do the high or low spots, so Roy does those. Dolores got a DUI when she skidded into a dumpster on her moped. She's classic."

Listening to my brother, I was surprised that I wasn't happier for him. For the first time I realized that I always took a lot of comfort in his delinquency.

"And Roy," he continued. "Roy's married, but his wife is a total bitch. She left a laundry basket full of Roy's shit on the porch the other night. Didn't knock, didn't leave a note, just that basket of clothes and a bunch of mail—probably bills. Roy was a binge guy. Three months he's super dad, super husband—you know, takes the kids to the zoo, the wife to JC Penny's, goes home mows the lawn. But put some sauce in him and he falls apart. I'm not talking about six whiskeys and a little back talk, a little ding in the fender. No, no. I'm talking about waking up in the Mexacali jail. Fist fights on business lunches. Getting *caught* nailing hookers in his garage. Hall of shame material."

"Jesus."

"Exactly. It's why we drink, Stan says, to forget that shit. It's a cycle."

"I suppose it makes you feel better about your own problems."

"One guy wet his pants at the office Christmas party."

"C'mon. That's bullshit."

"He says there's a video."

"And what, did he just volunteer this information to you?"

"We have a men's-only group therapy session. So by the way, this is all confidential."

"Yeah, no problem. I don't think we have any mutual friends anyway."

"You never know. These cats got around."

Of course, I never should have returned to Clarence's apartment three days later. I told myself that I was going to give it one final comb-through, make sure there were no secret panels or incriminating documents taped to the bottom of the cabinets. And I could take his television and set it up on my cardboard dresser. I wanted to take it the first time, but my arms were full of papers and bottles.

I had a bad hunch when I turned the key and walked through the door. I sat at his little plastic table, and drank a bottle of beer. Clarence's space was larger and cleaner than my tiny room, though there was a familiar feeling that I couldn't quite place the first time I was there. By the time I realized it was loneliness, the police were through the door.

CHAPTER 36

I don't mind prison. I've lost some of my baby fat because I'm doing push ups all the time, and I walk around the track when they let us out into the miniature yard. Gordon was partially right—that the jails in Spain are known for "easy time." But from what I gather he was talking about Quatre Camins, or Can Brians. I unfortunately was sent to Presó Model, Barcelona's notoriously run down city jail, which is allegedly haunted by the political prisoners who were executed following the Civil War.

At least it's easy to have visitors here. Kylie came last Sunday in a floral print dress and a straw hat—it's getting warm again, though she seems to be trying to exaggerate the image of her freedom. She may have the idea that I am going bad in here, learning how to be a real criminal, warming up to some lifer who's giving me the notes of all the jobs he'd cased but never finished. But the idea that I am an actual criminal has never seriously been considered by anyone. The prosecution bandied the idea about at the beginning of my case, but they soon seemed as eager as my defense to arrange a plea deal. The other junkie went MIA, so the only real evidence was the *Sic* "murder issue" that I had foolishly brought to work and left on the copier. Isabelle said it was her "civic duty" to give it to the police. I plead guilty to something like "criminal mischief resulting in death." The charge carried a maximum of thirty years, though my attorney negotiated for only one. And the only way he was able to get such a sweet deal was if I agreed to testify against Clarence should he ever find his way into a Spanish courtroom. I know he never will.

Gordon visits once in a while, but mostly he has written letters describing the increasing likelihood that he is going to marry his Catalan girlfriend. He's spending his Sundays with the family, playing card games and watching rented movies. "My Catalan is becoming passable," he says, "though helping me pass into what mad realm I cannot be sure."

Paz and Wichitom visit together. Wichitom moved into the apartment, into Enrique's room a week after Enrique moved to Madrid to finish his dissertation. Wichitom must have been plotting his move since our night at the party, and patiently waited for his opportunity. "We're keeping your room empty for when you get out," he said. "We can be a nice, happy family."

My only other visitor has been Gemma. She came with some dried fruit and some of Dmitri's old books—Camus and Kafka mostly. Gordon and Kylie were not able to get so much as a magazine past the guards, but Gemma explained that she knew one of them from her school days. She told me Dmitri had responded well to rigorous chemotherapy in South Carolina, and a recovery was not out of the question anymore. I had become resigned to thinking of Dmitri as an invalid, and I could hardly imagine him otherwise. Gemma spoke to him a lot on the phone, and she said that he asked her to pass along some notes. He had always racked his brain, she reported, for the best way to help me, and he realizes now that a year in prison was the perfect prescription all along. "Don't ruin it by masturbating all the time," she read from a piece of paper.

I sometimes think about the kid that Clarence killed. He and Clarence had some things in common: the estranged family, the appetite for intoxication, a calendar of empty days and nights. And it's funny how close they were to being in each other's shoes—after all, the kid approached Clarence brandishing a bottle, though I doubt that he ever intended to use it. The kid had been able to fool and elude everyone in his life until he found someone just like himself, only more so.

No one is getting raped in here, at least as far as I can tell. That's the question in the back of everyone's mind when they talk about prison. It may be because there are enough gays running around giving it up, or giving it up at a discount. There is a man in here with a very large rack, and a very large band of admirers, myself not among them.

And I stopped drinking of course. I could buy contraband wine in here, but it's pretty expensive. Hash too, though a single gram can run two thousand pesetas or a month of breakfasts. I'm taking a cue from my brother, whose letters arrive a month late, the most unlikely of mentors.

After my arrest, Reese flew over and paid for my lawyer. I'd like to say that that was the worst part, that having nothing less than the rest of my life and my very freedom depend on this guy who I never liked or respected, was worse than an extended incarceration. But of course this is not true. In fact, being so heavily indebted to him has felt like a kind of freedom. Being in jail has given me a peace that I never knew existed.

My mother couldn't make the trip, Reese said. She wasn't up to the long flight, the foreign courtroom, the inevitable sentencing of her first son. Reese insinuated a kind of disapproval in my mother's absence, but I understood. How much grief should one woman have to absorb in a lifetime? An estranged husband found dead one very cold morning outside a Boston soup kitchen. The bad son in and out of jails and rehabs, pawning her crockery. The good one charged with what amounts to accidental murder, and on his way to a Spanish prison.

Tyrone, Reese said, was nearly manic with desire to come, but he would have literally needed a signed document from the Governor of California.

I mostly pass the time in here sketching a prison newsletter like *Sic*, except I've titled it the *Thief's Journal*. "Man in Jail Eats Unidentifiable Meats; Melodramatic Movie without Subtitles Playing Again; I Think the Chaplain Is Naked beneath his Robe; etc." I'm trying to tap into the nervous edge that I used to blunt with my drinking. I think I've discovered what Clarence meant when he said that writing the paper was a way for him to figure things out, a way to get control of the world, just some place to begin making sense. I told that to Ramón, one of the few Catalan friends that I've met in here, and he said it sounds like a place to make *seny*, which is a Catalan word meaning something like understanding, judgment, sensitivity. It's funny that I had never heard that word before, Ramón said, after so long in Catalunya. I'm teaching him English, and he's teaching me Catalan. He says I have to learn it in order to stay in Barcelona. He's almost finished his two-year sentence for robbing a DIA with a plastic gun.

Tomorrow I Might Be Far Away

The fugitive boarded an afternoon train at Estació de França. Heading north, the track ran for a while alongside the sea

The first major stop was Perpignan. The fugitive bought cigarettes from a kiosk, and stared at the cover of a glamour magazine: the model's brown hair was sleek like the fur of an otter emerging from an autumn pond. He bought wine from a shop for twenty-one francs.

Winston Churchill once said that Russia is a riddle wrapped in a mystery inside an enigma. France is a hackneyed image, the fugitive thought, wrapped in a cliché inside a platitude.

The fugitive entertained the idea of going to Russia. He had read about their abundance of vodka. There he could settle into his role of foreign drunk, sleeping in stairwells, blunting his imagination, relying on sympathy for an occasional sandwich.

Or he could wander onto the steppes. He could wear an animal skin that feels like sandpaper on the inside, that still smells like deer, or badger, that still has chunks of clotted blood on the edges.

As the train rolls on to Montpellier, the kilometers pass and the fugitive tries to read but he can't. The sound of the wheels falling on the tracks, the shriek of wind, the sighing of the cars rising and drifting—all these things distract him.

The night before my sentencing, I stayed with Reese at his hotel near Park Güell. That afternoon, I had cleared my few belongings from Paz's apartment. Throughout my ordeal, I sensed a strange uneasiness about her and I wonder if it touched a nerve close to her own tragedy. Enrique was holding his position on the couch. He told me to read a lot, said a year in prison is perfect for that. "It will change you," he said. "But it is up to you if it will change you for the better or for the worse." He stood up as we were leaving. He and I shook hands, and I'm pretty sure it was the first time we ever physically touched. "Have a nice life, Ferry," he said.

In the morning, Reese and I took a taxi to the courthouse. We entered the Eixample, and drove down Carrer de Lepant. We crossed Diagonal, Còrsega, Roselló. And then suddenly, in a moment that I was not prepared for, we came upon the Sagrada Familia. My heart fluttered in my chest like a minnow in my palm. I never imagined it so massive, those weird towers jammed into that little area of sky. Guys in big coats were selling Christmas trees in the adjacent lot, and there was a cold but glittering mood about the place. "The Secada Familia," Reese said. "It's the biggest church in the world." Some nine months after I arrived, I finally saw it, and I saw it by accident. And now that I had seen it, I imagined that I might never see it again.